A DARING PURSUIT

The Clandestine Sapphire Society
Book 2

Kathy L Wheeler

ARE YOU SIGNED UP FOR DRAGONBLADE'S BLOG?

You'll get the latest news and information on exclusive giveaways, exclusive excerpts, coming releases, sales, free books, cover reveals and more.

Check out our complete list of authors, too!

No spam, no junk. That's a promise!

Sign Up Here

www.dragonbladepublishing.com

Dearest Reader;

Thank you for your support of a small press. At Dragonblade Publishing, we strive to bring you the highest quality Historical Romance from some of the best authors in the business. Without your support, there is no 'us', so we sincerely hope you adore these stories and find some new favorite authors along the way.

Happy Reading!

CEO, Dragonblade Publishing

**Additional Dragonblade books by
Author Kathy L Wheeler**

The Clandestine Sapphire Society
A Silent Accord (Book 1)
A Daring Pursuit (Book 2)

PROLOGUE

London—Winter 1827

S TIFFENING HER LIPS, five-year-old Geneva Wimbley covered her ears with her hands and begged some unknown being to keep her mama from dying. She didn't know what was wrong, but since she'd been confined to Mrs. Cornett's abode, she knew it was bad. Mrs. Cornett lived in the flat beneath hers and Mama's.

"She's going to die, isn't she?" she said in a voice that didn't sound like her own.

Mrs. Cornett patted her hand, leaving an imprint of flour from her bread-making. "Now, now, Geneva. You mustn't be so odious regarding these matters."

Geneva brushed off the flour and went to the grimy window that looked out over the street below, where debris blew about. The rain was welcome because it washed away a lot of the muck. "What will happen to me?"

"Your papa is expected back soon, dear. You don't need to worry none."

A shudder went through Geneva. Papa didn't much like her. She would have to run away from home if Mama died. She couldn't stay with her father. Every time he returned, the overpowering stench of being unwashed and that stinky gin reeked through the flat—she knew what it was because she'd overheard Mrs. Cornett telling Mrs. Barding, who lived across the hall.

Months ago, the smell had had Mama casting up her accounts. Eventually, she'd been able to hold down her piddling dinners. But her suffering now was worse. Much worse.

Geneva had to be ready. She'd have to take the ruby locket Mama had promised her without Papa knowing. Geneva had no doubt that Papa would toss her in the streets or sell her to one of the pickpocket handlers who ran the neighborhood's really horrid places. "Do you have any books, Mrs. Cornett?"

"Books! Lordy, Geneva." The rolling pin she held landed on the table with a thunk. "What do you want with books? Girls have no need for such nonsense."

Geneva turned from the window, stunned by the hurt curling through her. "But my mama has shown me my letters and is teaching me words." She planted her hands on her hips. "She told me I shall attend the same school she went to when she was a young girl."

Mrs. Cornett came from behind the table, her flour-covered hands landing at her ample hips. "Why, I never! You shouldn't tell lies, Geneva. It's unseemly." She shook her head and pushed back a strand of steel-colored hair from her forehead, leaving a streak of white. "And with your sweet, little mama on her deathbed."

"*Deathbed!*" Geneva ran out the door and pounded up the stairs in the dank, narrow hall to her own floor above.

A huge man in a vast, swirling greatcoat swept by her and pounded on the door of Mama's and her small flat. He didn't even wait for Mama to open the door—just kicked it in and slammed it in Geneva's face. He hadn't even seen her. Fear hurt her tummy.

He didn't come back out like Geneva thought he would, and after a few minutes, she crept forward, cracked the door open, and peered in.

"Can't ye see she's in pain, ye blackguard?" It was a woman's voice Geneva didn't recognize.

The other voice was low, a gravelly timbre that would haunt Geneva forever, even though she had trouble making out his words.

Mama was panting. "I-I know she doesn't belong to you, my lord, but please, have mercy... take her too, my lord. She deserves a better life than what that bastard I'm married to will give her."

"Bah. It's sufficient to say you didn't have the sense to keep from letting things get this far and now *I'm* stuck with the consequences. I shall take this, however, for compensation. Send the girl to the Black Widow when she's of an age. Hell, I'll pay the exorbitant fees it'll require." Then he laughed.

It was a laugh that sent chills of black ice inside Geneva. Blinking back tears, Geneva forgot about Mama being in bed, about wanting a book, or about anything but dashing back down the stairs to the warmth and safety of Mrs. Cornett's flat.

The older woman stood in the door with her arms opened.

Geneva dove straight into them. "You were right. Mama is on her deathbed." Her voice was muffled against the older woman's scratchy, woolen frock.

"No, child. I should'na said any such thing. It ain't her time. Ye jes wait 'n see. Don' fret now. Soon ye'll have a playmate o' yer own." She patted Geneva's shoulder. "Now, chin up, me sweet. Come an' have a nice, warm piece a bread right from the oven."

Northumberland, Winter—1827

A BLISTERING WIND swept through Stonemare that was more in line with the Earl of Pender's sudden appearance than the open door behind him saturating Mrs. Knagg's freshly polished floor with slashing rain.

Ten-year-old Noah Oshea, second son of the Earl of Pender, peeked through the crack from the library where he'd been immersed in *The Sceptical Chymist* by Robert Boyle. It was an old text in which Mr. Boyle introduced chemical elements. He'd already tried reading William Harvey's *De Motu Cordis* on the motion of heart and blood in animals. Yes, the words were too hard to figure out, but he would read anything to blot out his mother's screams that bellowed the halls. They were harsh sounds that echoed against the castle's old stone covered with threadbare tapestries.

He hadn't seen Mama. Not since she'd fainted at some pain growing in her stomach two days ago. Every time he approached Mrs. Knagg, their housekeeper, or the butler, Winfield, he'd been shooed away. The old castle was drafty and not in ideal condition for anyone, let alone someone not feeling well. Mama was likely to contract the ague. It wasn't fair that Lucius, his older brother by three years, could live at school instead of home tasked with taking care of the estate that would be turned over to him as heir apparent. Noah firmed his lips and prepared to step back but made the mistake of looking up.

Papa was staring straight at him with a wicker basket hanging off his forearm. "Have a gift for you, boy," he growled.

"I have a name," Noah muttered under his breath as the familiar resentment pulsed through him. He didn't dare back away, as Papa's fist could fly out at will in a wallop that would leave his ears ringing.

A small, minute squeal emitted from the… basket? Hope swelled through Noah. *A puppy? A kitten?* He'd never been allowed a pet, no matter how he'd begged throughout the years.

Papa turned to Mrs. Knagg. "Don't disturb us."

She was a pillar of Stonemare. Her robust build and commanding presence held an air of stern efficiency. A few wisps of ash-brown hair had escaped the severe bun, but the usual sternness softened in her brown eyes. "Of course, my lord. But wouldn't you care to see Lady Pender first?"

He turned toward the library, his strides long. "Later," he barked—then paused. Papa turned back to the housekeeper. "Is the wet nurse in house?"

"Certainly, m'lord. We shall have need of her at any moment.

"And the midwife?" The minute the words were out of Papa's mouth, Mama let out another bloodcurdling scream.

Noah couldn't see Papa's expression, but Mrs. Knagg's wince was quite clear. "We've sent for her, m'lord, but in this weather…" Her voice trailed off.

Papa nodded and entered the library, shutting the door behind him.

The click was ominous and resounded throughout the chamber.

Papa strolled over to the chair near the fire where Noah had been sitting earlier. He lifted the tome left there after Noah had rushed away minutes earlier. Papa grinned, his teeth gleaming white through his unshaven face in the gloom like the devil himself. Glancing at Noah, he lifted one brow. *"Sceptical Chymist,* eh?"

"Well, you won't let me attend school," Noah said, kicking at a sliver of paper, not bothering to raise his head. All he'd see was the regular criticism besides.

"I've told you a hundred times, boy, you aren't old enough. You'll go when you turn thirteen, just like your brother." He set the book on the nearest table. At least he hadn't tossed it in the fire.

"But that's three whole years."

Papa dropped into the chair. "Enough. Now, sit down. I need your help." He placed the basket on the floor between his feet.

Noah did as he'd asked. First, because Papa had never needed his help before. Second, because he really wanted his own pet. Not a puppy that was forced to stay in the barn on cold, stormy nights like tonight.

Papa reached down and lifted the lid off the basket, then drew out a bundle wrapped in a dark blanket. It wasn't moving and Noah's hopes dashed. Papa leaned forward and set the bundle in Noah's lap.

Noah tugged gently at the corner of a scratchy blanket, curious despite his displeasure. "What is it?"

"Don't let it fall, for God's sake." At Papa's harsh tone, the bundle jerked and rolled, bound for a worn-through rug that wouldn't protect a flea from the hard wood beneath but for Papa's quick reaction. He plopped it back on Noah's lap and another less bulky package wrapped in brown paper slipped to the floor, exposing a delicate, gold chain. Papa swooped it up then stuffed it into his vest pocket then stood.

"What is that?" Noah asked him.

"Nothing that concerns you. Your duty is to the infant, god-dammit." He started for the door.

"What? A baby?" He sputtered. "You're giving me a *baby?*" Noah's gaze fell to the bundle across his knees. All thought of that small parcel flew from his head. "What am I supposed to do with a baby?"

"I don't want it. Throw it in the lake, for all I care. But if you do decide to keep it, you'd best feed it soon. Once it starts hollering, it's not likely to stop."

Well, Papa had been right about one thing. Once the baby started crying, the thing hadn't stopped. Noah lifted it, trying to imagine a scared puppy or a sickly kitten, but nothing worked. He struggled to set it back in the basket, but even with the top of the basket closed, the ear-shattering sound could not be softened.

Noah was ashamed that even a fleeting thought of tossing it in the lake had occurred to him.

"What do I feed it?" he asked his father before he had reached the door. "Cream, like a cat?"

"Something like that." At the door, his father looked over his shoulder at him. "And, Noah—"

Oh, no. Papa never addressed him by his given name. Mama had once told him she'd overrode Papa's preference for Devlin because it sounded too close to "devil." His brother Lucius hadn't been so lucky, having been named after Lucifer. Noah looked up, still holding the howling child that indeed blotted out his mother's screams.

"No one is to know the child is not your mother's. You understand what I'm saying?"

"No," he said bluntly.

Papa let out a tired sigh. "Your mother is giving birth as we speak. Everyone is to believe your mother birthed this one at the same time."

"You mean like a dog or cat has more than one?"

"Exactly like that. I want no questions, son. The only people who will know the truth is you, me, and the wet nurse. Now, it's time I see your mother. Find the wet nurse. She can help with that parcel you're holding."

Noah sputtered. "But, is it a boy or a girl?"

"I don't know and I don't care. The wet nurse can tell you. Just give it a name and keep it out of my sight."

London—1838

GENEVA DRUDGED UP the stairs, three flights, to No. 26 Berwick Street. She entered the flat she hadn't lived in for the last two years, having been at Miss Greensley's School of Comportment for Young Ladies of Quality. She unpinned the black veiled hat and tossed it on the scarred piece of wood that served as a table for her, Mama, and Papa on the rare occasions he was home.

With Mama now gone, the place felt almost haunted. The dreary London weather did nothing to dispel the notion. Mrs. Cornett still lived on the floor below, but she was feebler now and Mrs. Barding, whose husband had expired long before Geneva had left for school, was now Mrs. Cornett's constant companion. Neither had been able to make the miserable trek to Mama's services.

Papa had, of course, but he'd opted to stop at The Rat and Bull for a "quick" drink. Geneva suspected he wouldn't return home for the remainder of the evening. Something for which she was innately grateful.

Geneva set the kettle on the stove to heat and changed from the dreary, black dress to something more comfortable. She was due to catch the coach back to school over the weekend.

The door flew back and Papa stood in the doorway, his small, beady eyes glittering—with fury? Madness?

But Geneva knew better than to cower, allowing him the upper hand.

His meaty hands clenched and flexed with ominous intent. "Where is it?" he demanded.

Level head, she told herself, turning and pulling a cup from the cupboard. "Where is what?"

"The locket."

Geneva reached into the back of her mind, memories swirling. Just like the greatcoat of the mysterious stranger who'd haunted her dreams since the age of five. "I've no idea to what you are referring."

He started toward her, the thick-knuckled fist rising. "Don't be usin' that highfalutin' tone with me. Yer mum ain't here to protect ye no more."

But Geneva's reflexes were sound. She managed to contain her flinch and snatched up the closest weapon.

The knife used for carving mutton on the rare occasion meat was in the house.

CHAPTER ONE

1847

"GENEVA, HAVE YOU completed the *Call to Arms for Education Reform?*" Miss Hannah Ruskin, sister of Baron Ruskin, and also fellow Miss Greensley's Academy graduate, as well as one of her dearest friends, looked up, her blue eyes questioning.

Geneva Wimbley and her group of cohorts from Miss Greensley's had created their own secret club: *The Clandestine Sapphire Society*, and they were on a mission: to further education for the masses with training for teachers, as well as a demand for better working conditions that included factory workers and others in need of basic human rights, food, shelter, clothing. The objectives also included promoting social justice and equality. Geneva, Hannah, along with Lady Abra Washington, and the Duke of Rathbourne's only child, Lady Meredith Jephson—now Lady Perlsea, Geneva reminded herself—had tired of those who stole from the poor to raise their own statuses, only to mock those they treated so abhorrently. Meredith had wed three years prior and her arrogant, overbearing husband had banished her to Cornwall due to some sort of agreement their fathers had struck when the viscount and Meredith had been just children. It was so archaic.

Geneva missed Meredith terribly and it had been quite some time since she'd heard from her friend.

"Of course. How else am I to pay the rent? I'm just wrapping up. How does this sound?" She set down her pen and picked up the sheaf of paper and read, "*In the quest of superiority in education, 'tis crucial we recognize the vital roles of educators. Instructors are not merely conveyors of information; they are the future of this great country. Mentors, guides, and inspirers of young minds. I implore you to support the quality of education, as it can only be as strong as the caliber of those from whom they learn. 'Tis with this conviction that the entire British population advocate for greater training across the board.'"*

Hannah put her hands together, wheat-colored curls bouncing and infectious grin curving her lips, exposing a playful dimple in her left cheek. "Bravo! Bravo!"

Geneva rose from her chair and gave a grand bow from the waist, grinning back. "Thank you."

Her friend took her cloak from the peg near the door, then set her bonnet on her head and tied the ribbons beneath her chin.

"Where is your maid?" Geneva worried about causing trouble for her friends. The baron in particular could be an issue.

"Downstairs, waiting in the carriage." Hannah tugged on her kid gloves and strolled over.

Geneva signed the document with their standard signature of "CSS" and, after sanding the carefully worded papers, she folded the small stack and tied them with a piece of twine. She rose from the table and made a great show of officially handing the small packet to her friend.

"Excellent." Hannah slipped it into her oversized reticule. "I'll stop by the printer's on my way home. What's next?"

"An article on supplying instructors with more beneficial tools and resources. I vow it's a shame women are not allowed in Parliament. The world would be a much better place, I'd wager."

With a scowl, Hannah said, "Yes. I do believe it would." She paused a beat, studying Geneva until the hair on the back of her neck raised.

"Is something wrong?" Geneva asked slowly.

"A date has been selected."

The breath escaped Geneva in a rush. "I know he's your brother, but Abra—"

Hannah touched her arm. "I think they'll be happy, darling."

Another scowl touched her lips. "It's that blasted stepmother of hers who's kicking up the fuss."

That was true enough. Abra was the daughter of Marquess Westbridge. Her mother had been from Jamaica. To hear Abra speak of her parents' marriage, it had been a love match for the ages, but sadly, her mother had perished in childbirth along with an infant sister some years ago. Long before Abra had begun attending Miss Greensley's School. Her death had devastated both her and her father.

Certainly, it had been natural for Lord Westbridge to remarry, but his current wife was determined to marry Abra off to the Marquess of Martindale. The man had recently inherited his title. He was a horrid man.

Hannah was convinced that her brother, Lord Ruskin, and Abra held an attraction for one another and were perfect together. Geneva wasn't so sure and feared for her friend being treated less than she deserved. Baron Ruskin was decidedly the better of the two.

Clutching her reticule, Hannah opened the door. "We'll talk soon. Get some rest, my friend. Those dark circles beneath your eyes will not cure themselves. *Au revoir, love.*"

The decisive click of the latch behind her friend reverberated through the flat, leaving exhaustion—mostly from her own thoughts and unending expectations—hitting her full force. She slid from her chair at the scarred table to the hardwood floor and stretched her body out, closing her eyes. Abra's stepmother was nothing but a social-climbing, bitter woman who resented Lord Westbridge's first wife's child.

With a deep breath, Geneva drew in the ancient smells that permeated the walls. The fragrance wasn't what she would call *pleasant*, per se. More like... familiar, bringing to mind Mama's and her gentler times together when Papa had been away at sea. She basked in the quiet—

From the flat next door, Mr. Pickler yelled at his poor wife. *Again.* Her own walls vibrated with his fury—*almost* quiet, then.

She slammed a fist on the plank out of frustration. There was something odd in the sound. Hollow. Her heart tipped in an erratic thump, but Mr. Pickler's words were spiraling into a widening cone.

With tired determination, Geneva came to her feet, taking up the knife she'd brandished against her father eight years ago. She held it within the folds of her skirts before slipping out into the darkened corridor and pounding on the Picklers' door.

The yells came to an immediate stop. Seconds later, the door crashed back and Mr. Pickler's large, bulking form blocked her entry. The stench of gin nearly felled her to her knees. "Wot do ye want?"

She clenched her teeth and spoke through the putrid smell. "To see Mrs. Pickler."

"We're talkin'," he growled.

Standing her ground, Geneva had learned early on, was the only way to deal with such bullies. "Still, I insist on speaking with her. I suggest, sir, you sleep off your stupor." She shoved her way past him, her fingers tightening on the wooden hilt of the knife.

To Geneva's greatest relief, Mrs. Pickler was none the worse for wear. The stubborn compression of her lips was reassuring. She stood at the table wielding her own knife over a loaf of freshly baked bread. "Ah, Miss Wimbley, I expect you're hungry," she said, slicing into the loaf, releasing a stream of steam.

Geneva's stomach grumbled in a most convenient and timely manner. "I am, indeed, Mrs. Pickler." She took one of the two chairs. More like collapsed in to.

Mr. Pickler glared at the two of them but muttered something unintelligible before disappearing into the curtained-off, makeshift bedchamber. Within seconds, his snores filled the flat.

"He'll sleep it off and be back to his charmin' self in no time," Mrs. Pickler said with a sharp grin. Her thin, wiry frame belied a lifetime of hard work. The hazel eyes were clouded by weary dullness and her graying hair, streaked with white, was pinned up in a messy bun, though stray wisps had escaped to frame her face, softening her prominent cheekbones. "I 'preciate yer angel-like tendencies, dear." Her bony fingers held up the knife.

Geneva took her own knife from the folds of her skirts and laid it on the table with a small laugh. "Thank you, Mrs. Pickler. I am relieved to hear that."

Mrs. Pickler pushed a plate in front of Geneva then plopped a jar of currants down. She took the chair across from her guest. "Ye work too hard, gel."

"Work too hard?" she murmured. Perhaps she did.

"Ye think the women in this buildin' don' know wot yer about?" She shook her head, smiling. "I see yer titled friends a comin' an' a goin'."

"Oh." What was she supposed to say? "I, er, wasn't aware…" Her voice trailed off.

"'Tis a good thing yer doin'. Ye'll git no arguments from me. Now, eat up. Yer thin as a rail."

Thirty minutes later, Geneva reentered her flat bearing a nice, warm gift.

"Good. You're back. I let myself in," Lady Abra Washington said unnecessarily. Geneva had given her friends keys to the flat due to the clandestine nature of their endeavors.

She stood in Geneva's tiny kitchen with one hand on an open cupboard door. Her maid, Pasha, was seated on the sagging settee near the windows that overlooked the street below. Abra glanced over her shoulder, her hazel-brown eyes going straight to the borrowed plate from Mrs. Pickler with another large slice of bread slathered with currant jam. She dropped her hand. "Fresh bread? Is that"—she swallowed—"for me?" She glanced at Pasha. "I mean us?"

"Of course it is. That stepmother of yours is a horror acting as if you hoard every crumb you put in your mouth." Geneva strolled to the table and set it down, then dropped the knife with a *clunk*. "I vow, if I ever have the opportunity to drag that woman into an alley—"

Abra's eyes shot to Pasha then back to Geneva with a lifted

brow, cutting her off. "Ah. Mr. Pickler was drinking, I take it?"

"Yes." Geneva tilted her head, considering the knife she'd plunked down. "You know? I don't believe we need worry over Mrs. Pickler any longer. That woman is resourceful and can take care of herself."

"You doubted her? I never have. Not for a moment." Abra cut the bread in half, then strolled over and handed the plate to Pasha. She took a large bite and her features relaxed into pure ecstasy. "I would kill the man myself if she promised us bread on a daily basis."

Geneva grinned. "I feel the same." She knelt on the floor and began lightly tapping the planks in a systematic manner.

"What are you doing?" Abra asked around another bite.

A grim smile touched Geneva. "I thought I heard a hollowing earlier."

"Really?" Abra's chair scraped back and she went on her knees too, starting in another area, mimicking Geneva's actions. "When was this?"

"Right before Mr. Pickler began his rantings. Hannah had just left for the printer with the Education Advocacy pamphlets. Which reminds me—she mentioned a date had been set—"

"Listen," Abra interrupted urgently. "Here."

Geneva stilled and Abra tapped again. "That's it."

"You think it's a secret compartment?"

It was the only hope Geneva could harbor after all these years. To prove having a legacy, the promise from her mother, had perhaps been wishful thinking. "Let's see. It's an odd place if it is." The flat was on the third floor of this Berwick building. But where else could her mother have hidden a ruby locket? At times, her mother's words and the man in the swirling, black cloak seemed nothing other than some reoccurring nightmare. And perhaps it had been. Still, her heart thudded painfully against her ribs.

Abra jumped up, quickly returning with an oil lamp set at its brightest setting. "Look, there's a space between the slats." She retrieved the knife, pried the plank open, and set it aside. "There's something there," she whispered.

Geneva's hands shook with disbelief and longing. "Truly? After all these years?" She reached in with trembling fingers and pulled out a wooden keepsake box. Carved leaves bordered all four sides. Etched atop in an elaborate design was *Emily Renee*. "Good heavens. I-I didn't dream it," she whispered. Dust filled the carved-out crevices and came off on Geneva's fingertips. "My mother's name was Emily." There was even a key in the keyhole. She ran a fingertip over the dull metal.

"Open it." Abra's impatience jarred her.

"Oh. Right." She turned the key and lifted the lid. The creak sounded more like a squeal. It was the most precious sound Geneva could ever remember hearing.

Inside, she found a delicate, lace handkerchief yellowed with age. Silk ribbons that were stiff and almost unbending, faded pink and a blue one softened to grayish purple. A distressed sachet that had long since lost its scent and an empty perfume bottle. Geneva pulled the stopper and put it to her nose. Lemon verbena. "I-It still smells like her." Overwhelming emotion stung the backs of her eyes. She grappled for control.

There were no trinkets. Or if there had been, they'd likely been sold off years ago. There was also… "No ruby locket," she said. At the moment, she couldn't have cared less. This was a legacy of sorts she'd never expected to have. The gravity of that manacled her chest.

"That top part is just an insert. Perhaps the locket's underneath," Abra said.

Nodding, Geneva lifted the wooden insert. Abra was correct. It was another compartment designed to hold letters, she supposed. There was only one. As if handling the queen's jewels, Geneva took the note and unfolded it. She'd never seen her mother's writing before, but whose else could it have been?

Lord Pender,

I beg of you, please. Things have turned most dire. My husband

The words were marred here. By tears?

is a violent man. You must do something to save my Gen…

Again, a blur.

All that is precious to me is in your hands. Everything in my posse—

That was where the letter stopped. Geneva lifted her head, her own vision obscured, and met her friend's eyes, which were filled with concern. She looked down at the letter. A splash plinked on the paper. Geneva flipped it over, but the backside was blank.

"What does it say?" Abra asked.

Geneva handed it to her and brushed away a tear. Now was not the time to blubber like an infant.

"At the least, we have a name," Abra said. Then, scowling, added, "Lord Pender is a scoundrel along with that libertine son of his. Every time I think how he deserted Meredith in the wilds of Cornwall, I'm angry all over again. I vow, their reputations know no bounds." She folded the missive over and handed it back. "What do you wish to do?"

Geneva's determination firmed. "Find my locket, of course. Now that I know it truly exists." At least, she hoped that was the case. She came to her feet, swooping up the box from the floor, then stopped. "Is there anything else in there?" She waved at the floor.

Abra dipped her head, then looked up. "Nothing. Oh, wait." She reached down then brought out her hand and opened her palm. "A pearl earbob."

Black edged Geneva's vision. She fell back to her knees, hardly able to catch her breath.

Abra grabbed her hand and plopped the pearl into it. "The other one must be here somewhere." She bent over the opening, blocking it from Geneva's sight. "Blast. There's nothing—wait. There is something." She reared back and traded the earbob for another key. This one, small and rusty, left marks on Geneva's hand. Abra held the earbob to the lamp, studying it from all angles. "I don't know much regarding the value of jewels and such, never having so much as a chain to wear about my neck, thanks to my dear stepmother, but... this appears significant to me. What do you propose to do with it?" She held the earbob out in the flat of her hand.

It was a singular piece of delicate yet striking craftsmanship; its age was evident in the faint patina and whispered of a storied past. The pearl itself was lustrous though slightly irregular in shape with a soft, creamy sheen that caught the light and glowed with an otherworldly beauty. Its surface bore the subtle mark of time with tiny imperfections that only enhanced its authenticity and rarity. Geneva couldn't pull her eyes from it and responded without hesitation. "Sell it. We shall need the blunt."

A searing hatred pierced her that was ages old. If she had to describe it, it would have resembled something like a large, black greatcoat smothering her senses, blinding her, muffling all sound. Suffocating her ability to breathe. "Let's set this plank back in place. We've plans to make." She tightened her fist around the piece of metal she still held and stopped, peering at her very good friend. "If you... will you accompany me?"

Abra's straight, white teeth gleamed in a huge grin. "Just try to stop me."

"What about the evil stepmother?"

"I'll tell Papa we are to visit Meredith. He trusts me implicitly."

"But... if he learns the truth, he might quash our friendship."

"You let me handle Papa," she said with a wave of her hand.

A rush of gratitude filled Geneva. "Of course, Pasha—"

"Adores you." Abra glanced over to Pasha who was watching

them, eyes wide. "Don't you, Pasha?"

"Of course, my lady," she dutifully responded, though Geneva detected a gleam of excitement in her eye.

It wasn't as if they hadn't managed to fool Abra's parents before. They could now as well. "All right," Geneva said softly. She leaned over and gave her a fierce hug. "Thank you," she whispered. No one had a better friend.

CHAPTER TWO

THE SCIENTIFIC FORMULA converged in a blur that made Noah's eyes ache. He dropped his pen and whipped off his spectacles. With his forefinger and thumb, he rubbed his eyes then stood and raised his arms over his head in a stretch that cracked his spine one vertebra at a time. Over the last fourteen years, his study in chemistry had migrated to attempting to understand the musculoskeletal anatomy, his main focus being the foot and ankles. It was complicated research that involved observing gait and balance and functional limitations. He lowered his arms then pinched the bridge of his nose, drawing in a deep breath.

Besides downing several cups of strong Brazilian coffee, he'd yet to breakfast. He tugged out his watch and flipped it open. Only eight-thirty. An ungodly hour of the morning. He'd been in his laboratory already over two hours.

Uncle Sander and Aunt Verda were due home any day from their long-deserved holiday on the Continent. His youngest brother, Julius, was on Grand Tour and scheduled to return home with them. Noah couldn't have been more thrilled. He missed his family.

Smiling, he snatched up his spectacles. After securing the wire handles behind his ears, he leaned down and scribbled a few more observation notations in his journal then closed it. He was weary to the bone. Admittedly, he'd been able to focus on his research uninterrupted, but there were hitches in Noah's well-ordered life outside the last month. One was his father's behavior, which was growing disturbingly erratic. Inconsistent at best, and worst? Unstable...

The other was his eldest brother, Lucius, who hadn't recovered his fury upon learning he hadn't been free to marry Miss Docia Hale. Father had apparently signed that right away as part of a gaming vowel. According to Uncle Sander, in 1827, Lucius's hand had been tied to the Duke of Rathbourne's only child, Lady Meredith Jephson. At the ripe old age of thirteen. His brother had every right to his anger, of course. But the wedding had been three years ago. And unfortunately, Lucius had directed his anger at Lady Meredith by consigning her to the Cornwall property, Perlsea Keep, within days of their nuptials. Meanwhile, Lucius had maintained his residence at the Pender mansion in London year round, doing God knew what.

As far as Noah could tell, Lucius hadn't returned once to Cornwall. He let out a sigh. And, yes, he missed him too.

Since Lucius's unavailability, Docia had been dropping less than subtle hints of accepting an offer from Noah. Sadly, Noah couldn't think of a single reason to keep ignoring those hints. *Sadly?* An odd way to consider the possibility of one's own lifetime union. Therein lay the rub... a lifetime. With Docia. He shuddered.

God, he was tired. He dropped his spectacles on the table and rubbed his eyes again.

Across the chamber, the door flew back. The velocity of wind created threatened the stability of the charts pinned to the walls.

Docia rushed in, blonde curls escaping the chignon at her nape. The taffeta silk she wore—marigold—caught the sconced lighting with a subtle sheen. The fabric whispered softly with understated elegance. Her sudden appearance brought him upright. She *never* entered his laboratory, having mentioned on more than one occasion it was like stepping back into the Middle Ages with the narrow windows, smelly chemicals, and dungeon-esque atmosphere.

To which he always replied, *"That's because it used to be a dungeon."* For some reason, he always returned to his ten-year-old self when she was about. Marrying her did not seem wise. But Stonemare was isolated and, at times, was quite lonely.

"He's dead."

Noah blinked away the cobwebs, but that didn't clear the confusion and she did have a way with dramatics. "What?"

Baldric, the old stablemaster, who was a hundred if he was a day, ambled in behind her. Polar opposite of theatrical. Unflustered—that described Baldric—yet tense—that did not describe Baldric. "His lordship." His voice was as gravelly as his skin was wrinkled.

Noah came to his feet, disoriented and disbelieving. "I don't understand."

Docia was standing before him, clutching his lapels. "Your. Father. Is. Dead." She spoke pointedly. Succinctly. Knowingly.

Her hands had to be the only reason he was still standing. Noah hadn't seen his father in months. As long as he could remember, one minute he'd been there and the next, he'd disappeared with no word, rhyme, or reason anyone could fathom.

Docia led him to his makeshift desk and pushed him to sitting.

An instant later, Baldric thrust a glass of brandy into his shaking hands.

After tossing it back, Noah looked up into Baldric's black eyes, vaguely noting his tightly compressed lips. "But how? Where?"

"On the moors. Not far from where yer grandfather was found."

That sounded too much of a coincidence to be believed. The details regarding Grandfather's demise were sketchy at best, but the whisperings were that he'd frozen to death. Ancient history, having happened long before Noah and Lucius had come along. "How?"

"Stabbed. In the heart."

Docia spun around, facing Baldric, and gasped.

"Fletcher and Hicks are gittn' the body now," Baldric finished. "What do ye want me to do wi'thm?"

"The parlor." Noah's voice shook. "Contact the magistrate—" No. His father was the magistrate. He hauled in a breath and started over. "Contact the parish constable. Dear God." He stood, took Docia's arm, and urged her out the door and up the stone steps. In the study, he moved behind the desk and pulled out a sheet a vellum to write the first of many missives. He took up his pen, then blew out a harsh breath and then dipping it, he scrawled out the first and most important one.

To the new Earl of Pender: his brother Lucius.

AN HOUR OR so later, Noah pulled off his spectacles. He flexed his cramped fingers and looked up. Docia sat in one of the wing-backed chairs near the fire. He'd forgotten her presence—not all his fault, surely, as she usually chattered like a magpie. Yet, she hadn't uttered a word since Baldric's departure. He rose from the desk, poured out a couple of brandies, sauntered over, and handed her one. "You're especially quiet."

Docia's curls gleamed like the sun in the fire's light. Her frock was of the brightest marigold, cast orange reflecting the embers from the hearth. She was a year older than his twenty-nine years. She should have married years ago; instead, she'd counted on marrying Lucius, none of them having realized Father's reckless actions when Noah, Lucius, and Docia were but children.

"If we are to marry, it will have to be now and in Scotland. To call the banns will take too long and no parson will marry us now. Not when word gets round that your father's perished. Let alone *how* he perished." She turned dark-blue eyes, pooled with tears, on him. "Then, perhaps that was your intention all along."

Noah shoved a hand through his hair. "That's not fair."

She shrugged then leaned back to where her profile was hidden from him, raising her glass for a dainty sip. She never gulped. Everything about her was feminine, above convention. Except for this blasted proposal.

"I never promised to marry you, Docia." A bitter smile escaped him. "If I recall correctly, you said marrying me was a step down for you."

"I spoke the truth. But I also said, such a union was a step up for you."

She had indeed. He'd been ten at the time. So pretentious she'd been. What could he say? *Fine, we'll leave for Scotland first thing in the morning?* He opened his mouth, but nothing came out. He didn't love her. He wasn't certain he could love anyone. Inside, he was just... empty.

The chair moaned and her face appeared around the chair's wing. She glared daggers.

"All right," he said, capitulating. "One week from today. We shall escape to Scotland. That should allow me enough time to have Father's body prepared for viewing. I daresay that doesn't give the family enough time to arrive to throw a wrench into the works." His lack of enthusiasm left him guilt-ridden, but she was getting what she wanted, wasn't she? It was the most he could muster at the moment.

Her features softened and a smile curved her lips. "Thank you." She finished her brandy, stood, and handed him her emptied glass. She shook out her elaborate skirts, leaned in, and brushed his cheek with soft lips. "I'll be ready."

Noah stared into the fire, listening to the rustle of silk, aware of the door latching behind her. Aware of his lack of response to her chaste kiss.

That click rattled through the vast spaces in his chest. He held up his glass, the fire turning the color to a dark, murky shade he couldn't name. So, this was what impending nuptials felt like.

A prisoner of one's own body with no hope for reprieve for the rest of one's sorry, vacant life.

CHAPTER THREE

THE PRICE WAS hell and Geneva was on her way to collect. With her dear friend Abra at her side, of course.

Geneva stared out at the passing landscape from the newly christened East Coast Main Line and let the anger roiling inside carry her determination to fruition. The Earl of Pender had stolen from her one too many times. The most important? Her mother.

The rail coach's jerking motion left her feeling somewhat ill, but not enough to derail her mission. Besides, they'd been on this blasted train for ten hours. "I don't see much hope for a future in passenger rail travel."

"You need to calm down, Gen. This is the fastest mode of travel available, as you well know. Rail travel is here to stay, you mark my words. You're just scared," Abra added softly. "The earl you're planning to confront is a very powerful man." She pointed to Geneva's tapping foot. "That hasn't slowed once since we boarded. Did you even nap?"

Geneva's foot stilled, knowing her friend was right—she *was* scared. She glanced to the corner, where Pasha dozed without stirring. "No." She turned a glare at her friend. "I did try."

Abra moved her attention back to her periodical. "Mmm."

A tap sounded on the door and a stiff porter looked in. His glance went to Abra with a frown then turned to Geneva. "Ten minutes to Alnmouth Station, miss."

"Thank you," Abra said. At which point the door shut a little too hard.

The unexpected episode struck the perfect degree of lightness Geneva required in the moment. She grinned for what felt like the first time since discovering her mother's half-written note. "They hate when you do that, you know."

"What they hate is my Jamaican heritage," Abra returned.

"Yes." Geneva took her hand and squeezed. "I just wish you managed your peers with such aplomb," she added, scowling.

Abra sighed. "I know and I love you for it."

As promised, the train pulled into Alnmouth ten minutes later. The station bustled with activity, travelers hugging loved ones, children running in all directions on the concrete platform. Geneva stepped onto solid ground, her body still vibrating from the train's rough rhythm.

The early morning air was fresh and damp with dew. She drew in a bracing breath as she, Abra, and Pasha made their way past the small ticket office, through the moderate-sized, brick building. It appeared to serve as a waiting area of sorts with large, mullioned windows that lined the ceiling, the walls, even the doors that let in loads of natural light. Benches lined both walls of the long, echoing building, but hardly anyone was sitting through the mass of chaos.

They carried their own portmanteaus and once out the doors on the front side of the station, Geneva located the livery stable instantly. "This way," she said. Cloaking herself in sheer determination, she threw her shoulders back and marched right up to the stablemaster. "I'm in need of a carriage."

He looked her up and down, frowning. "Where ye headed?"

Abra answered in her poshest Lady Abra voice. "Stonemare."

Geneva nodded. "We have urgent business with the Earl of Pender."

The grizzled man tugged at his old-fashioned pointed beard, reminiscent of the Guy Fawkes era. "Won't be seein' the old earl, I reckon'." His eyes grew calculating. "Ye drivin' yerself?" To his credit, he didn't appear to find umbrage with Abra. A sign Geneva took as encouraging.

"If I must," she returned, impatience prickling her. She was so close, she could taste it.

"Ye ever handled the ribbons?"

She flashed a quick glance at Abra, whose eyes widened. "Yes," Geneva lied. *How hard could it be?*

Harder than it seemed, she soon learned. The nag he'd let them was more inclined to graze alongside the road they traveled, based on the directions the stablemaster had provided, than remaining on the compacted, narrow dirt path. But Geneva was nothing if not persevering.

The hazy sun with which the morning had begun was disappearing behind darkening clouds. By the time Stonemare materialized, its turrets obscured in parts, exposing only battlements. The scene leaped from the pages of a Mrs. Radcliffe novel, complete with a pile of crumbled stone that may have actually been one of the turrets. The surprise was that the roof appeared intact atop tiles that should have withstood the elements. Even for Northumberland.

Though still early, even by country standards, a carriage was parked in the sweep.

She drew her dilapidated cart to a stop and hopped down.

An ancient man manifested from the gloom. His gnarled hand took up the reins. "Surprised ye didn't end up walking with this old bag o' bones." His voice reminded her of a sack of rocks. That was all he said before ambling away with her horse and cart.

The motion startled her. "Wait! Our bags."

He just lifted a hand, acknowledging she'd spoken, and kept going, the slight breeze stirring the gray-streaked, scraggly hair that hung down his back.

"This place is terrifying," Abra whispered.

"We'll see about that." Geneva strode to the open doors and peered inside, startling another ancient man she assumed was the butler. "I'm here to see the earl." Her voice echoed sharply in the vast foyer.

Before he could respond, a much younger man entered the

hall from another door. He was large. Tall, as muscular as a Scot, but with black hair and eyes that were as gray as a storming sea. He was dressed to the nines, or at least he was to Geneva's decided lack of knowledge of men's fashion. "I'll handle this, Winfield."

Oddly, the butler melted away, leaving the younger man to pierce her with a gaze that made her skin tingle.

"And, who might you be?" His mildness took her aback.

"Miss Geneva Wimbley of London to see the Earl of Pender."

His gaze flicked over her that appeared almost dismissive, but for the hard swallow given away by his bobbing Adam's apple. "My brother is not due until the week's end." His voice, however, remained firmly in control.

She wasn't certain how she felt about that... *Wait...* "I'm sorry, did you say...*brother?*" That didn't seem right. She tilted her head to one side with the wavering image of the man in the black greatcoat sweeping through her. She'd been five. That man would have been considerably older by now. Wouldn't he? By some twenty years. "I'm speaking of the *earl,*" she reiterated, slowly, *enunciating* clearly. Truly, was she *not* speaking English?

Amusement in the form of twitching lips met her eyes. "Yes, that would be my brother, Lucius, formerly Viscount Perlsea. He is the current Earl of Pender."

"But..." Geneva shook her head, flabbergasted, and glanced at Abra, panic welling in her chest.

"We were made to understand the earl had returned home last week. To Stonemare," Abra said pointedly.

The man's eyes narrowed and his voice hardened. "That's not possible."

"Isn't it?" The new voice came from behind.

Geneva spun, surprised, to face a man who was startlingly similar to the other.

"Blast it, Lucius," the first man muttered. "You spoil all my fun."

Fun? The word felt foreign to Geneva. It wasn't *fun* that she'd lost her mother at the age of fifteen. It wasn't *fun* that her father had threatened her life hours afterwards. And, that train ride—certainly hadn't been *fun*.

Like molasses, the man's words wove another thread of shock through her.

The Earl. Of Pender. *Lucius?* This was Meredith's husband? Geneva hadn't attended the wedding. The duke hadn't allowed it. She glanced at Abra, who gave a barely discernable nod. She recognized him, then.

Geneva turned back to Meredith's husband. His dark hair, almost black, was disheveled with the first sign of gray touching his temples. Sharp, angular features appeared prominent due to the high cheekbones. She met Abra's widened eyes again, the two women reading one another's thoughts as they so often did. Something had happened to the earl.

As one, Geneva and Meredith turned, their gazes out the huge, wooden door with its black, iron brackets, that stood open. But, no. Meredith wasn't there. Their friend hadn't accompanied her husband? And why should she have? According to Meredith, he'd deserted her three years ago and hadn't once returned to Cornwall.

Geneva forced her attention back to the new earl.

He was looking at his brother, ignoring Geneva, Abra, and Pasha. "Yes, I'm home. And I have good news. Sander, Verda, and Julius are but a stone's throw behind me." A devilish smirk tipped his lips.

A young woman of considerable beauty—flaxen hair, navy eyes—peered around the first man's shoulder. "What?" Her voice reminded Geneva of champagne bubbles floating from their delicate flute and blinking out before they reached the rafters. She wore a frock that was obviously of the latest fashion. French, perhaps. The lemon-yellow of her full-skirted silk dress looked soft as butter. Draping lace of cream, embroidered red flowers outlined the godet with touches of green leaves. It was a lovely contrast. The expression on her face, however, contradicted the overall impression. "What are you doing here, Lucius?" Her pretty face twisted into one of shock—her mouth hung open and tears shimmered before she quickly blinked them away. She stomped her foot like a small child.

Geneva took a step closer to Abra and Pasha out of the proverbial line of fire.

Again the smirk appeared from Meredith's errant husband. "Apologies, my dear. I feel I've interrupted some interesting... incident."

So did Geneva.

Man Number One winced, while the new earl's eyes seemed to devour the woman in yellow.

Blood rushed Geneva's ears at the daunting implications, obliterating any exchange between the two. How was she to find her locket now? The sickness she'd experienced toward the end of the train ride was nothing compared to the now sudden nausea. "But... the old earl..." she whispered.

With an elegant bow worthy of Prince Albert, "Lucius" rose back to his full, impressive height. Arrogance emitted from him like a fog. "Is no longer. As of two days ago."

Her stomach cramped. "Two days..." She'd missed the earl, the answers she craved, by just two miserable days.

Loathing, hot and furious, curled through her, watching Meredith's horrible husband wave out a hand toward his brother. "Where is Father's body?" The stark, frigid demeanor of this new Earl of Pender struck Geneva anew. This... this unfeeling *brute* was whom her friend was tied to for life! Oh, to have her trusty knife—

Man Number One spoke. "The parlor, of course."

More shock—or was it dread?—complete *shock* pumped through Geneva's blood. Panic. Panic too. That sweltering greatcoat. Swallowing hard, she gripped Abra's hand. "What am I to do?" she whispered.

Abra's hand squeezed back. But her eyes were locked on the younger earl, seething venom. Outright fury, near hatred that was so unlike her friend. Even in their darkest days at Miss Greensley's, Geneva had never witnessed such unbridled contempt from her. Geneva, yes, as she was unrefined. Not Abra. Never Abra.

A footman moved into the vestibule and held out a dark greatcoat to Man Number One, but he waved him off. "Never mind, Fletcher." He glanced at the pretty woman in the yellow dress and winced again. "I'm afraid plans have changed. I'm sorry, Docia."

The pretty woman drew herself up, donning her own cloak, albeit an invisible one. "Yes, I can see that." She stormed past Geneva and Abra, leaving a cloud of expensive perfume on her way to the door. "And it's *Miss Hale* to you."

Within minutes, the sound of horse hooves pounded the ground. But they went on forever and seemed to grow closer rather than farther away.

But then there was the sound of carriage doors opening, followed by people chattering, then crowding the entry as they pushed their way inside. The butler reappeared and Geneva stepped farther into the shadows, pulling Abra along with her.

Now that the Earl of Pender she'd sought was dead, locket aside, it was clear the answers she desired with every fiber of her being were lost to her forever.

CHAPTER FOUR

Miss Geneva Wimbley's blood-drained features had Noah taking a step forward, if only to catch her from a dead faint. But Uncle Sander and Aunt Verda's entrance amid Lucius's untimely arrival blocked his effort. Miss Wimbley had moved into the shadows and was clutching her companion's hand. She had her own pillar of strength, it seemed. Her white-knuckled grip deepened the contrast in the pigment of the two women's skin. The rich, amber tone of her friend's complexion and striking hazel eyes that leaned toward green was an arresting combination that spoke of an interesting heritage.

Not quite as interesting as Miss Wimbley from London, however, with her deep, dark-chestnut shade of hastily gathered curls at her nape. The quaint, upturned nose, and stubborn chin teased him with an interwoven thread of discomfort. He was a bastard for the relief plowing through him at her sudden appearance. Not in the literal sense, of course. He was definitely the son of the former Earl of Pender and his countess. And they had been legally wed.

No, the sense of liberation solidified Noah's earlier misgivings that a union with Docia would have led to catastrophic failure. Of course, he would have to deal with the fact that he'd promised his hand to his childhood nemesis. But there was plenty of time for that later. First and foremost was handling the nature of his father's demise. Elaborating on the nature of his death in a letter had been out of the question.

Aunt Verda rushed forward and hugged him. "Oh, darling, how awful for you"—she turned to Lucius, including him—"both, regarding your father. We decided not to stay the night in London after all and rushed home." Her voice boomed against freshly waxed floors that resembled nothing of the dilapidation of 1827 when she'd entered their lives nineteen years ago. The echo startled him into action.

His Uncle Sander appeared next. "Are we to gather in the doorway all day, Noah?"

"Sorry," he mumbled then looking around, he frowned. "Where's Julius?" After all these years, the protectiveness over his younger brother hadn't waned in the least.

"Here." Julius appeared in the door with a scraggly ragdoll on his shoulders.

"Me, too." Said ragdoll was fourteen and much too old for such antics. Her bright-red hair matched her mother's, but her gray eyes were Oshea through and through.

Noah shook his head. "Honestly, Isabelle." He strode forward and lifted his fragile cousin from Julius's shoulders, set her carefully to her feet, and held her until she balanced herself. An infected snake bite at the age of four had left her foot in a condition no specialty doctor could fix, at least to Sander and Verda's satisfaction. Not in a manner that outweighed the risks involved. The imp's vastly independent nature would have them all bound for Bedlam by the time the chit married.

Isabelle wrapped her arms around Noah's waist and hugged him tightly. "I missed you."

"I missed you too, poppet."

"It's starting to rain," Julius said, urging everyone inside. He stopped, coming face to face with Miss Wimbley and her companion. "Oh, who have we here?"

The entire family stopped and all eyes turned to the new-comers.

Noah picked up the introductions. "This is Miss Geneva Wimbley of London and…" His voice trailed off.

"Er, yes." Miss Wimbley recovered and color returned to her cheeks in an engaging blush. Something he suspected didn't happen often. "This is my friend, Lady Abra Washington."

Washington. English, then. The name was familiar, but Noah rarely moved through society and instead tucked the information away.

"The library, then," Noah said. "Father is laid out in the parlor for viewing. I expect the next few days will be quite hectic. The castle will be overrun with visitors."

The family filed down the hall, leaving Noah with Miss Wimbley, Lady Abra, and their maid.

Baldric's shadow darkened the entry. He tossed three valises inside. "The ladies' baggage," he rasped out, then faded like the apparition Noah always believed him to be.

"We had no notion Lord Pender…" Lady Abra's voice faded. "Of course, we shall remove ourselves to an inn in Alnmouth immediately. This will be a trying time for your family."

Miss Wimbley's spine straightened and her jaw tightened. She met Noah's gaze with a direct one of her own and he couldn't tear his eyes from eyes so deep a blue, he expected to see stars reflected from a night sky.

Winfield emitted a small cough. "Master Noah?"

Noah started, but his gaze remained captive. "Inform Mrs. Knagg to have their bags brought to the Blue Suite in the west tower." He was not about to turn them away. There were too many questions surrounding the women's sudden appearance. Perhaps it was the determination in Miss Wimbley's stance. Certainly, it was not the color of her eyes—navy eyes that didn't belong in Northumberland's rare, sun-filled days. Eyes that color were indeed out of the ordinary. "If you don't mind a visit with the family?"

A wrinkled creased Miss Wimbley's forehead, as if she hadn't comprehended the question.

Her friend cut her gaze to Miss Wimbley then answered for them. "Truly, we don't wish to intrude. Perhaps a quick freshening up? That's all we require if it's not too much bother, of course."

Noah caught the swift squeeze of Miss Wimbley's fingers on her friend's. *A silent thank you.* There was definitely more to their visit than met his eyes. He sensed a challenge, and it fired his blood as nothing had in some time. Smiling, he said, "Nonsense, Lady Abra. I insist you stay. Many of the ton will be arriving soon. I expect you'll know most everyone. Winfield, where *is* Mrs. Knagg?"

"The kitchens, sir. I'll retrieve her—"

"No. No, Winfield. Don't bother. Have Hicks retrieve their bags. I'll show the ladies up myself. Ladies?" He led the way up the grand staircase that gleamed under Verda's care over the years, pointedly ignoring his aunt's, uncle's, and both brothers' raised brows. Thankfully, Isabelle hadn't learned that intricate and annoying move as of yet.

Once on the landing, the walk was short down the main corridor to the back portion of the west tower.

Now that his father was gone, the earl's suite would naturally go to Lucius and his bride if Lucius ever saw fit to release her from another Pender holding—the Cornwall property's Perlsea Keep—imprisonment. Ah, well. No one held a grudge more effectively than his eldest brother. Noah took another sharp turn to the right.

At one time, long ago, the Blue Suite had belonged to Uncle Sander, but after he and Verda had wed some twenty-three years now, they'd adopted the eastern wing of the castle, which had initially housed Aunt Verda, as their main residence. It allowed for plenty of privacy.

After the difficulties of a horrid event when Isabelle had been but four, she too, had rooms near her parents rather than residing in the nursery above stairs. Even after a decade, guilt still gripped him with the capacity of the teeth of an iron trap.

Noah was wildly curious as he considered the friends and their maid from a covert gaze. He pushed open the door to the sitting room and ushered them in.

"The suite holds three bedchambers," he explained as they strolled down a wide corridor. He opened the door to the renovated sitting room that was more than suitable for his unexpected guests.

He indicated two doors to his right, meeting Lady Abra's hazel eyes. "The larger one and a smaller one, convenient for your maid."

She indicated her thanks with an incline of her head.

Miss Wimbley strode across the chamber to another door and peered in. "Ah, this shall do nicely for me." Pure excitement gleamed from her dark eyes. For the first time since learning of his father's passing, something hard, and… and large, odd, shifted in Noah's chest. He couldn't seem to pull his gaze from hers.

A long pause ensued until the air was fraught with an undeniable awkwardness.

"Sir?" Miss Wimbley's voice seemed to echo through a long tunnel, startling him.

He cleared his throat. "My apologies." His hand swept out. "Your bags should arrive soon. I'll have hot water sent up immediately. We keep country hours at Stonemare. Luncheon is served at one, and dinner at seven." He backed from the chamber, closing the door on his exit, pausing momentarily, and contemplating what had just happened.

An explosion of muffled feminine laughter sounded from behind.

Chuckling to himself, Noah found one of Stonemare's two footmen, Fletcher, and ordered water for his guests, then made for the library to face the multitude of questions with which his family was surely bursting.

AT THE DOOR, Noah forced himself to enter the library. The

chaotic scene was both familiar and annoying. Julius teasing Isabelle; Aunt Verda standing back but watching with hawkeyed alertness; Lucius, with his typical broody aura, staring out at the sudden downpour; and Uncle Sander? He pierced Noah with a steady gaze. "Where's Docia? It isn't like her to not be in the thick of Pender business. Her carriage nearly ran us to ground."

The chaos around him shifted to avid curiosity.

"Are you going to marry her?" Isabelle's question was a gut punch worthy of an opponent from Mantons.

Resentment colored Lucius's hard expression, with a tightened jaw and sneer curling his lip. "Why wouldn't he, Issie? She's his for the taking." He stormed out, slamming the door behind him.

Verda turned shrewd green eyes on him. "Are you?"

Noah hedged. "We've talked about it."

His aunt shook her head but refrained from saying anything. She didn't have to. As governess to Docia and Noah, his aunt hadn't been a fan of Docia's. However, over the years, they'd come to a tolerable understanding, and Aunt Verda would never allow harm to come to her. Nor would Docia harm her. He was almost positive.

"Who is Miss Wimbley?" Isabelle asked. "Her friend is quite interesting."

"*Lady* Abra is the distinguished daughter of Westbridge. He's a marquess and quite powerful," Aunt Verda said, surprising him.

"How knowledgeable of you, Aunt. In any event, I expect you all to respect their presence." Noah was adamant. Also intrigued.

"But what are they doing here?" Isabelle insisted.

Since Noah had witnessed Miss Wimbley's shock at hearing of his father's death, the same questions nagged him. "Father's services, of course. What other reason could there be?"

"Noah," Uncle Sander said. "A word, please." He glanced at Isabelle. "Run along, my dear. I have business to discuss with your cousin."

Aunt Verda's brows lifted, but she didn't say anything, just took Isabelle's hand and left the room. The door latched softly behind them.

"All right, Noah. Let's have it," Sander said. "The truth. What happened to Damien?"

Noah took in a deep breath and let it out slowly. There was no way to soften a blow with a blunt object. "He was stabbed. In the heart." Saying the words aloud still wounded Noah to the core. Such a shocking end to an earl of Father's rank.

"Gads," Sander breathed. "I suppose his notoriety's finally done him in."

"There'll be no keeping the facts from the gossips," Noah told him. "I didn't dare relay details in a letter. I wanted to warn you before word got about. The parish constable has cooperated thus far. You may as well prepare yourself. We'll be descended upon within days, if not hours."

✦—————✦————✦

CHAPTER FIVE

"**H**OW DO YOU expect to explain your presence, Geneva? Lord Pender is dead."

Geneva watched as Pasha tugged out an array of colorful frocks from Abra's portmanteau and hung them on the pegs, then stuffed the bag at the bottom of the wardrobe. "I'll think of something," she muttered, hoping that would be the case.

"You should unpack," Abra told her.

Pasha walked to the door, obviously prepared to do just that for Geneva, but Geneva stopped her.

"Don't bother, Pasha. I have my doubts on the length of our welcome. Go settle yourself in your chamber." Geneva waved her hand in the direction of a discreet adjoining door.

The maid nodded and silently took her leave.

Geneva paced the plush carpet. "I cannot believe Meredith's husband did not bring her!" She turned, facing Abra, planting tightened fists on her hips. "That cur. That *libertine*." She couldn't think of a term harsh enough for the viscount—no. He was *earl* now.

Abra's expression took on that fiery fury it had had when she'd first laid eyes on the new earl. Her lips compressed and her hazel eyes flashed again with unadulterated contempt.

"What?" Geneva asked. "What is it you know that I don't?"

"I was *at* St. George's for their wedding," Abra bit out. "The bishop had to *remind* him to speak his vows. It was a horrid act to pull on a young woman who had been forced into such a situation. None of which was Meredith's fault."

Geneva strode over to the settee that faced a low fire in the grate and dropped beside her friend, remorse suddenly gripping her. "We really should have gone to Cornwall."

Abra clasped her hand. "No," she said earnestly. "You have every right for answers. Mr. Oshea has handed us an opportunity we can't possibly pass up. We're here to find those answers. You deserve them. I wouldn't be anywhere else."

"But your father," Geneva said. "There's still time. We could leave here today. Take the train straight to Cornwall, and he would never be any the wiser."

"And what if we get there, and she's on her way to Northumberland? Surely, word is out regarding Pender's death. I expect a good many of the ton are headed here now."

"Lud." The palm of Geneva's hand slapped her forehead. "I didn't even think of—oh, no. Your father and stepmother could—" She swallowed hard. "Oh, dear," she whispered. "Martindale." The Beau Monde was full of scoundrels who were insensitive, and worse, deliberately cruel.

Despite the amber tone of Abra's skin, it paled.

"Lord Martindale can't hurt me. Not any longer. Lord Ruskin…" Her voice trailed off.

"Has he asked you yet?" Geneva spoke gently.

Abra's eyes widened, but then welled with tears. "No," she whispered. "How did you—"

"Hannah mentioned yesterday before you arrived. We were finishing up the Education Reform article. She said a date had been selected."

Her eyes dropped to her lap, where her fingers interlocked so tightly, her knuckles lightened. "Perhaps he's decided on another." Her friend suffered from a belief of inadequacy in her social status. Completely invalid concerns in Geneva's view. Abra never considered how her hazel eyes evoked her father's heritage and how proudly he viewed his daughter, daring anyone to speak ill of her. The man was a crack shot with a musket and a pistol and swords.

Something Geneva's own father would never have considered. Even sober. He'd just waved his emptied bottles of gin about then fallen over in the process.

Abra's lips firmed again. The stubbornness unfamiliar to those who didn't know her well, or *chose* not to know her well, set in. "We're staying. Stepmother hates leaving London." But she didn't sound so sure and surveyed the chamber, effectively avoiding Geneva.

Geneva followed her gaze around the lovely room with its paper of pale blue, sprinkled about with posies of pink, that reminded one of a summer day in Hyde Park. The coverlet was snow white and covered with fluffy pillows.

Geneva hugged her. "All right, if you're sure."

"I'm sure." With a small smile, the tension faded from Abra's shoulders. She speared Geneva with her usual pragmatism. "How shall we go about locating your medallion?"

Geneva stood and scowled. "I certainly can't mention it." She pursed her lips. "Mr. Oshea seems a reasonable enough man. Perhaps I can casually show him Mama's half-written note and go from there." She strolled over and looked inside Abra's case. Then, testament to the friends they were, Geneva pulled out Abra's jewelry box as well as her silver-handled brush, a wide-tooth comb, matching mirror, and arranged them atop the vanity.

Abra rose and went to the vanity. She straightened the already straightened hair instruments then turned to Geneva with an air of excitement shining from her eyes. "So what shall we do first to find your locket?"

"Don't be daft, *Lady* Abra. There is no *we*, my dear. You know your stepmother is gnashing her teeth to acquire Martindale for you. Bah, I should just toss in the proverbial towel and crawl back to London. It's just a shame I haven't the temperament for it."

"At least you admit it." Abra grinned. "All right. Let's enter the lion's den. See what we are up against."

"Sooner rather than later is my usual adage," Geneva agreed.

They moved to the sitting room and Abra leaned in Pasha's chamber. "We'll return shortly, Pasha. Mr. Oshea has promised hot water."

Geneva waited for Abra then led the way through to the main corridor. "I wonder what's down that hall." She spoke in a low, barely audible tone.

Excitement shimmered between them reminiscent of their school days. Missing only were Hannah and Meredith.

"Let's look," Abra whispered back.

Curiosity drove Geneva and she nodded. Together, they followed the length of the hall to a set of double doors. Geneva set her ear against it, but all was silent. She glanced at Abra with a small smile, but her friend, even with a small shake of her head, knew Geneva's largest failing was her obstinate way and curiosity that kept her in trouble more than out. Geneva clasped the latch and pushed down.

Abra gasped and Geneva shushed her.

For such an old castle that from the outside looked so dilapidated, it appeared ready to fall around their ears, the door didn't squeak when she pushed it inward. Geneva peered inside. In the corner, a pianoforte of mahogany polished to perfection with graceful cabriole legs tied by brass casters sat on a raised platform. It's awfully huge for a music room," she whispered. The one at Miss Greensley's wasn't near this size.

Large, mullioned windows with triangular, metal strips covered the far wall from the ceiling down to hip level. Beneath them was a cushioned bench that stretched the full length of the wall. Enormous mirrors rather than artwork graced the other walls. Overhead, ornate moldings edged the ceiling and an old-fashioned chandelier held some fifty unlit candles. They were currently unneeded, as the rain had stopped and the sun reappeared in its hazy glow.

"Don't—"

Ignoring her timid companion, Geneva stepped inside, awed

by the chamber's vastness. "This must be the music room."

Abra's muffled huff and light footsteps followed Geneva. "No. It's a ballroom. Much larger than those I've attended in London," she said in a hushed tone.

"How can you tell?"

Abra pointed to a raised recessed area. "That's the musicians' gallery—so they don't interfere with the dancing."

"Goodness. They host balls here?" Geneva's voice seemed to echo and bound against all those mirrors.

She shrugged. "Doubtful. We're in Northumberland. I suspect the *ton* rarely travels this far north and east much." She strolled over to the pianoforte but clasped her hands at her lower back. Abra was quite the accomplished musician in her own right and was likely tempted to touch the keys. "Someone plays," she said. "It's dust free."

"Interesting," Geneva murmured. "Perhaps you'll be allowed to exercise your skills while we're here."

Abra straightened and stalked back to her. "As I mentioned before, my dear, like you, I don't anticipate a long stay." Her annoyance was in full form. "Don't you have some pamphlets to complete for Hannah?"

"When have I ever left anything unfinished?" she returned. "Surely, they have mail service from Northumberland to London."

"You know how dangerous it is to put such information through the post. And to her home? That isn't wise." Her defensiveness was most telling. "If Ruskin—" But she stopped there.

Geneva studied her friend, reminded by Hannah's words of a date being considered. "You're frightened he'll learn what we are about," she said gently.

Abra's eyes widened, revealing exactly that.

Geneva took a leveling breath. "I don't believe the baron reads through his sister's correspondence. If it makes you feel better, I shall just write and ready the articles for our return." A relieved *whoosh* swept the air. "Thank you," she whispered.

Geneva couldn't pull her eyes from Abra. "You really care for him, don't you?"

Her eyes shimmered and she quickly turned away. "I don't wish to speak of it." She mastered her emotion, went to the door and pulled it open. "Are you ready for the lion's den?"

Noah Oshea appeared in the arch like a dark, avenging angel. "'Lion's den'?" He echoed as he moved inside. His younger brother and the niece whose name escaped Geneva came into view.

She wanted to sink through the floor. But she was not one to back away from awkward situations. She raised her chin. "I was curious." She spoke a little too staunchly and caught Abra's small flinch. "Apologies. I'm not nearly as refined as my friend."

The young girl had bright-red hair, framing an elfin face with a stubborn chin of her own. She grinned.

"It's, er, Miss..." Geneva floundered, mortified she hadn't paid closer attention.

"Isabelle, my lady." The girl didn't appear to mind in the least. She dipped a curtsey and gave an infectious smile instead.

"It's just Miss Wimbley," Geneva told her. "The 'lady' is my friend. Lady Abra."

Miss Isabelle's mouth formed a perfect "O."

Geneva rescued her. "Who is the musician?"

Miss Isabelle's smile turned shy. "Me."

"Ah, as is Lady Abra," Geneva said in a conspiratorial whisper.

Miss Isabelle swung her gaze to Abra. "Truly?"

Abra nodded.

"Oh, may I hear you play?" Abra's flinch this time was much more pronounced.

Mr. Oshea could have worn a cloak of feathers for all his bristling. "Perhaps after luncheon, poppet. Our guests are surely famished."

"Oh, yes." The child's face turned an engaging shade of pink that clashed with that red hair. "Of course."

The younger brother grinned, his gray eyes flashing with mischief. "I'm Julius Oshea," he said. "We came to show you the way to the dining room."

"All of you?" Geneva nearly moaned. "I, er, mean…"

Julius Oshea went to Abra and held out his arm and bailed Geneva out, saying, "It couldn't be helped. We were curious."

Abra shot her a helpless look, but Geneva pressed her lips together in an attempt to suppress a smile. The attempt failed and she basked in her friend's perturbation. Such times were so rare, after all. She gave a little shrug.

Noah Oshea did not offer his arm to Geneva, instead taking Miss Isabelle's, leaving Geneva to follow. Within seconds, the reason became ultimately clear as he walked with great patience due to a slight limp that exuded from Miss Isabelle's left foot.

Something decidedly odd regarding the household touched Geneva. No one seemed particularly sad or disquieted with the passing of the previous Earl of Pender. But then, considering the content of the note Geneva had happened upon from her mother, she suspected that shouldn't have come as a surprise.

NOAH THOUGHT LUNCHEON would never end and after the fifth course, he pushed back his chair. He'd never gone in for port and cigars. Lucius hadn't even appeared for the meal. "Would you care for a tour of the grounds, Miss Wimbley, Lady Abra?" Noah asked.

Miss Wimbley's expressive face lit up with curiosity, stirring something remotely odd and unfamiliar in Noah's chest, and he caught the minutest wince in her friend's expression. "I'd be delighted, sir," Miss Wimbley breathed. A fiery warmth spread over his skin and felt as tangible as if that breath had breached the clothes he wore.

In the foyer, Hicks assisted the women with their cloaks. He swept his own about his shoulders and watched as she donned her straw bonnet and aging kid leather gloves. Whatever else Miss Wimbley was, she was not steeped in funds. Not like Lady Abra.

Miss Wimbley had been lively company throughout the meal. Much too forthright for polite society. After all the years around Docia, Noah found it quite refreshing. She had nothing of Docia's dainty measure. Miss Wimbley's steps were purposeful, her laugh just this side of boisterous, the look in her eyes bold and captivated by her surroundings.

But another thought took hold, raising Noah's hackles. If she thought to go after Lucius, the woman was in for a shock. Surely, she knew Lucius was married to the Duke of Rathbourne's only daughter. News of their nuptials had been in all the broadsheets, the clubs, the ballrooms—if his brother was to be believed. The notion of Miss Wimbley parading around London as Lucius's mistress pricked Noah with biting discomfort. He'd only offered a tour of the grounds to learn the reason for her appearance. At least that was what he told himself.

The wind was gusty on this spring day. More times than not, low, dark clouds hid the sun. The weather along the coast this far north was predictably unpredictable. Downright dangerous if one didn't know the moors well.

He escorted the ladies down the portico and he paused, trying to determine the direction he wished to take.

Miss Wimbley didn't wait on them, however, turning toward his most monumental youthful lapse of judgement: the fallen turret.

Noah glanced at Lady Abra, who just shook her head as if reining in Miss Wimbley were an impossible task, her eyes saying, *Much luck to you, sir.* With their roll toward the heavens, Lady Abra took a seat on a bench within watching distance, leaving Noah to sprint after her fleeing friend.

Miss Wimbley stopped before his failed experiment, her head

cocked to one side. "What happened here?"

Lucius strolled up from around the pile. "One of Noah's disastrous experiments." Noah did not like the smile on his face. More surprising was her reaction to Lucius. As if he were infected with a contagion, she stepped away from him, the smile on her face so razor-thin, her lips went bloodless.

She turned her back on him, cutting her gaze to Noah. "What sort of experiment?"

Red crawled up Noah's neck. He rubbed a palm over it. "I thought I could turn lead into gold. It's, er, not possible."

Miss Wimbley spun around, facing him outright, her lovely mouth agape, completely appearing to have forgotten Lucius. "You blew up a part of your—" She swallowed. Loudly. "Your castle?"

"Technically, it's mine," Lucius said.

Her eyes flashed with some seething emotion, but she never turned her head, still staring at Noah. "A little too much saltpeter," he muttered.

Lucius stared at the pile of rocks. "Why haven't you had the rubble cleared?"

"I'm allowing the locals to make use of it. What do you care, besides? This is the first we've seen of you since your wedding."

Disgust covered Lucius's brooding features. "I don't wish to speak of that harrowing event." He bowed at Miss Wimbley. "Until later, miss." He sauntered off, leaving Noah with Miss Wimbley looking after his older brother.

"He didn't like his wedding?" she asked not quite so nonchalantly as she'd likely intended.

The undercurrent in her tone had Noah turning a sharpened gaze on her. "Our father promised his hand when he was a lad of thirteen. We didn't learn of it until Lucius was all set to offer for Miss Hale a few years ago."

"The woman who dashed out this morning? She's quite beautiful." This came out somewhat grudgingly.

Noah paused, struck by the dulcet melody of her voice. It

flowed like a gentle brook over rocks. Even with its stingy tone, the sound was soft, soothing, pleasing to the ear.

A long pause ensued and he realized he was staring. Her plump lips mesmerizing him.

He started, warmth crawling up his neck. "Er, yes. Lucius is still quite angry at how the events unfolded." His brother had never been more excited than he had been at the prospect of wedding Docia. More than Noah had seen him in years.

It had seemed Lucius had finally decided to take an interest in the earldom's holdings. He'd rushed to London, met with the solicitors, purchased a ring, then run into Father and the Duke of Rathbourne at White's, according to Lucius, or at least as far as Noah had been able to piece from Lucius and their father.

Later, Noah had been called into Father's study by Uncle Sander, who had sat behind the desk with Noah in the chair across, where he was informed that Lucius refused to be counted on for their future. Lucius's resentment, while understandable, would affect them all.

From that day on, Noah was tasked on assisting his uncle in looking after the earldom's funds. Sander had built a brilliant strategy going from the small-scale home-based handwoven cloth the villagers had produced to more beneficial means with the land's natural resources for quarrying and processing decorative stones. Even more so when the Berwick Railway had expanded from Newcastle to Tyne into Northeast England.

With his hands at his lower back and a brisk, cool wind in his face, Noah allowed Miss Wimbley to lead their path. They walked in companionable silence around his chemistry-experiment-gone-bad. He'd been fortunate he hadn't leveled Stonemare into the sea below, sitting on the edge of the cliffs as it did.

Miss Wimbley came to a stop, plucked the ties of her bonnet free, and tore it off as if it choked her. The winds whipped her skirts into a frenzy, giving him a tantalizing view of slim hips and shapely calves. In build and coloring—but for her dark hair—she was similar to Docia. Unlike Docia, there was a vibrancy about her that shimmered in the muted sunlight. The band confining her hair was no match for a sudden updraft gust. The light-colored leather strip seemed to suspend in midair then floated down and disappeared long before it hit water. "Oh, dear."

The dark-brown curls barely draped past her shoulders in a surprisingly unfashionable length. But the shorter style suited her delicate, pixie-like features. She turned then, facing him with an impish grin.

The sight mesmerized him and refused to let go.

"I expect you're wondering why Lady Abra and I showed up on your doorstep," she said. Her frankness shouldn't have surprised him, but it did.

The melodic timbre again held him spellbound. She looked up and squinted into the sun with no care for her complexion. He caught sight of a sprinkle of freckles across her nose that teased him to distraction. Her deep-chestnut curls had an unnerving effect on his libido. She was like a dark avenging angel but for her startling navy eyes. The perfect illusion, he suspected, as her words penetrated. He'd almost forgotten his own mission to learn what she was about. "Er, ah, I... Yes, I admit to a certain interest," he said slowly, welcoming her entry to the conversation.

She gave him a sharp nod. "I have reason to believe your father seduced my mother."

A slow chill seeped into his bones. "I don't understand." Yet he was afraid he did.

"Your father is a known libertine." Of course, it didn't occur to her to use a more polite word. Her boldness shifted from refreshing to an irritation that set his teeth on edge.

"Was."

Her brows lifted. "Pardon?"

"Was. My father is dead. Perhaps that fact escaped your memory. It was this morning, after all, when the topic was raised in the vestibule."

Once the words penetrated, her face blotched a fiery red. "Oh, I'm—" Her voice cracked.

Noah winced, instantly regretting his forthright harshness. He hadn't meant to embarrass her. Not really. "Where is your mother? I can't imagine she gave you leave to travel here on your own to confront a known libertine."

"No. She would have been suitably appalled," she said with another of those razor-sharp smiles that did not reach her eyes. She lifted her delicate shoulders. "She died in '38 and left no instructions on how to conduct my life." She glanced over her shoulder, but they'd drifted from Lady Abra's line of sight.

He was struck with a bolt of lightning. Such fortitude masked other emotions, he'd guess. Fear? Vulnerability? Anger? Which was it and, why? She was a woman virtually alone. He speared her with a depth usually reserved for one of his experiments. No, she didn't appear frightened, but that didn't mean she wasn't. This went deeper than she was revealing. "My condolences on your mother's passing, Miss Wimbley. That must have been most difficult for you."

His words didn't turn her into a simpering miss. She ignored his acknowledgement as if he hadn't spoken. No, his words had a whole other unexpected effect. Her spine straightened, her shoulders squared, her chin lifted. Her eyes met his unwavering-ly. "I happened upon your father's name not two weeks past. As I mentioned, I came here for answers from Lord Pender. Your father," she clarified. Her shoulders fell. "But now he's dead." Then she speared him with those oddly shaded blue eyes as the genuine despair in her voice dug into his chest with the force of a dull spoon.

The briny-scented wind whipped her cloak about while he considered how to handle her. But then, he doubted anyone knew how to handle such an obstinate ball of fire. It was her vibrancy that held him enthralled, but he'd never been one ruled by absurdity and certainly not by his emotion. He forced his thoughts into their normal realm of analytical common sense. His scientific process of thinking, he insisted silently.

In that scope, he reluctantly asked, "What kinds of answers?"

She looked back over the jagged edges of the cliffs and didn't speak for a long moment.

He followed her gaze farther out to a small island that jutted from the ocean's floor. He'd always dreamed of boating over, but the Northumberland seas were too violent for any sort of safe crossing. Not with weather that changed on the flip of a shilling.

"I believe it was your father who visited my mother when she was ill. For years, I believed it a dream. I was just a child, you see, but the memory is too vivid."

Noah waited.

"I-I heard her beg him to take me with him."

Startled by that notion, his head shook, balking at what she was inferring. It wasn't possible. "You believe my—" He swallowed. Hard. "The earl is, was, *your* father?"

"I know she doesn't belong to you…"

She jerked around, facing him. "No!" She shuddered. "Absolutely not. My father is—was—a sailor. Hardly ever home. Addicted to the perils of gin, I fear. But he was definitely my father," she said, looking as if it pained her in admitting so.

Her adamant denial sent a shot of harsh relief through him for reasons he refused to examine.

Miss Wimbley inhaled as if bracing herself to continue. "But your father took something from Mama," she said fiercely. "And I want it back."

Julius. She wanted Julius. She'd learned Father's secret somehow. What else could it be?

CHAPTER SIX

"WHAT EXACTLY IS it you believe my father stole?" Mr. Oshea spoke slowly, carefully. There was no defensive stance or immediate denial that his father had indeed stolen anything. And he had. Geneva was certain of it.

A sudden current cut across the cliff, knocking Geneva off her feet. Her arms flailed and for a second, she was horrifyingly airborne. Then her feet were back on solid soil and her arm scorching where Mr. Oshea still held her in an iron grip, dragging her from the edge where she'd stood. "Are you all right?" His words came out in a rush of fearsome brutality.

Her hand splayed her chest. Her heart pounded through the layers of her frock, her cloak, her gloves. She feared the blasted organ would fly from her body if she removed her hand. "Yes. Yes, I-I think so." She'd never been so frightened in her life. Not since she'd taken up the carving knife against Papa's threat all those years ago. She shut out the memories and moved a few more steps from the cliff's edge, hugging herself.

Perhaps Mr. Oshea wished her ill.

She cut her gaze to him. "We should head back." Damn, the tremor in her voice. Showing weakness was not her forte and certainly not in her best interest. A sharp gasp escaped her—perhaps he wished to keep her locket for himself.

"What's wrong?" His words came out amid abrasive, pointed breaths.

Notably, he didn't re-ask his question on what his father had

51

stolen. A question she wasn't inclined to answer. Not yet. Not until she learned if her legacy had indeed been confiscated by Lord Pender. Those memories in her past—her five-year-old self—were so vague and obscured by that sweltering greatcoat that had seemed so ominous at the time, hovered over her, and felt as intensive as to bury her alive.

In silent, mutual consent, they turned as one to the front of the castle. They rounded the corner and Mr. Oshea let out a gurgled sound. "Damnation." The low growl whispered over her skin, raising bumps.

Geneva stopped beside Mr. Oshea and lifted her glance from the path. Abra remained near the bench, standing halfway between the front entrance and the corner where Mr. Oshea and Geneva now stood. Her gaze moved to the shiny carriage she'd pulled behind that morning. Mr. Oshea's words from the hall that morning pushed Abra's presence from her mind. "Isn't that Miss Hale's rig?"

"Er, yes. It is." He edged back from the line of sight.

The action touched Geneva with amusement. "You don't wish to see her again?"

Other carriages began lining the drive.

"She's considered family and has the devil of a temper. Storming out in a huff is hardly unusual for her. I just don't wish to deal with her at the moment. That's all." Now *that* sounded defensive.

Geneva hid a smile that tipped quickly into a frown. "Are you in love with her?" The instant the words left her mouth, she wished to snatch them back. But there they were, floating on the breeze.

He didn't answer right away. Perhaps the words had been carried out to sea and he hadn't heard them. His eyes were stormier than the crashing waves with which she'd nearly experienced an intimate proximity.

An unlikely scenario, however, watching from the corner of her eye as he shoved a hand through his dark hair.

"Forgive me. I tend to be a bit too forthright," she said.

His grunt came out sarcastic. Yes. She was absolutely positively certain she'd heard sarcasm.

His lack of verbal response prompted her further. "It's especially annoying when improper things emerge with no thought on my part."

He cleared his throat. "Think nothing of it." His unreadable tone said it all. She'd overstepped common propriety. As usual.

Gads, it was the story of her irregular life.

"It appears the viewing of my father's body is underway," he said with a resigned sigh that tugged at her sympathies, surprising her.

Geneva straightened her spine and firmed her resolve. She hadn't made the trek to Northumberland only to get distracted by the intricacies of the remaining Oshea clan. "I'd best check on Abra. She's really quite introverted, you know. Thank you for the tour. Oh. And for saving my life."

He inclined his head with a cool smile. "It was the least I could do."

"Of course. An accident while walking might do harm to the family name and all that rot," she muttered, marching away. She started in Abra's direction and stopped. Her friend had moved and was disappearing through the front door among those emerging from carriages. One in particular—shiny, black, outrageously costly—Martindale. Quickly, Geneva turned back to her host. "Is there, um, another entrance? I prefer not"—*facing*—"fighting the crowd."

For the first time since she'd met Noah Oshea, genuine amusement glinted in his eyes, turning his irises from storm gray to something that hinted at dark steel. He took her arm and led her back around the fallen turret to another less visible door. "Right this way."

NOAH DIDN'T BLAME Miss Wimbley for wanting to avoid the throng at the entrance. He rather wished he could as well. After all, he'd been the one to issue the invitations for the service. But if she had aspirations in angling for a husband—

He barely restrained from dropping his head in his hands and groaning aloud. She'd told him why she'd shown up on his doorstep. The danger lay in him, not her. Besides, it was not as if they were likely to run into other guests in this portion of the castle.

With a sure hand on her arm, Noah led her through the rubble to the one door that led to his laboratory. Conundrum that she was, it would be fascinating to gauge her reaction to the various charts and skeletal bones lying about. He pulled the key from his waistcoat pocket, unlocked the door, and lit a candle from one of the sconces.

"What is this place?" Curiosity, not fear, shaded her voice. "It's cold."

"The stairs down lead to my laboratory," he said, assessing her carefully.

To his surprise, her lips twitched. "Dr. Frankenstein?"

His response mirrored hers and then, he couldn't refrain—he grinned outright. "Not quite."

"I've never been in a laboratory. Might I see?"

The stairs were original to Stonemare. Concrete and cold. As a safety measure, he descended before her. "Take hold of the rail, please. The descent is treacherous." His boots echoed compared to the scuff of her kid-leather-booted heels. She was light on her feet. That was a surprise because despite Miss Wimbley's ethereal and waiflike appearance, her presence seemed larger than life. She did not present to him as someone prone to fading into unpainted wainscoting.

He opened the door then went about lighting the lamps within, feeling the heat of her gaze with his movements about. He *never* left candles burning, not a single one and not for a single moment. Too much could go wrong. He'd learned much from the turret distastefulness. The thought touched him with a wry smile. He returned near the door. "Do you wish to remove your cloak?"

In response, she slipped it off and handed it to him.

Noah hung it on a peg near the door, then slipped off his own. He leaned against the wall with one ankle crossed over the other, his arms folded over his chest, and observed her. She kept her hands clasped at the lower back of the cheap, muslin frock she wore. Its dark-blue color matched her eyes to perfection. She moved around the chamber like a graceful woodland nymph, stopping and leaning in when he reached Isabelle's infamous—among *family only*, of course—Bug Board. Frankly, some of the species sent shivers up his spine.

"This area seems different," she said.

"Isabelle's interests lean toward entomology." He smiled. "I gave her an entire corner."

"Unusual for normal girls."

The truth had finally revealed itself. Disappointment crashed over him. "She is a normal girl," he ground out.

Her face raised, her eyes darting to his. Her brows lifted, her expression questioning, before her eyes widened and then narrowed on him. "You misunderstand me, sir. I attended school with a group of young, overprivileged women whose only accomplishments were stitching a straight line in their embroidery or painting a presentable landscape. Neither of which I ever perfected."

"Oh."

Her boldness would drive him mad, he decided, if he dissected every statement uttered from her. With a deep breath he let out slowly, vowing to listen and to restrain his assumptions. She was different. He just had to work out the rhythms and directness rather than assigning subtext to her. "Isabelle wishes to become a doctor."

A soft smile tilted her full lips. The sight blasted him with unbridled desire. "I have no doubt she shall succeed. It's a daunting path she is choosing for herself. Dorothea Erxleben is the only woman physician I've heard of and she hailed from Quedlinburg of the Holy Roman Empire. And that was years ago. She received her medical degree in 1754."

"My, you are a fount of knowledge," he murmured, stunned.

She flashed him a quick grin. "I remember because it was the same year Lord Hardwicke's Act was enacted. You know, the one where a marriage was not allowed unless parental consent had been obtained for anyone under the age of twenty-one? Since Scotland did not adopt that law, a man could hie off with an heiress and force her to marry him. Hence, Gretna Green." She wrinkled her nose and went back to her perfusing. "As I said, 'tis a difficult path that lay ahead. I, however, greatly admire such aspirations." The genuineness coming from her set forth a rush of something ancient in his blood.

"It sounds as if you have a few aspirations of your own," he said.

"Mmm," was her only response before pausing near his microscope and examining the bottles of various chemicals. Miss Wimbley then moved on to the middle area before coming to an abrupt halt.

Her eyes flashed to him literally sparkling. "Tell me these bones are not human."

"I guess I could *tell* you that," he hedged.

"Oh, my," she breathed. She brought up an index finger and traced the line of one of two talus bones that lay side by side. "What is it?"

His skin tingled, and he could swear he felt the heat of that breath from across the chamber. The very large chamber. "They are ankle bones."

"May I hold one?"

In an instant, he was crossing the room. "No, er, I mean—"

"I'll be gentle," she said with a smile directed at the table, not at him, that nonetheless had the ability of stealing his breath.

With the forthright audacity she'd already exhibited on at

least two previous occasions, she lifted one of his bones.

No one touched his bones. They were too difficult to obtain. Especially the one she currently held. He suppressed the urge to snatch it from her delicate fingers and forced himself to inhale. She ran a fingertip over an inverted rotation that raised bumps over him as if touching his person and not an inanimate object.

His skin quivered.

"This one is different from the other one. Why is that, do you suppose?"

With another deep breath, and an alert eye on her handling of his most prized possession, he answered slowly. "It's a deformity—here, I'll show you." He took both taluses and moved down the table to where the tibia and fibula lay side by side. "These are the bones in your calves." He watched her from the corner of his eye in a constant assessment, asking himself if her interest was genuine or artificial. "When I align the normal talus"—he held up one—"see this? How perfectly the pieces fit together. When I attempt to align the deformed bone, the discrepancy is quite obvious."

She leaned close and he got a whiff of soft orange blossom. It was as if a burst of spring exploded over his senses. How the devil had he missed that before?

"Goodness," she breathed. "I had no notion."

"Not many do." He ran his own fingers over the damaged talus. "This one grew inward. As such, it creates a misalignment that, depending on the severity, can impact an individual's mobility and balance."

Her eyes snapped to his. The intelligence he read there affected his own balance in that moment. "Miss Isabelle," she whispered.

Noah frowned, damning himself for imparting so much information. The familiar tightness banded his chest and restricted his airflow. The recollections of that long-ago day crashed over him, stole the very breath from him in agonizing waves. His hands flattened on the table that weaved through a darkness he'd yet to completely conquer. That summer day when he'd taken his young cousin with him about the countryside. Ten years ago, when he'd been home from his studies and she'd surprised an adder sunning on a low rock. The recollections that still had occasion to haunt his nights.

What an idiot he'd been to invite Miss Wimbley into his private sanctuary. He didn't even *know* this woman. Suddenly, the impropriety of this visit to his lab twisted parts of his body, low in his abdomen. Quickly but carefully, he gathered up the bones, moving them back to their initial places. He was infuriated with himself. "I fear I must return upstairs." He spoke sharply enough to draw her steady contemplation, feeling as if he resided on one of his own glass slides for study beneath his own microscope. "Lucius will pummel me if I leave him to deal with the incoming visitors arriving to view our father alone." He guided Miss Wimbley to the door then taking her cloak from the peg, he held it out.

Shockingly, she refrained from arguing with him as that was surely her nature. She nodded, throwing him soundly off-balance. "Of course. Thank you for allowing me in," she said softly. "It's truly fascinating."

"Yes, well, I've come a long way from my chemistry experimental days. Too much volatility," he muttered, taking up his own cloak.

Her head tilted to one side. "What of the lamps? Don't you fear—"

Blast it. Red-hot embarrassment covered his body, tempting him to dash up the stairs and back out the door for a dive off the cliff into the cold water below. "Of course. I'll be just a minute." He went about snuffing out each and every flame before leading her out the door, shutting and locking it behind them, chastising himself for getting caught up by the distraction of... *her.*

$$\text{\textreferencemark}$$

CHAPTER SEVEN

GENEVA CLIMBED THE two flights to Abra's and her suite. She entered and collapsed onto the settee in the sitting room with a sense of disequilibrium. Her head spun. Turmoil twisted her insides. She was the most insensitive person on the face of the earth. The image of Miss Isabelle sitting high above the ground on Julius's shoulders and the careful handling by his next older brother, Noah lifting her down and setting her so gently to her feet plowed through her. Errg. When the devil would she learn to internalize her immediate impulses instead of blurting out the first thought that invaded her head?

The door opened and Abra strolled in from the corridor. "Oh, there you are."

"Just as we returned, you'd left." With concerted effort, Geneva pushed the unsettling images from her mind, which denigrated to the other disturbing incident of the morning.

"Miss Hale insisted I walk with her. You left *me* behind. You know I don't walk as quickly as you. Besides, walking off alone with him is unwise," Abra admonished her.

Geneva rolled her eyes. "Ugh. You sound like your father."

"At least you didn't say 'stepmother,'" she returned, wrinkling her nose. "Where *did* you get to?"

"If you must know, the wind nearly sent me flying over the cliffs to my demise. And that wasn't the worst of it."

"Mr. Oshea kissed you?" was her wry retort.

"*What?*" Geneva scowled at her friend. "No. What a ridiculous notion." A vision that didn't repulse her. She swallowed a groan. "Don't say such things. I'm trying to tell you I almost fell to my death. Over. The. Cliffs."

"Yet here you are."

She couldn't believe it. Abra didn't believe her. She was tempted to raise her sleeve and see if there was a burn mark from his valiant grip on her. But if there were, she'd prefer to check it in private. She clamped her lips tightly.

Abra grinned. "Hmm. All right, then. I had an opportunity to speak with Mr. *Julius* Oshea. He's very sweet."

"Are you certain that was wise? What of your plans for Lord Ruskin? And *young*. He can't be over fifteen."

"Nineteen. He's nineteen. That's almost of legal age."

Geneva speared her with a quelling glance. "Oh, how you jest. Well," she said, adopting a too-casual tone. "Your stepmother would adore you marrying into an earl's family, would she not? I suggest you not entangle yourself with these people, Abra. It's quite unfashionable to marry one so much younger than oneself."

"Ha. It's only a few years. Why, when I'm forty-nine, he shall be forty-four or five." She waved out her hand. "Hardly any difference at all."

Genuine humor erupted from Geneva in a full-bellied laugh. The first since she and Abra had boarded the train north. "Oh, all right. You win. Besides, he *is* untitled."

Her bottom lip poked out in a pout. "True." She dropped beside Geneva on the settee and laid her head back and swiveled, facing Geneva. "What are your plans?"

She clasped her fingers together, laid her palms open across her ribs, and stared up at the ornamental plastered ceiling. Tastefully arranged grasses topped with sparsely placed flowers in ivory tones took the place of decorative corning that embossed the top portion of the walls into the ceiling and edged the rectangular chamber. The calming sight allowed her to pull her thoughts together. "The family will be occupied with all the pomp and circumstance that goes along with an earl's passing."

"I don't think I care for the direction of this conversation," Abra mumbled. "I'm part of the peerage, you know."

"Oh. You act so normal I tend to forget."

"Well?"

Geneva lowered her voice, and even glanced at the door behind them to make certain it was closed. "I need to search the earl's chamber."

Abra jolted to sitting. "Blast it, Gen. Don't you dare. They'll run us out of here with our heads on pikes."

"That's much too old-fashioned."

"Don't be flippant," Abra snapped. She dropped her face in her hands. "Papa will kill me."

"Nonsense. If anything, he's likely to help us. If you deign to ask him, that is."

A sly look glinted in her friend's eye. "I suppose I could ask him to make enquiries."

Well, that jest was a spectacular misfire. "Don't you dare. Then the evil one would be involved." Geneva tapped her fingers on her thigh. "I think I can search the earl's chamber during the service."

"I sincerely hope you mean 'former earl.'" Her teasing remark dripped with wry amusement.

Geneva rolled her eyes then eyed her thoughtfully.

"Don't even think such a thing." Abra groaned. "Searching the former earl's chamber is too risky. Besides, we shall have to make an appearance."

"*You* have to make an appearance," she corrected. "I do not. I practically live in the slums."

"You do *not* live in the slums. I would never visit the slums. Besides Papa already investigated your residence and deemed it acceptable as long as I am accompanied by Pasha and a footman."

"You never bring a footman."

"He doesn't have to know everything. You are missing my point, Gen. If Papa hadn't approved, I would be locked in my chamber."

Geneva released a sigh. "That's neither here nor there. I don't believe Lord Perlsea, rather, *Pender,* has moved into that chamber and it might be our only opportunity."

"I suppose I can act as a decoy," she said reluctantly. "But Mr. Oshea seems highly observant to me." She narrowed her eyes. "Especially where you're concerned."

How utterly annoying. "Truly?" Geneva certainly hadn't detected anything of that sort when he'd shown her his laboratory. He'd just watched her with a hooded gaze from across the room. Only when she'd touched his precious bone had he displayed the passion that seemed to simmer beneath the skin. She shivered.

"You gave them my suite?" The feminine fury vibrated outside the sitting room door.

Geneva met Abra's eyes and by mutual consent, they looked at the closed door, remaining silent.

The low, deeper response was indiscernible but set Geneva's nerve endings afire. Why did Abra have to put the picture of a kiss from him in her head?

"How could you?"

Another rumble of Noah Oshea's incoherent words.

"Of course, I was coming back," she snapped. "And no. I refused being banished to the East Tower."

The two went back and forth until Miss Hale appeared to cave with the promise that her companion—fine! Mr. Oshea— would fetch her each morning.

"She has a carriage," Geneva whispered.

"She's staking her claim," Abra whispered back. "I've met her before, you know. In London. She attended my debut." Abra grinned. "She reminds me of you."

"*What?*" Geneva smacked her friend's hand. "What a horrid thing to say."

"It was quite the scandal," Abra went on. "She'd put it about that Pender's son was to marry her."

Geneva's mouth dropped, and she'd never be able to explain

the manacle squeezing her chest.

"Not that one. The other one. Viscount Perlsea, *Lucius*. The current earl." She emphasized his name and titles as if Geneva were an imbecile of low intellect. "It was all before Meredith learned her father and the previous earl had contracted a betrothal agreement."

Geneva scowled. "I know that. But the bastard sent her to Cornwall and won't let her leave. She's a prisoner."

"Don't be so dramatic. You know as well as I no one can force her to remain in Cornwall. She's chosen to remain due to the school she's set up for the children."

"That was a couple of years ago. Something else is going on. We haven't heard from her in months." Geneva jumped to her feet and dashed to the windows. "Lud, all we can see is the sea from here." She spun back to Abra. "Surely, she'll accompany her father to the memorial service."

Abra drummed her fingers on her knee. "It's difficult to say. The duke, as you might recall, has a reason behind everything he does. She'll be here if it suits him."

Geneva paced from the hearth to the window and back, her head down, the thoughts pricking her skin like a ping of arrows from Caligula's massive army. Abra wasn't wrong. "We should ascertain what chamber they assign Miss Hale. If it faces the drive, perhaps we could offer to trade."

"Geneva!" Abra's exasperation brought her up.

She stopped, her eyes shooting to her friend. "What?"

"I'm in a horrible position here."

Geneva hurried over, lowered next to her, and took her hands. "What do you mean?"

"I know this will come as a surprise, but as a debutante, I was not well received." Abra's attempt at being witty, of course. Geneva understood in a way different from Hannah and Meredith. Abra had been singled out from the moment they'd met because Abra was not lily-white like other English debutantes, and Geneva hadn't peerage on her side.

The night after Abra's come-out ball—which Geneva *hadn't* attended—the four friends had stayed the weekend at Lord Westbridge's mansion in town with Abra, where she'd cried her heart out at the injustices of it all. How petty all those other young women were. Geneva had spent the weekend thinking how fortunate she'd been at her own lot in life. It had taken all her resolve in not voicing that stroke of luck.

"You must have forgotten the weekend after," Geneva countered.

"No, I haven't forgotten." Abra spoke softly. "Some of the *ton* will likely be making the trip north to acknowledge the late earl's passing." She leaned in. "That includes my father and stepmother."

Groaning, Geneva dropped her face in her hands. "Your stepmother?" She adored Lord Westbridge. Lady Westbridge not so much. The woman could have stepped straight from the tale of *Cinderella*. The heroine's stepmother personified.

"He could hardly leave her behind," Abra bit out.

Geneva's shoulders slumped. "And that means—"

"Yes. Lord Ruskin will likely be among them. So, you see? I can't possibly get caught up in the least bit of scandal."

"If indeed they appear, perhaps Hannah will be with them?" An inkling of hope trickled through Geneva. Hannah would help stave off any looming fiascos.

"Doubtful. Ruskin is too traditional. He wouldn't allow Hannah to attend the funeral." A frown furrowed her forehead. "If Papa and Stepmother do attend, Stepmother will insist on accompanying Papa, and she'll drag me along for sure."

Blast. Her foot tapped the floor, more thoughts inundating her. "How are we to explain we're in Northumberland and not Cornwall?" Geneva's voice trilled higher with each word. "I shall ask to be removed to a smaller chamber. Your father shouldn't know I'm here. Or that we are here together." That went double for Lady Westbridge. The woman hated Geneva.

"Geneva, think! How do you propose I explain *my* presence in

Northumberland? No. Like it or not, we are in this debacle together. Papa will never cause a scene. *If* he shows, I'll speak with him. You know he will forgive me anything." She heaved in a deep breath. "Almost, anyway."

She stood and took Geneva by the upper arms and shook her. "I came here for you and I shall tell Papa so. If Lord Ruskin can't accept you as my dearest friend, he may find himself another woman to take as his wife. If he even bothers to request my hand," she whispered with a sense of hopelessness that broke Geneva's heart.

"He can't possibly be that daft," Geneva assured her. Abra's loyalty and friendship brought tears to Geneva's eyes. "He'll ask. If he doesn't, the fault shall lie at the feet of your stepmother. Hannah is certain of her brother's regard for you." She squeezed Abra's hand. "You are the dearest friend one could ever have and I shall do my utmost to be worthy. Now, about Meredith…"

NOAH TOOK DOCIA by the arm and hauled her down the corridor to another hall as far from the Blue Suite as he could get. He opened the door to the Yellow Suite and peered in. There were bags on the floor and he quickly backed out. There was no other option; he dragged her to the East Tower, where they could talk without being overheard. Unfortunately, all of his ancestors would be there to witness this ridiculous scene.

Docia jerked her arm from him. "There is no call for brute force! You know? I don't believe we shall suit one another for marriage, after all."

Something with which he wholeheartedly agreed. The relief rushing through him was monumental. "All right," he said slowly. "Why the change of heart? You've been badgering me for months."

"I've seen how you look at that… that *woman*."

This was not a conversation he was prepared for, and certainly not with Docia. With a mental step back, he studied her elfin face—the delicately proportioned features, the small, upturned nose, and high, well-defined cheekbones. The blue eyes were reminiscent of someone else's he preferred not thinking of in this moment. But one couldn't deny Docia's attractiveness with another of her brightly-colored frocks that was likely French. Whether it was the latest fashion or not, he couldn't say.

When Noah considered their past, his brain had apparently been absent. He should have remembered the two of them had never been true friends. How they had clashed at the onset. Docia had announced at the age of eleven her intentions of marrying Lucius.

From the time they'd been children, she'd been enamored with, obsessed with, all that was proper, including behavior, but she'd never been quite able to quash that self-serving side of her personality. In the right mood, it could be engaging. In the wrong mood, it was downright irritating. The whole family felt sorry for her, he supposed. Her father had gone to London one weekend and had never returned.

So, Verda and Sander had welcomed her into the Oshea fold.

Currently, her eyes were narrowed on him, her arms folded over her chest with her nose in the air. "I'll reserve judgment for the time being, however."

He let out an impatient breath. "Oh, for God's sake."

She strolled over to him and touched his arm.

The move surprised him.

She frowned. "I don't know how I feel about Miss Wimbley. I'm almost certain she is not for you. Perhaps you could take her as a mistress." Her hand fell away. "With discretion, of course."

And just like that, every hackle raised the hair on his skin. "I'll be sure to let you know if she accepts my proposal," he bit out, his insides trembling with outrage.

She turned on her fashionable heels, their clicks echoing against the chamber walls. He glanced up at his father's portrait.

The resemblance between Lucius, Noah, and their father didn't jump out to Noah. The artist had captured his father's weak chin and pouting lips. There was also a bleakness in his eyes that Noah had seen in Lucius's since his marriage to Lady Meredith. Still, that did not mean Docia was for his brother. Which was certainly an impossibility besides.

The previous Earl of Pender's lips seemed to twist in the mocking smirk that Noah had experienced his entire life. He was half-afraid he'd see that same expression on his father's face even as the coffin box was being nailed shut.

God, Noah's morbidity knew no bounds. Too much time in his laboratory and working with bones, he supposed. He blew out a deep breath, scowled at his father, and strode from the East Tower. He needed to speak with Lucius. Docia would drive him into an early grave and Noah wanted to warn him. She was up to something, and it did not bode well. Her schemes never had.

◆—◆══❧══◆—◆

CHAPTER EIGHT

M ISS ISABELLE TWISTED back and forth with her hands at her back, a delicate chain against her neck reflecting the lighting. "I don't know why everyone keeps calling this the Blue Suite," she informed Geneva and Abra. "I renamed each to something, um, more enchanting."

"Ah, enchanting. What did you name this one?" Geneva asked her. The girl was truly a delight.

"Morpho."

Geneva met Abra's eyes before turning back to Miss Isabelle. "I..." She had no idea what *Morpho* meant.

"I've seen pictures. We have a most extensive library, you know." Miss Isabelle limped over to one of the lower paintings and straightened it, stood back to gauge her work, then adjusted it again.

Geneva was at a loss.

"I believe it is an interesting and extremely beautiful butter-fly," Abra said.

Geneva's mouth dropped.

Miss Isabelle spun quickly around and Geneva's heart nearly lopped from her chest, fearing the girl would lose her balance. She didn't. "Yes!" She clapped her hands together. "They are quite famous for their blue wings. They shimmer," she said with a dreamy smile. "I think they are mostly found in an enchanted forest."

"Morpho..." Geneva repeated. "It doesn't sound like a—"

There she went again, nearly blurting out how unappealing the name sounded for something that belonged in an enchanted forest. "Like a species one would find near Scotland," she finished weakly.

Miss Isabelle's nose wrinkled. "You are right, of course. They are mostly found in South America. The Amazon, I suppose. It's much warmer there."

"What other rooms did you name?" Abra asked her.

"Let's see," she said slowly. "The Yellow Suite is now the Brimstone. The Rose Room is now the Red Admiral, the Green Suite is Banded Peacock." She ticked off a finger for each one she listed. "That is the name I assigned Noah's chamber."

A burst of unexpected laughter erupted from Geneva picturing Mr. Oshea in a chamber called the Banded Peacock.

She caught Abra's smirk and a flush of heat crawled up her neck. Geneva turned her narrowed gaze on Miss Isabelle. "You're bamming us, aren't you? There couldn't possibly be a butterfly called 'Brimstone.' And it's yellow, you say?"

She grinned and the sweetness of her expression sliced through to Geneva's heart. "Yes. There are all sorts of butterflies. The pictures are beautiful. I've even composed songs about them."

"Oh, I should love to hear that," Abra told her.

"Shall I play for you now?"

"That would be delightful," Geneva and Abra said at the same time.

Lucius hadn't yet moved his belongings into their father's chamber, but Noah couldn't fault him for that. There had never been any desire from Noah to hold the title of earl. He relished his position in assisting Sander in managing the numerous Pender properties. Sander seemed thrilled with the partnership, as it kept him from having to travel so much.

Noah raised his fist to tap on his brother's current chamber door, but the muted voices stopped him.

"Don't you see, darling? This is our chance. You haven't even consummated your marriage yet." The words spilling from Docia stunned Noah. Never had he heard her speak so frankly. "You haven't, have you?"

"No," his brother murmured.

"That's settled, then. You'll return to London and file for an annulment."

"It's not that simple, Docia. There must be grounds for such a claim. Her father is an extremely powerful man. He's not known for his subtlety when he's crossed." Lucius had that right. "I suppose I could visit Perlsea Keep and speak with her. Perhaps Meredith hates me and will be willing to work together. What a blasted conundrum."

Noah expected the duke to attend Father's services *if he hadn't already arrived*. They were related through marriage, after all. And his reaction to his daughter not being in attendance was sure to be noticed and remarked upon by more than just her father. Noah gave two sharp raps and entered the room without awaiting an invitation.

Lucius's hands were on Docia's upper arms and he leaned forward as if he had just kissed her.

Or was about to.

"What are you doing here?" Lucius demanded in a low growl.

"Did you know that Docia and I had intended on leaving for Scotland this morning?" He glanced at her. "To be married?"

"What?" His brother's ears turned red. He pierced Docia with a hard look. "Is that true?"

In Docia fashion, she lifted one shoulder. "I also told Noah I didn't believe we would suit."

A true statement, if somewhat out of context. "She's been badgering me since your wedding," Noah said. "I gave in and we were to leave this morning, but then—" He shrugged. "Well, plans were interrupted." Another thought occurred to him and he grinned. "*You* interrupted, showing up when you did." Actually, it was Miss Wimbley who'd arrived first, but Lucius had been right on her heels.

Lucius grunted but eyed Docia with a glint of... suspicion? *One could hope.* Being wed to the daughter of one of England's most powerful men required delicate handling. Attracting the duke's ire was not wise, but as usual, Docia was up to her old tricks, stirring up a pot of trouble with no thought to the consequences.

There was another tap at the door and Winfield poked his head in. "Apologies, my lord, Mr. Oshea. But the Duke of Rathbourne has just arrived. Where shall we put him?"

Docia froze and Lucius's groan matched Noah's own.

"I suppose it's too crass to place him in Father's bedchamber?" Lucius said.

Winfield cleared his throat. "It *is* prepared, my lord."

Noah met Lucius's eyes and the connection they'd shared since Lucius had accepted Julius when they'd been but children stretched between them. Noah nodded.

"That shall suffice," Lucius said.

Winfield inclined his head. "Very good, my lord." He ducked back out.

"Well, if the earldom hadn't hit you at this point, that should do it," Noah told him with a half-smile and shaking his head.

CHAPTER NINE

GENEVA HUDDLED IN her bedchamber, mulling over the past hour when Miss Isabelle had given Geneva and Abra their own private concert. Miss Isabelle may have struggled to a degree with walking, but it certainly had not affected her talent and skill with the pianoforte.

The girl was fanciful in the most feminine and dainty way possible. On the diametric end of the scale of Geneva. *Heavens.* Naming Mr. Oshea's bedchamber with the word "cock" in it! She was still laughing. Notably, with an edge of hysteria. Geneva was no green girl, having grown up in Soho. One could not walk down the street without some drunken sot offering his endowed manly parts by whatever name. Geneva could name at least five off the top of her head. *Penis, cock, prick, staff, rod.* The labels were endless.

She took a sip of a most excellent oolong tea, set it down, and paced her bedchamber. With each pass of an English mantel clock over the hearth, the slow-moving hands appeared stuck. Abra's and her entire strategy was based on timing. Suppers were notoriously long, and country dinners, Abra had said, were no different than those held in town. The plan required Geneva to enter the late earl's chamber at the second course. Because no one dared leaving the table at a second course and as such would give Geneva plenty of time to search with a minimal chance of being caught. Their strategy set, Geneva and Abra feigned megrims. Abra would remain in the sitting room and wait for the promised tray to be sent up.

On her fifth or twentieth pass—she'd lost count, though she did not care—impatience finally got the better of her and she hurried to the sitting room. Sheer determination surged through her. She stalked to the door and peered out, then cast a last glance over her shoulder at her friend.

"Be careful," Abra whispered, worry creasing her forehead.

"I will," she promised. Geneva slipped into the corridor devoid of servants and guests alike.

Thankfully, the master suite was nearby. Just down the hall, closer to the stairs, running the length of the windows to the west in the direction of the stables, she surmised. On stealthy steps, she rounded the corner to elaborate double doors and a raised threshold that marked its importance for master and mistress of the castle. Doors of heavy oak with black, decorative hinges brought to mind something out of *Historia Regum Britanniae*.

Rather than the current style of an actual doorknob or even a lever, to enter, she clasped a thick, iron, circular handle and turned. The stout door was heavy and took concerted effort, but she took comfort in the well-oiled hinges for their lack of creaking. It was easy convincing herself she wasn't trespassing, as no one was occupying the suite since the old earl's death. She pushed inside and stopped—

"What are you doing here?" Miss Hale demanded. She came to her feet and shook out her skirts, attempting to hide the bag she'd been rifling through.

Geneva glanced behind her then stepped inside, closing the door behind her, and smirked. "I could ask you the same. Whose bag is that?"

Miss Hale scowled. "The Duke of Rathbourne's."

Geneva gasped.

"I see you've heard of him."

You've no idea, Geneva didn't say. "Yes." She surveyed the bedchamber, taking in the rich, velvet curtains in forest green over the windows that matched the bedcurtains. Dark-paneled walls lacked artwork. This was a man's room and Rathbourne, Meredith's father, had been handed the honor of lodging in it. She willed her heart to slow its pounding and brought her gaze back to Miss Hale. "Why aren't you at dinner?"

"Why aren't *you?*"

Geneva indicated her frock. "I've nothing to wear and I am untitled. I shan't be missed. You, however…" She let her voice trail.

"Being untitled has nothing to do with anything as you well know." Her eyes flickered over Geneva's unflattering dark blue muslin then rose to her face. "I must concede regarding the dress, but all right." Miss Hale's sputter spelled out her frustration. "I thought to… to. Oh, what does it matter? You are correct. I must go, as I will *certainly* be missed." She stalked around Geneva to the door. "This isn't over."

"No. It's not over," Geneva said evenly.

Miss Hale opened the door and glanced out, then indicated Geneva precede her, and with no other option, she did. In fact, Miss Hale walked Geneva to the "Morpho" Suite then followed her inside and again, Geneva stopped so suddenly, Miss Hale bumped into her.

Abra stood near the hearth, and Pasha sat at a table near the windows, as unobtrusive as ever. "There you are. Oh, dear," she ended on a whisper when her gaze landed just beyond Geneva's shoulder.

Mr. Oshea, Noah Oshea, turned from his place near the window.

Miss Hale stepped around Geneva and strolled to the hearth. "Well, isn't this an interesting tête-à-tête."

"What are you about, Docia?" Mr. Oshea knew her quite well it seemed.

"It's *Miss Hale*," she hissed back.

Geneva's lips twitched and she bit the bottom one upon catching Abra's mirth. There was certainly no love lost between Miss Hale and Mr. Oshea.

"I've been visiting with Miss Wimbley. She's agreed to accompany me to Chaston tonight," Miss Hale said with a sly smile.

Geneva drew in a sharp inhale as apparently she had lost the ability to forge *any* other response when it came to *any* comment the woman deigned to make.

Miss Hale turned to her. "Isn't that right, Miss Wimbley?"

Geneva gathered her wits and narrowed her eyes on the woman, attempting to fathom this unexpected action. The motive was vastly clear. Miss Hale wished to silence her and knew that Geneva could out her just as quickly. "Yes. Yes. That's right."

"What?" Abra's shock, of course, was not a surprise, but with Mr. Oshea's piercing, gray eyes trained on Geneva, she couldn't even send her friend a pleading glance. Could only look in her direction and give her an innocent blink and hope.

It was enough. Abra's lips tightened and she remained quiet.

"Yes," Miss Hale went on. "Miss Wimbley has confessed she didn't have the wherewithal to bring an appropriate wardrobe with her." Her nonchalance grated.

Suspicion fleeted Mr. Oshea's face. "And, you, uh, so kindly offered to assist her." He raked a gaze over Geneva. "Hmm."

Her face burned. She lifted her chin. All she had was her pride, but, blast it, it was hers.

"That's enough, Noah," Miss Hale snapped. "Miss Wimbley cannot help her circumstances."

"You know nothing of my circumstances, *Miss Hale*." Geneva's jaw ached. It was clenched so tightly, she barely managed coherent words.

But the woman was an expert in redirection and acted as if Geneva hadn't spoken. "Pack an overnight bag—" She stopped, eyeing Geneva's frock so critically, it was all Geneva could do to not storm to her chamber and slam the door. "I retract that. Don't bother packing, Miss Wimbley. You shan't need a thing." She turned to Mr. Oshea. "We shall leave for Chaston and return in the morning."

"Meaning two in the afternoon?" Mr. Oshea retorted.

Miss Hale shrugged.

"No. You'll stay for supper and I shall drive you to Chaston tonight and return for you in the morning by nine as we discussed." He spoke pointedly.

Her eyes went over Geneva's day gown again. "Fine."

This time, Geneva did send Abra a pleading glance regardless of who witnessed it.

And, of course, Abra came to Geneva's humiliating rescue. "I'm certain I have a fitting garment Geneva can don for supper."

Mr. Oshea inclined his head in a sharp nod. "We meet in the library at seven." His gaze swept over the three of them. "I'm thrilled to see no one is upon their deathbed."

With that, he took Miss Hale's arm in a firm grip and they departed.

"But I don't wish to go to dinner," Geneva wailed before pulling herself up. "Did you know the Duke of Rathbourne has arrived?"

Abra groaned. "Are you sure?"

"When I snuck into the earl's suite, Miss Hale was in there going through his belongings," she said, nodding.

"What the devil was she doing going through his belongings? Why does she want you to stay the night with her?"

"An excellent question. And I don't know."

"You take my word for it, Gen, Miss Hale is trouble and does nothing if there is no benefit in it for her."

"I take your point." Geneva tapped her chin, seeing Miss Hale's smugness and Mr. Oshea's near-to-fraying temper. "I expect I'll learn something from this idiotic turn of events."

"Perhaps. Don't dawdle." Abra went to her bedchamber door and opened it. "I've been dying to rid you of those ill-fitting frocks you seem to favor. We must hurry. You too, Pasha. We require your expertise."

A grin split the maid's face and Geneva decided it was a con-spiracy. "Yes, milady."

"I was hoping you'd forgotten," she muttered.

Abra pierced her with a smug look over her shoulder. "Unless you *want* to make an entrance."

Geneva hurried after them. "My worst nightmare."

ORCHESTRATING A SUCCESSFUL supper was completely out of Noah's repertoire. Even Aunt Verda, who'd once lived in London, professed her own inefficiency at such matters. Docia, of course, would excel at such a task even without experience, but Mrs. Knagg, thankfully, had been cognizant enough to add staff—and he used the term loosely—from Alnmouth. Winfield could be counted on to keep things in order.

The parlor held his father's body, so pre-dinner drinks were served in the library, where Mrs. Knagg and Hicks—Stonemare's other longtime footman—moved unobtrusively about. So far, no one had dropped any trays of sherry, madeira, ratafia, or brandy.

The conversation was a low hum due to the solemnness of the occasion and the crowd being relatively small. Curiously, Aunt Verda and Uncle Sander maintained a large distance between themselves and Rathbourne, and despite that gap, the air between them shimmered with hostility.

Noah had forgotten Aunt Verda's father, Baron Krupt, had wanted her to marry—*snag* was the term she'd used—when referring to Rathbourne. The duke had desired her as a mother to his only child. A child who was now tied to Lucius. The families were intertwined in a most inconvenient way. Lucius stood with Sander and for the moment was resigned to glaring daggers at Rathbourne's back.

Those of the *ton* who hadn't made it to Northumberland would be sorely disappointed, as supper should prove worthy of an "event of the season" marque. And not in a gracious way.

Impatience rippled through Noah. He tugged the fob from his

waistcoat pocket and flipped it open. Ten past seven.

"Don't worry, darling," Docia taunted him in a low voice. "The little bird will fly from her nest and arrive before you know it and dressed to the nines. One minute detail regarding Lady Abra Washington is her resourcefulness. Astonishing, given—"

Noah snapped the fob shut and slipped it back in its pocket, piercing her with a sudden hatred that surpassed all the resentment through the years. "Just what are you getting at?" he hissed. The sense of having been there before made him dizzy. As if he and Docia were back to their ten- and eleven-year-old selves, prepared to tear one another's throats out. A blazing fire of fury tore through him. "Say more about Abra's character and I shall haul you out of here by the delicate lace of your fichu for all the guests to witness."

Eyes flashing, she turned her back on him and sauntered to the duke. Perhaps they could claw one another's eyes out. "Good evening, Your Grace. I thought perhaps Lady Pender would have accompanied you," Docia said, loud enough to fill the chamber.

Noah chanced a glance at his brother, whose white-knuckled grip threatened the heavy glass he held.

"She's unwell of late," His Grace returned smoothly. "An unfortunate side effect of being with child, I suppose."

The sudden stillness that crowded the room didn't do justice to Docia's gasp and her face draining of color. Glass shattered behind Noah and he turned to see the same shock on Lucius's expression, and his hand now bloodied with shards of glass amid brandy dripping on the toes of his Hessians.

The door to the library swung wide with Winfield entering and announcing, "Lady Abra Washington and Miss Geneva Wimbley."

Rathbourne's entire body jolted as if prodded with a blacksmith's iron.

Abra entered, and while her dark skin glowed against her burgundy gown and the draping shawl that looped her arms, his gaze was riveted to the woman behind her in deep bronze. She was a vision with her almost-black hair swept up but for a few wispy curls that framed her face, giving an ethereal halo effect. Her full lips had more color than he recalled. Unsurprising, the gown was a tad too long but appeared to fit across her nicely shaped bosom.

His Grace let out a gasped curse worthy of a rookery gaming hell.

Neither young woman flinched. So, they knew the duke, it appeared.

"What the hell are they doing here?" Rathbourne demanded. Truly, there was not a subtle bone in the man's body.

Noah quickly took two glasses of sherry from Hicks and hurried forward. "They are here for the same reason you are, Your Grace. To pay their respects." The little white lie would serve its purpose—he shot Miss Wimbley a telling look—if she didn't argue outright with the statement.

Miss Wimbley skirted Lady Abra and strolled right up to the duke. She was as foolhardy as Docia.

It was his urge to shield her from Rathbourne that had Noah starting in her direction.

Miss Wimbley tilted her head just so and a small smile curved her lovely lips as she fell into a deep and perfect curtsey. "Your Grace. How nice to see you… again."

She obviously didn't realize the havoc such a man could wreak on those who mocked him. And, mock him, she did. It was right there in her tone.

A snicker from Docia, who'd appeared to recover from her previous shock, sounded under her breath.

Noah shot her a glare and started toward Miss Wimbley, but Winfield's timely manner announced dinner, thankfully, staying any further fireworks. Noah wouldn't have been surprised had a second turret on the property collapsed.

Rathbourne's reputation preceded him and no one was fond of the pompous ass. For a minute, no one moved.

"Did I misunderstand the man?" the duke barked, spurring

the sudden clink of glasses being set aside in various parts of the room. With Lucius's wife not in attendance, Abra was the highest-ranking lady, but the Duke of Rathbourne pointedly ignored her. Instead, he offered his arm to Docia and escorted her out. It was a direct cut, but Lucius's brooding went on hiatus as he stepped forward without hesitation and approached Lady Abra. Other parties moved out of the library. And, as inappropriate as it was, Noah slowed Miss Wimbley with a hold on her arm, forcing them both to lag behind the others. "You are either the boldest person I've ever met or the reckless."

She bristled. "Your point?"

He let out a harsh breath. "Rathbourne does not make a favorable enemy, Miss Wimbley."

She had the audacity to laugh. A high, tinkling sound that ran over his skin like a babbling brook. "No. He doesn't."

There was something so unique about the color of her eyes—he couldn't pull his gaze from her. The fire's light indeed reflected the night sky dotted with stars within their navy hue. That afternoon, they'd taken on a mix of the crashing sea and the muted sun, lending a tint toward sapphire. He was no artist, but sapphire seemed exactly right. A deep, rich blue jewel with a starburst in their center.

Christ, he was a poet now? "What makes you believe you can escape the duke's wrath?" He truly was interested.

"I went to school with his daughter." She grinned and the effect momentarily stunned him. Her hair was dressed in a similar style to Docia's. The deep bronze of her gown matched the streaks of mahogany in her hair. Wispy tendrils caressed her nape and the tips of his fingers tingled. "I know all sorts of interesting things about the mighty duke." She patted his arm. "Don't worry over me." Her brows wrinkled. "Are we going to eat?"

"Why haven't you worn your hair like that before?" He lifted his hand, intending to touch. See if those curls were as soft as they appeared.

She put her fingers up as if she couldn't believe it herself, her cheeks taking on an engaging blush. "It's amazing what a skilled lady's maid can accomplish with hair as unruly as mine."

"I think it looks beautiful," Isabelle said.

His whole body jolted as if struck by a bolt of lightning. He glanced at the door and found Julius appearing to restrain a grin.

"Come on, Belle. I'm famished," Julius said.

A strangled sound caught in Noah's throat and he squeezed his hand into a fist, dropping it back to his side.

Miss Wimbley turned her impish smile on Isabelle. "Thank you. Heavens. Do you know how many pins are in there? I'll be lucky if my skull is not pricked for my brains to leak out overnight."

His lips twitched.

"Perhaps you could donate your remnants to Noah," Isabelle said. "He studies bones, you know. I should think the brain loads more interesting."

"Er, after the fact, if you don't mind," Noah said. "Though I suspect, it's Belle here who studies live beings."

Miss Wimbley shrugged. "Certainly," she said to Isabelle. "I give him full leave. I shall be dead, after all." She tapped Isabelle's hand. "But only if you supervise."

She grinned back. "I shall indeed."

Miss Wimbley's gaze surveyed the library. "I'm hungry."

As was he in that moment—but not for food, quite suddenly. "Right." The familiar rush of embarrassment plundered him. "Shall we?"

Isabelle laughed. "You're silly, Noah." She looked up at Miss Wimbley.

"You'll accompany us?"

"I'd be honored," she returned in a voice that Noah would swear choked with emotion.

Noah held out his arm, anticipation rippling through him. "Shall we?"

Nodding, Miss Wimbley set her hand lightly atop his sleeve. He and Miss Wimbley followed Julius escorting his cousin to the main dining hall, where all eyes turned upon them.

CHAPTER TEN

DREAD THROBBED AGAINST Geneva's head that didn't just have to do with the pins stabbing her in multiple places. It was also the clopping hooves of Mr. Oshea's retreating carriage. The wind might also have been a contributing factor. And seeing as how it blew dark clouds over a full moon—with the briny sea air and impending rain—she was quite ready to pull her hair out along with the pins.

"Well, what are you waiting for?" Miss Hale's tone was almost strident. If anything, it put the pain of the prickling pins from her mind. Miss Hale stood in the open doorframe with a hand on her hip. "Lady Abra will be furious if you ruin that gown. I happen to have been in the shop when she ordered it. The madame was quite rude to her for obvious reasons." Miss Hale slipped off her cloak and hung it on a peg.

Geneva whipped up her skirts and followed her inside. She was spoiling for a fight. "And what might those reasons have been?" she said, her voice low and even.

Her host's brows pinched in, as if confused. "Madame did not believe that Lady Abra was one of the peerage. I enlightened her. I may not have cared much for your friend, but her father is a marquess and he would have run the woman from town. No one wanted that—she is extremely skilled—so I let her know what she was up against if she mistreated Lady Abra in any way. Take that abhorrent cloak off and come along."

With compressed lips, Geneva flexed her fingers and surveyed the spacious entry hall, giving herself time to rein in the temptation of letting her tongue rule freely. No one greeted them and Miss Hale was already halfway up the stairs.

"We don't have much time," she said with an impatience that did not seem out of character. "Noah will return in the morning at eight and it's already ten-thirty."

Geneva doffed her bonnet and ratty cloak then hung it next to Miss Hale's. "Is this really necessary?" she mumbled.

"You saw how the duke reacted when he saw you. And there will be much more than him to contend with before the week is through."

Swallowing a groan, Geneva followed Miss Hale up the stairs to a roomy chamber. "Where's the butler? And the housekeeper?"

"Oh, I pensioned them off years ago." Her muffled voice came from inside the wardrobe.

Geneva gasped. "You live here alone? Where are your parents?"

Miss Hale reappeared, her arms ladened down with an array of brightly colored gowns. "I'm one and thirty. I daresay, no one cares if I live alone or not. Besides, the only time it's a real issue is when my cousin visits. And those occasions are as rare as seeing a full moon in a London night sky."

A quick burst of laughter erupted from Geneva, acknowledging the irony. "So, never." London's night sky was notoriously obliterated with coal smoke in winter.

"Exactly." Miss Hale moved to the bed and dropped the load of them.

The mounds of fabric caught Geneva by surprise and she blinked.

"We don't have all night, you know. Strip."

Startled, Geneva jerked then shook her head. "What the devil?"

"That is an impolite word," Miss Hale chastised her. "Are you completely uncouth?"

Geneva chuckled, surprised she could manage it. "Is it? I

suppose it is." She eyed the stack of gowns. "Why so many? We're not attending a ball."

Miss Hale lifted one shoulder. "Ha! Even if there were, there wouldn't be any dancing. Sander and Verda don't allow it."

"Ah, Miss Isabelle." The words came out before she could swallow them.

Miss Hale paused in her sorting and turned, facing Geneva, her gaze intense and speculative. "Surely, you didn't say anything to Noah. He's quite sensitive regarding the subject."

"Oh?"

But Miss Hale did not deign to answer. A long silence ensued and Geneva shifted under her scrutiny.

"He showed me his laboratory," she said, feeling a tad defensive. "I saw the bones."

Miss Hale shuddered. "I hate that place. He spends all his time in that horrid hovel. I vow, I can hardly breathe when I enter that chamber of torture."

"Truly? Hmm. I thought it fascinating." Geneva clenched her fingers until her knuckles showed white, refusing to touch the lovely silks her ink-stained fingers would likely mar.

"You would." Another tremor, delicate, rippled over Miss Hale. "In any event, you're right. Isabelle is a sweet girl. Vastly independent, though, without a care for her own well-being. Hence that deplorable limp. Or how she looks to the unsuspecting public."

"So altruistic you are," Geneva said dryly. It took a second for the impact of Miss Hale's words. "'Deplorable limp'? What do you mean? I thought she was born with the infirmity." In fact, she was almost certain it was Mr. Oshea who'd used the word 'deformity.'

Miss Hale didn't bother with an answer and turned back to the gowns she'd piled on the bed. "How do you know Lady Abra?" Apparently, that line of conversation was not to be.

But Geneva knew the answers would be forthcoming at some point and opted to let the matter slide. "We attended school together."

"You?" Miss Hale's amazement grated over her skin.

"Subtle, aren't you?" Geneva was heartily sick of the insinuations. She rubbed her forehead with the heel of her hand. And tired. She was fatigued beyond words and just wanted to lie down. The possibility of sneaking away occurred to her and she eyed the huge pile of gowns then glanced at the door.

"Your friend wasn't at all well received." The nonchalance with which Miss Hale spoke nearly impaled Geneva with a searing blaze of fury.

Her attention abruptly fired back to her host. "Stow it, Miss Hale. Abra is my friend and I shan't listen to any untoward regarding her."

But once again, Miss Hale acted as if Geneva hadn't spoken. "I attended her debut. It was appalling."

As Geneva well knew. "So she mentioned," she gritted out through clenched teeth.

"I mean…" Her voice lowered as if the entirety of the *ton* had their ears to the door. "Her mother was… was from… the West Indies—"

"You're an idiot," Geneva snapped. "Her mother was from Jamaica. A fact that does not shame her father, else he'd never have married her. I swear to you, if you say another dreadful thing about my friend, I shall walk all the way back to Stonemare. Tonight."

Miss Hale stopped and turned, her jaw dropped, red dotting spots on her high cheekbones. Over her arm was a lovely lavender gown. "I-I'm sorry. I… suppose I envy your relationship. I have no friends. Not among ladies." Her brows furrowed and her voice softened. "Or among gentlemen, for that matter. I'm quite self-centered. I suppose it's from living on my own so long."

Geneva drew in a breath. If anything, she was a fool for a self-deprecating tale. She considered Miss Hale for the longest time before her shoulders caved with acceptance. Geneva believed her. "I'll let it go this time, but no more. Abra is one of my dearest friends and she's been snubbed and cut for the most awful of reasons. Her stepmother is downright hostile and I won't stand for someone like you disparaging her."

A small smile touched Miss Hale's face, transforming it into awe-inspiring beauty. "'Someone like me.'" She shook her head. "I supposed I deserved that set-down. All right, Miss Wimbley. I apologize. I shall treat her as good a friend as you do."

That was doubtful, but that was the best Geneva was likely to receive from the annoying, over-aged debutante, she thought with a stab of vindictiveness. "So, you never see your cousin?"

"When my father… disappeared, he petitioned for the viscountcy. It was granted, of course. And no, I don't see him. I hate him. And he hates me. It's a mutual hate." Miss Hale punctuated the statements with a sharp nod as if that settled the matter. The discussion was obviously over. She held up the lavender gown. "Here, try this one." She assisted Geneva out of Abra's bronze gown and donned the new one. "It's perfect. I knew it would be." She led Geneva to a tall, free-standing mirror in the corner. "Look."

Geneva couldn't believe her eyes. With her hair pulled up in its similar style and, despite the contrast in color, they could pass for sisters, but for Miss Hale's rounded chin. Geneva's was more pointed, stubborn—not an attractive trait and certainly off-putting to others. Focusing on her flaws, however, was not her way and she shoved away the unwanted introspection. "Why were you so upset to hear that Meredith, I, er, mean, Lady Pender is with child?"

"W-What?"

Geneva's gaze shot up. The red flush had drained, leaving Miss Hale's countenance positively pallid. Her lips trembled, but true to her nature, she rallied, lifting her chin in more reminiscent defiance.

Excellent. It was past time being at the mercy of Miss Hale's indirect hostility. Her show of good faith, while nice, seemed less than genuine.

Geneva pounced. "Earlier. When Rathbourne announced his forthcoming grandchild. You were beyond shocked." She watched the woman's reflection in the mirror. Yes, Geneva had heard the duke's announcement just before entering the library and she didn't believe a word of it. According to Meredith, her husband hadn't returned to Cornwall once since abandoning her there three years before. While Meredith hadn't put actual words to paper the wedding had not been consummated, she had intimated it by writing: *their connection had stopped at the altar.* And the duke was cunning, not above using crafty methods for means to an end. His own.

Miss Hale's face remained the same ashen pallor it had that afternoon and Geneva almost felt bad for her, just not enough to take back her words. She couldn't squelch the notion that Miss Hale meant Meredith harm. No one hurt Geneva's friends. Not if she could help it.

Her eyes took on flecks of ice, her expression coy, her voice nonchalant. "I told Noah he should consider you, you know." The underlying steel sent waves of chill swirling down her spine.

Geneva's head snapped from the mirror to face her. "For *marriage?*" Her squeal could have shattered glass.

"Certainly not. That would *never* do." Her eyes flashed and Geneva caught the glint of malevolence. "I suggested he take you as his mistress."

The words coiled about her like a serpent, swift, constricting, and spreading through her chest—a dark tide pulling her under, only to release her and batter her against a rocky shore. "You—" she choked out. But Geneva drew in a harsh breath, remembering she'd learned more at Miss Greensley's than academics. She was the epitome of survival tactics. "You've made it abundantly clear why you've no friends, Miss Hale," she said gently. "And I, for one, am sorry for you."

CHAPTER ELEVEN

T HE NEXT MORNING, Noah was wakened by a harsh rain and a
fierce wind rattling the windows. He crossed the icy floor to
the hearth and stirred the embers before tossing on more fuel,
then rang for coffee. The water in the basin was as frigid as the
floor, but being the mighty Northumberland man he was, he
splashed his face with nary a flinch.

More of London's elite had appeared at the castle last night,
some as late as midnight, and he didn't expect it to let up
throughout the day. Father's service was scheduled for the church
in Alnmouth the next day.

Noah swiped his face with a linen towel and dragged on his
clothes. A glance at the mantel clock showed seven and he'd told
Docia to be prepared by eight. He had no intention of being late
and it had *nothing* to do with a desire to see Geneva Wimbley or
brushing a fingertip over her plump bottom lip—

The effort to put that image out of his head was futile.

He wrapped his cravat in a simple knot and donned a dark-
blue waistcoat that reminded him of a certain pair of navy eyes.
On a whim, he picked through his wooden jewel box and located
the sapphire stick pin, and with a grim smile, poked it through the
starched fabric. Snatching up his coat, he stepped into the
corridor, nearly bumping into Julius. Noah frowned. "What are
you doing up at this hour?"

"I couldn't sleep. Are you for Chaston? I thought to accompany you."

That was the last thing Noah wanted. "Why?"

"Why not?" he drawled with distinct mockery. "I'm awake and desire to accompany you. Is there some reason I shouldn't?"

Yes. "No." Noah ran a critical eye over him. "You might consider wearing your boots. The roads will be all muck." He could only hope they didn't break a wheel, or worse, an axel. "I'll meet you in the dining hall."

With a sharp nod, Julius slipped back into his chamber.

By the time Dermid brought the carriage around, the rain had lessened. The wind, however, remained a stubborn, brutal reminder that spring in the northeast was as unpredictable as a failed chemical experiment. Exhibit A? Fallen turret.

"You seem unusually enamored with Miss Wimbley," Julius said. The darkened interior hid his expression, but Noah detected the grin in his voice.

He responded with a grunt.

"There is something unusual about her, isn't there? I mean, she's friends with a woman of… of foreign ancestry."

"Of which there is nothing wrong." Noah's tone was hard and unrelenting.

"Oh, I didn't mean that," Julius hastened to say. "Lady Abra is very interesting as well." There was a beat of silence, then, "But what are they doing here?"

Noah stared out at the swaying trees. A question for which he had no answer. "Exactly what I intend to find out," he murmured.

"So, you don't believe they are here to pay their respects to Father. I thought as much," Julius said with a nod in his voice. "Still, it's quite curious. Does she remind you of anyone?"

"Lady Abra? No." He refused to speak of Miss Wimbley. Not when thinking of her shifted him so off-balance.

From across the confines, Julius's snort filled the limited space. "It won't work, you know. I have eyes. I see how you look at Miss Wimbley."

Noah leaned against the squabs, folding his arms over his

chest. "And just *how* do I look at her?"

"Like she's an experiment you are determined to evaluate under your microscope. Only she won't fit on one of your little glass slides."

That didn't sound so bad—

"But then your expression changes," Julius went on. "As if you hadn't eaten a decent meal for years and she has transformed into a rare delicacy you cannot wait to taste."

Christ, what a conversation. Noah flattened his palms on his thighs and smoothed them down his legs, gripping his knees and digging his fingers into the trouser-cover flesh. His younger brother was much too observant. The skin at his neck tingled beneath the layers of his clothing. It itched where the wool touched him, stuck to sudden dampness where his lawn shirt clung. And his cravat? Downright choking. "How fanciful you are," he said, unable to keep the roughness at bay.

"Ah, we're here."

The carriage slowed near the portico then stopped. It shook with the removal of the steps. Julius clapped him on the shoulder, his smile gleaming as he moved into the light. He jumped down, bypassing the steps altogether, and dashed inside Chaston Manor without so much as a knock.

Noah shook his head and followed his brother inside, half-wondering if he'd find Docia's body sprawled from a shove in the back at the foot of the stairs.

Instead, Viscount Chaston, all disheveled six feet of him appeared from the drawing room. "What the devil?"

"Gads, you devil. When did you arrive?" Noah shook his old friend's hand.

"Barely an hour ago. What's going on?"

"Julius and I are here to escort your cousin and... er, her friend to Stonemare."

Chaston was a cousin some-number removed of Docia's. He rarely bothered with Northumberland, preferring the London residence. He'd given up on domesticizing from the onset. The man waved out a hand. "I'd offer refreshments, but I doubt there are servants in this blasted house." He turned, inviting Noah and Julius to follow him into the drawing room. The fire had been stoked to blazing. "Hell, my bedchamber is a disaster. My valet is setting it to rights before I can even make use of it."

"I believe she hires women from Alnmouth to clean weekly," Noah informed him wryly. "I take it she doesn't include the master chamber in their duties?"

"I wished she'd get herself married," he muttered, dropping into a wing-backed chair near the fire. "Unfortunately, she's too old."

Docia strolled in from the hall. "We're all set—" She froze. "What are *you* doing here?" she demanded of her cousin.

"I'm here to pay my respects to my neighbors," he bit out, his eyes flicking over her latest frock of shimmering emerald.

Noah gave up on following the conversation as anticipation rippled through him. Slippered feet sounded from the hall, and Miss Wimbley entered. He swallowed hard. An urge to study her under a microscope warred with desiring an artist to capture the vision she presented in light-purple chiffon with its violet, satin sash. Her skin had been scrubbed to a rosy blush and her hair was still pulled up, much as it had been the night before.

While Noah didn't consider himself the least bit fanciful, as he'd accused his brother, he could swear a swirling mix of colors muddied her aura. Grays, purples—except for her eyes. They were clear and brilliant. Sharp and all-seeing. And sapphire, the exact shade of his stickpin. Just as he'd remembered.

He set his squeezed fists at his back and inclined his head. "Ladies."

A small snort emitted from Docia and Noah could swear his cravat tightened further about his neck.

Chaston came to his feet so quickly, Noah was tempted—and he may have taken a step—to shove him back down. But Julius had his arm.

"Lord Chaston, allow me to introduce Miss Geneva Wimbley

of London," he said. "Miss Wimbley, the Viscount Chaston."

"Charmed, Miss Wimbley. I would offer refreshment, but alas…" His gaze cut to Docia, he nearly sneered. "Er, of London, you say?"

"Yes, my lord." Miss Wimbley's lips twitched. "Berwick Street," she said lightly.

A frown, clearly disapproving, turned his lips. The man was as uncouth and rude as his cousin.

"We should depart," Julius intervened. "The ladies must be famished."

"Yes, of course," Chaston said the same time Noah murmured the same.

The party moved into the hall, where a stuffed portmanteau and a smaller case had appeared. He picked them up and stepped out the door, handing them off to Dermid, who stashed them in the boot. "Throw the tarp over them."

"Aye, sir."

Julius assisted Docia with her hooded spencer, leaving Noah to Miss Wimbley and Julius's smirk over Docia's head and at Miss Wimbley's back.

With a glare, Noah turned away and found himself being keenly observed by Chaston.

Noah ignored him, taking another hooded spencer of dark purple from the peg, abandoning the worn cloak. She smelled of something distinctly French that was much more to Docia's taste. In his humble opinion, the orange blossoms suited her bold personality that had nearly felled him to his knees the day before. He resisted an impulse to kiss the back of her neck where the wispy strands of her dark hair feathered his knuckles.

The spencer sported a hood and he lifted it to her hair. He dropped his hands and stood back, aware of Chaston's stare—that of a fire-forged blade slicing him between the shoulders.

"Thank you." She fastened the ties, her eyes meeting his. Eyes that had taken on the deep colors she wore that almost clashed with his waistcoat and stickpin.

Julius had led Docia out.

"What are you really doing here, Miss Wimbley?" he said low enough for her ears only.

A small, irritated smile tilted her luscious lips. "I believe your friend Miss Hale compelled the situation," she said. She spun on a satin purple slipper and escaped through the door and into the carriage.

She was as wily as he, it appeared. Still, he knew there was more to her sudden appearance at Stonemare. The thought trickled ice through him.

Firming his lips, Noah vowed he would have his answers in the end. He glanced at Chaston, who just shook his head and reentered the drawing room.

Letting out a long breath, Noah followed her out, securing the door behind him.

CHAPTER TWELVE

IN THE QUIET ride to Stonemare, amidst the lack of oxygen Mr. Oshea seemed to steal from everyone—her, leastways— Geneva just realized that Miss Hale had never answered the question of what had happened to her parents. She hadn't seen a personal maid, which Geneva found extremely odd, considering the amount of clothes the woman hoarded. The house was large and spotless. Someone tended to it. The sparse number of servants didn't mean there weren't any, but for one as pretentious as Miss Hale… Yes. Definitely odd.

"When did your cousin arrive?" Geneva asked her.

Her head was turned away as she appeared to be staring out at the passing landscape. "I've no idea."

"Less than an hour ago," Noah Oshea said for her.

Geneva wondered what she was seeing, as the rain had started back up after its short reprieve, rendering the view useless.

"And with no prior warning. Typically rude of him," Docia bit out.

Rain pelted the carriage, slowing their progress to the castle, but no one seemed inclined to speak. Geneva took the opportunity to study both Mr. Oshea and his brother. There was a similarity, but nowhere close to that of Mr. Oshea and the new earl. All had the dark hair, broad noses, stubborn chins. The youngest brother, however, didn't have the gray eyes the older brothers had. Julius's were more like the color of hers, a dark, indiscriminate blue.

"Finally," Mr. Oshea breathed.

It wasn't just that the sound that set her skin afire—it traveled over her with the force of a flaming deluge.

"We're here…" His voice jarred Geneva back from her thoughts and she glanced out the window.

Oh, no. She wanted to sink through the carriage into the muddy ground below, recognizing the deep-green barouche immediately. She'd ridden in the blasted thing. Any lingering doubts were squelched when the door opened and the marquess's emblazoned coat of arms revealed the fact. She cringed as the trio emerged, along with a maid, and watched as they were ushered into the castle.

Abra's parents had arrived along with Baron Ruskin—and no Hannah. There would be no avoiding him or his evil marchioness. Westbridge wouldn't allow anyone to dismiss Geneva outright—*one could hope*—but Lady Westbridge had no such restraints.

"We shall have to wait until the other conveyances have moved," Mr. Oshea said unnecessarily.

"I have an umbrella," Julius offered.

But Mr. Oshea's eyes were on Geneva. He'd read her expression and was helping… *her.* She forced her features to relax. While his assistance was appreciated—truly appreciated, beyond words appreciated—it wouldn't save her from having to face Lady Westbridge.

Geneva studied the baron, worried anew, praying he was good enough for her friend. She didn't trust his intentions. But then, she acknowledged, whose did she trust but her own? She forced herself to recall Hannah's reassurances. It was right for someone to be concerned and she knew Lady Westbridge didn't harbor any such concern. In the end, it was Abra who would suffer. All because of her mixed heritage.

Geneva donned her own cloak of hostility. She could handle Lord Ruskin *and* Lady Westbridge. She nodded at Julius. "Thank you, sir. There's no need to wait on my account."

"There certainly is," Miss Hale bit out. "That is one of my best gowns you are wearing and your slippers will never survive the muck."

"Oh," Julius said, his eyes dropping to Geneva's feet. "I'm afraid Docia is quite correct."

"We shall wait," Mr. Oshea decreed, brooking no argument.

In the end, it mattered not. The Marquess of Westbridge and party were still in the vestibule when Geneva entered. "Oh, Lord Westbridge. How lovely to see you," she said with heartfelt emotion. Lord Westbridge was the personification of Geneva's idea of a loving father. The stately countenance, the stern look in the hazel eyes Abra had clearly inherited from him. He took Geneva's hand and bowed over it, leaving a sheen of guilt in its wake.

Raising his head and spearing her with a paternal narrowing of his eyes, one brow lifted, and spoke too softly for those around to hear. "Miss Wimbley. What are you doing in Northumberland, you naughty child? I must have misinterpreted my daughter's... words. I could have sworn she said you and she would be traveling to Cornwall for a visit with—" His eyes swept the hall. "Lady Perl—Pender," he quickly corrected with an admonishing look that heated Geneva's face to some ungodly shade she likely couldn't name. He leaned closer. "And the man I sent to travel with the two of you?"

Panic banded her chest; she swallowed back bile.

"Never mind. I shall deal with you later. Where is that elusive daughter of mine?"

"Upstairs, my lord. I-I'll let her know you've arrived," she whispered.

Lady Westbridge glared down her pointed nose. She had small eyes that always seemed too close together. The marchioness abhorred that the marquess treated Geneva with such respect as one of Abra's closest friends. She was older than the type of woman Geneva had thought the marquess would have wed, but Abra had told her he hadn't been looking for a child bride. By no means was Lady Westbridge in her dotage, as she was in her early forties, if memory served. The woman didn't speak, but her rancor seeped through every layer of Geneva's fine clothes.

"Lady Westbridge. Lord Ruskin." Contriteness had Geneva lowering her eyes. She dipped a respectful curtsey. Of no matter, however, as Lady Westbridge's lips tightened.

Lord Ruskin stepped forward, a puzzled look on his handsome face. He and Hannah shared the same wheat-colored hair and bright-blue eyes. But there was a seriousness about his demeanor that Hannah insisted had not been there before he'd left for the Continent.

"Geneva, you're back—" Abra's steps slowed on the grand staircase. "Papa? Mother?" Geneva feared her friend would faint and tumble the rest of the way down the stairs. But Abra was not so missish as to lose her comportment. Miss Greensley would be proud. Abra gathered her poise and continued her descent with grace, going to her father.

"Darling." Lord Westbridge leaned in and kissed her cheek, murmuring quietly. He was careful in making certain no others could hear, but Geneva imagined his edict: *Your mother warned me this friendship I've condoned would come back to haunt me.*

Abra's eyes dropped and she nodded.

Lady Westbridge looked as if her spine would splinter under such rigidity. "Lord Ruskin insisted on accompanying your father and me, Abra." The woman's words seemed to grind out of her.

Abra's head lifted quickly, her amber-toned face darkening with a deep flush. Geneva nearly groaned.

Granted, the baron was an attractive man, Geneva felt forced into admitting, but his staunchness concerned her for the future of the Sapphire Society should he learn of Hannah, Abra, and Geneva's endeavors. He didn't seem the sort to embrace change.

With Meredith gone and Lady Westbridge determined to marry Abra off, Hannah would be next. Where would that leave the Society?

Where would that leave...her?

Geneva started up the stairs, desperate for escape. Before she reached the top, Mr. Oshea called out. "A word, Miss Wimbley?"

She couldn't turn. If she moved her head an iota, the unshed tears blurring her sight would spill. She just couldn't. Not in front of Lord Westbridge. Not in front of Lady Westbridge. And most especially, not in front of Mr. Oshea. "Later, sir."

Even Lady Westbridge's gasp failed in cheering her. Though there would be a gossip bill for cutting the man in his own entryway. The thought didn't stop her. She quickened her steps.

Sadly, one couldn't outrun one's guilt.

Geneva escaped to her bedchamber and tugged off the lovely white kid gloves and tossed them on a chair. Oh, no. She'd forgotten to leave them with the footman like a true lady. Another breach of etiquette in the face of many. Her tears spilled over even knowing it did no good to brood over the lack of cultivated behavior. What a hopeless case she was. Raising her head, Geneva moved to the vanity with sluggish steps. She took a handkerchief and dried her tears. What a colossal fool she was.

Blast, it was cold. The chill in the chamber had her clutching the hooded spencer tighter about her, and she realized the fire was just embers, presumably because she'd slept away from the castle the night before. She took up a poker and stirred the fire, tossing on more fuel. The room was too cold for her to remove her spencer.

She paced the room slowly. Partly to keep warm and partly to pull her thoughts together. In the end, she considered, the Clandestine Sapphire Society stood for those who had no voice. For women, for children, for education, the poor, the abused. That would *never* change. Not as long as she remained on this earth and was a viable member of the population. She would never, ever give up the fight the CSS stood for.

Geneva strode to the escritoire in the corner of the room and lowered the desk portion. She sat in the hard chair and pulled out the latest article for Hannah. Anything was better than contemplating Lord Westbrook's disappointment in her. Perhaps worse:

Miss Hale's scathing words, suggesting Geneva would only qualify as a mistress to a man such as Noah Oshea.

The thought of putting herself in such a position sickened her—the lack of self-respect, the disdain of her friends. Her entire life, she'd fought to prove her own worth, from Mrs. Cornett's thoughtless remarks on a young girl's desire to read to exacting deference among her peers at Miss Greensley's.

Even in those days, when the excessively and unduly indulged ladies had mocked and treated her atrociously unfair all because she hadn't been born and bred in the illustrious confines of Mayfair, Geneva had still managed to find solace in her aspirations and penning them to paper. Those moments of solitude, of which there were many, had been where her dreams of equality for women and those of lesser fortune due only to one's circumstances had taken root.

That same need to lose herself in her cause raced through her.

She uncapped the inkwell, yanked out a sheet of foolscap, took up her steel nib pen, and tapped it against her lips. There were so many issues that failed the women, their children, and the poor, she hardly knew where to begin. But this was her life's blood.

After a moment, she set her pen to the paper.

To the Women of England (and men, if you dare to listen):
When women are entombed in the vortex of poverty and squal-
or, the mothers of all children, doomed in cycles of economic
dependence and exploitation, are denied your right to work,
your right to earn a fair wage, and your ability to participate in
the greatest economy in the world, you do all women, in fact, a
grave injustice. Women, you are undervalued and underpaid
for your labor. Women, you are relegated to menial and low-
paying positions, denied opportunities to care for your families.
This hurts and limits the entirety of economic welfare for all.
Therefore, I implore all of you: Demand equal pay for equal
work. Insist and create pathways presented to you for the same

economic empowerment afforded to men. We. Women. We carry, in our wombs, the future of the world. Without us, men would be left to pound their chests or one another, knowing the end of their world was upon—

Someone tapped at the open door, startling Geneva from her fierce scribblings.

"Miss Wimbley?"

She swallowed a groan. "Mr. Oshea." She stood so quickly, the chair toppled over. "This is my bedchamber, sir."

He appeared in the arch holding her bags, a wolfish smile tilting his lips.

A fluttering sensation in her stomach left her wondering if she'd ingested something disagreeable. The chill abated and the chamber grew unbearably warm.

His gaze surveyed her small abode that sent another quivering sensation through her.

"So it is," he said. "I'm not accustomed to being brushed off in my own home."

With a prim sniff, she tipped her chin up, her nose in the air, not unlike an expression she'd often observed in Miss Hale. "You should have sent a footman."

Mr. Oshea dropped the bags on her bed then strolled over and set her chair aright. He turned a grin on her that muddled her ridiculous brain, solidifying the notion of turning it over to scientists for studying after her time expired on this earth. "They are inundated with the flood of arrivals," he said.

She couldn't seem to pull her gaze from his curved lips. Her fingertips tingled—

"Miss Wimbley?"

Startled, she glanced down, surprised to find she clutched her pen so tightly, it dug into her fingers. Carefully, she turned and set it aside.

But once the eye contact between them had severed, Miss Hale's words roared back. *I suggested he take you as his mistress.*

Pride and fury curled through Geneva. She would rather die in the gutter than become any man's mistress. She gave him a wary look. "What is it you require, sir?"

He chose to ignore her question. "You're still wearing your cloak?"

Irritation flooded her. "What has that to do with anything? In case you've forgotten, I was not here last night and the fire was not tended." She marched to the small wardrobe, shucked the spencer, and hung it on a peg.

"Why are you really here, Miss Wimbley?"

"It's my chamber." Her impatience blasted through the room. "For the duration of my stay, leastways," she muttered under her breath.

"You have the most interesting ability to misinterpret a question," he returned. "You said you were here to take back what my father stole from you. What exactly did you mean? What did he steal?"

There it was: the bill.

She angled her head to one side, contemplating him for a long moment. She was not used to sharing her deepest thoughts, fears—certainly not her dreams. Not with many and certainly not with men. His shoulders looked broad enough to carry some of her worries, but trusting him was another matter entirely. He didn't wear his greatcoat, but he was big. An image of the man who'd visited her mother all those years ago appeared in her mind like an apparition. Ghostly and transparent. She shivered.

"What is it?"

Jarred back, she studied the concern etching his features in the creased forehead and lines bracketing his mouth. Rather than answer, Geneva went back to the escritoire and pulled a small, private case out. Quickly locating the yellowed, folded missive, she then strolled over to Mr. Oshea and held it out.

NOAH REACHED FOR the letter, not quite convinced it wasn't a venomous viper. But of course, a piece of paper that looked years old couldn't kill a person... Only, he knew that wasn't true. He hadn't known Julius's true origins. He had in fact, being honest with himself, avoided what he would learn. But there were lies surrounding his younger brother's arrival at Stonemare. Lies Noah had precipitated. Because, if he looked too deeply, he feared losing the brother he'd raised and so desperately loved.

With chilled fingers, he opened the note and read.

Lord Pender,

I beg of you, please. Things have turned most dire. My husband... is a violent man. You must do something to save my Gen... All that is precious to me is in your hands. Everything in my posse—

Nothing about Julius. Even in the areas impossible to make out, it was clear the author's concern was over Miss Wimbley. Not indicating a claim to Julius.

Relief rushed through Noah and blood worked its way back into his hands, his face. He looked up to find Miss Wimbley watching him with an intensity that stole his breath. "I take it you are this "Gen" she refers to?"

"Yes."

"I wonder why she didn't finish it."

"That's not all that difficult to understand," she said with a grim smile. "My father *was* a violent drunkard. I suspect she heard him coming up the stairs and hid it away before he entered and for some reason never got back to it. In any event, I'm here to find answers, Mr. Oshea. I believe it was your father who visited my mother when I was but five years old. He took something from her that belongs to me. Something invaluable and cannot be replaced. *That* is what I'm here for."

The coiling sensation in Noah's gut tied into hard knots. He calmly handed the note back to her, keeping a tight rein on his emotions. "And what might that be?"

"A locket. A ruby locket my mother promised was my legacy," she admitted, going back to the small desk and lifting the case.

Stunned by her words and at a loss for his own, he watched her slim, delicate fingers—stained with ink—gently take the case and replace the missive in its allotted place.

"I had hoped to speak with him, but of course, I arrived too late."

"I'm sorry," he said. *And relieved.* "I'm not sure how I can help you after almost twenty years."

She turned quickly, spearing him. "Twenty years? You have quite a memory for something you would have no way of knowing."

What a dolt he was. She was too shrewd by half. "I am at your service for any assistance you require," he said quickly as visions swarmed him of the small parcel hitting the floor and the fragile chain that had reflected the firelight that night nineteen years ago. For all he knew, Father could have sold that tiny chain to pay some gambling debt. Likely had so.

Surprise lit her features, and… gratefulness, perhaps. "Truly?"

"Of course." He failed to understand why he couldn't shut his mouth and take his leave. As quickly as possible. It was the fault of those dark-blue eyes. They begged for his aid. Her lips begged for something else. Something only he could give her. He moved closer, unable to bear the distance between them a second more. She was so lovely.

Slowly, she straightened and turned her body, facing his. The tip of her pink tongue touched her bottom lip. The shot of lust hit him like a dagger, piercing his chest with unfulfilled need.

"Th-Thank you. I didn't expect that," she said softly.

He reached forward, allowing her time to move away if she so desired.

She didn't.

He took her hands in his, leaned in, and brushed his lips over hers. They tasted sweet as a summer apple snapped straight from the tree. Her fingers moved up and clutched his lapels. His own hands gripped her by her upper arms. Over and over, he feathered her lips, touching the seam with his tongue.

Her lips parted on a surprised inhale. He didn't hesitate and slipped inside.

She stilled.

He explored the soft confines, reveled in the velvet stroke of his tongue against hers until she capitulated like warmed butter. There was an inherent need to stop, but the reasons to do so escaped him. Underlying guilt pelted him with a second bullet, but he couldn't stop.

She broke away, panting for air. "Sir?"

The urge to cover her mouth again hit him like the magnetic forces he'd spent years studying. *Not yet.* If he could but bottle the sensations. He wanted to howl at the moon.

"I-I don't think this is what you meant by your 'help,'" she said. "Was it?"

His hands fell away and flexed in and out of fists at his sides. "No," he said on a soft sigh. The current situation did not escape him. He was in the unique position of controlling what information Miss Wimbley acquired. He truly was a cad. He strengthened his voice. "No, of course not. I will do my utmost to assist you, Miss Wimbley." And he would... to the best of his ability. His decision firmed. Perhaps it was time to learn exactly where his younger brother had come from.

The band tightening his chest released, allowing him to breathe without choking. "You've nothing to wor—"

"Geneva?" Lady Abra's voice sounded from the sitting room. Loudly.

Miss Wimbley's eyes widened in sheer panic.

Noah flinched. He put a finger to his lips and moved quickly to the side of the wardrobe on quiet steps then indicated she slip out.

With a swift nod, she hurried to the door and left with a fleeting glance in his direction before disappearing into the outer chamber. "I'm here, Abra."

"What are you doing?"

"Writing an, er, observance for Hannah."

Lady Abra laughed. "Observance? Don't you mean a composition? Or an essay?"

Noah didn't hear Miss Wimbley's response but found the conversation highly enlightening, especially recalling the ink on Miss Wimbley's fingertips. He stole back across the room, ignoring their conversation and, indeed, found a paper right there on the flat. He lifted the paper and studied the tidy, efficient handwriting with its bold strokes, then read.

Each word entrenched the core of her beliefs and gave him insight to the mystery that was Geneva Wimbley. Her intelligence showed through her words like a goddess's flaming torch. Passionate words for a cause leaped off the page like a spray of well-aimed needles pricking his skin. Words that tugged at him. Showed clear purpose. Something of which was blatantly missing in his own life.

He. Had. No. Purpose...

Only, he did, as his vow to help her locate the answers she sought fleeted through him.

CHAPTER THIRTEEN

"I HAVE TO change."

Geneva scowled and, with a quick glance over her shoulder, followed Abra into her bedchamber. The situation had turned perilous. More than just Abra finding out Mr. Oshea had entered her bedchamber—it wouldn't matter that Geneva hadn't invited him. No, it was that blasted kiss filling her head with impossible possibilities. Such proprieties would only lead to ruin. More importantly, she couldn't bear the thought of losing the respect of her Clandestine Sapphire Society cohorts.

Abra stopped and skewered Geneva with one of her soul-searching, sees-too-much fixations. "What is it, dear? You seem out of sorts. That's not like you."

Panic prickled Geneva's skin. But she could not confide in Abra. From the depths of her corrupted reasonings, she searched desperately for some topic that would not give her away. Abra just knew her too well. The subject should have hit her at once. Gads, she was addlepated. "Why did Lady Westbridge have to come?" A rhetorical question if ever there was one. "I know, I know. It's an idiotic notion. Of course she would come."

Abra shot her a quick smirk, confirming the idiocy that required no answer. "I thought to assist Mrs. Knagg. She seems a little overwhelmed with all the guests. I suspect not much in the way of entertainment goes on in Northumberland."

Geneva laughed, for the absolute notion of Abra assisting with guests when she was a guest couldn't be borne. "You are not a servant, my dear," she returned. Still, her friend did have a way of trying to make herself smaller than she was. Something that drove Geneva to madness.

Abra grinned. "I'm only doing it to peeve Stepmother."

Geneva's hands flew to her cheeks. "Oh, the horror!" She shrugged. "That's all right, then. Should I order you about? She detests that."

"Certainly." But testament to the friends they were, she wisely added, "Only when she's about."

"You are the brilliant one of our little group," Geneva acknowledged with an admiring nod. They fell into a companionable silence as she went to Abra and assisted her with the ties at her back. "Do you think I'm unmarriageable?" she asked slowly.

Abra spun around. "What on earth put that notion in your head?"

She shrugged. "Just something Miss Hale said last night... It's nothing."

"Of course it's something. That *woman*." Her exasperation bounded against the walls. "She is nothing but a bitter and jealous feline, Gen. I should have seen it years ago, but I was too young and intimidated. Why, she must be at least thirty." She shook off her dress and let it pool around her feet.

"She told me when you ordered the bronze gown, the madame nearly gave you the direct cut, but she stepped in and told her you were Lord Westbridge's daughter."

"Oh. I'd forgotten that." Abra stepped over the silk at her feet. "Still, don't make the mistake of disabusing yourself that her actions were altruistic. The woman was known for more than one incident of that nature that season. I'm more interested in why you think you are unmarriageable. What exactly *did* she say to you?"

Geneva picked up the pretty dress and shook it out then went to the wardrobe and hung it inside. "She said she..." Tears blurred her vision. The second short burst of emotion astonished her. She *never* cried.

"Gen?" Abra had her by the shoulders, then turned her, jarring the tears loose. They dripped down her cheeks. "What did Docia Hale say? Tell me."

The hurt shifted to fury and she swiped the tears away. "She said she told Mr. Oshea he should *consider* me."

"A statement with which I happen to agree," Abra said gently.

"As. His. Mistress." Geneva's entire body shook with outrage. "She said marriage between me and Mr. Oshea would be completely unacceptable."

Instantly, Abra grew incensed. Her face flushed, her eyes flashed. "Well, she is wrong, my friend. Any man would be lucky to have you."

"Ha! What do I have to offer? There are no prospects, no connections, no dowry." Saying the words aloud should have lightened the load on her shoulders. Instead, it felt as if an iron manacle banded her chest and squeezed.

"Ah, but you have integrity, honor, passion. More so than Docia Hale has in her delicate little pinky finger!"

The kiss Mr. Oshea had leveled on her flashed through Geneva's mind and set heat searing her cheeks. "Passion," she squeaked.

"You've taken up a noble cause regardless of its popularity."

"Oh." How could she have forgotten? Blast it. Her post for Hannah lay on the escritoire for anyone—Mr. Oshea—to read. "I, um, need to run to my chamber."

"In a moment. Can you assist me with this frock?"

"Of course." Geneva eyed the dark dress Abra pulled from the wardrobe. "Goodness, I do believe you are truly determined to help Mrs. Knagg. I thought you didn't wish to embroil yourself in a scandal. Did you forget your baron is here?" Geneva didn't believe for a minute Abra was serious.

Abra froze. "Oh. I did forget… but… Blast it, I just need out of this macabre dwelling. I'll go for a walk."

Shaking her head, Geneva pointed at the frock. "It's raining and that dress is velvet." A thought hit her. "Perhaps we could do some exploring. Surely, there are unpopulated portions in a castle of this magnitude where no one would see us. We could search for my locket. Yes! That's perfect."

A second later, Abra's shoulders fell. "I don't have a more appropriate one for poking about in cobwebbed attics and chambers."

"I do." And sadly, she did. "Of course, but if we happen into Lady Westbridge... well, you know... anything I have will definitely 'peeve' Lady Westbridge."

Abra grinned. "Sounds brilliant."

"And might get back to Lord Ruskin, Abra. But if you absolutely insist—" She stopped and leveled the same contemplative gaze Abra had turned on her moments ago. "You're doing this to avoid your father, aren't you? Abra..."

Abra's chin went up and she grabbed the velvet dress. "Fine. If you don't want help finding your locket—"

Geneva strode to the door. "Just don't say I didn't warn you, blast it. I'll just be a moment." She pulled the door open and slipped through.

"Wait, I'll come with you."

Geneva spun. "No—" But it was too late. Much too late. Mr. Oshea stood frozen just outside Geneva's bedchamber door and Abra outside hers.

"What the devil?" Abra whispered.

"It's not what it looks like," Geneva said weakly.

Mr. Oshea's lips tilted on one end. "Perhaps you should don a wrap, Lady Abra."

Geneva gasped, and Abra looked down. "Oh, for the love of heaven." She dashed back into her chamber.

One disaster diverted until the outer chamber door opened and Lady Westbridge marched in as if fire were licking her heels.

Swallowing a groan that nearly choked her, Geneva donned the cloak that served her well in dealing with her editor at *The Flying Intelligencer*. She needn't have bothered.

"Miss Wimbley, I was able to repair the latch on your window," Mr. Oshea said.

Lady Westbridge's eyes pinned him. "Don't be ridiculous, Mr. Oshea. It's quite obvious what's going on."

Mr. Oshea straightened to his full, imposing height. "And just what is it you believe is going on, my lady?" His composure was beyond admirable. It was enviable.

How did he manage to remain so calm? Just being in the same room with Lady Westbridge raised the boiling point of Geneva's blood, and not in a fashionable way. She was ready to stalk to the woman and poke her in her overexposed bosom and tell her to mind her own affairs.

Lady Westbridge's eyes narrowed.

The door behind Geneva creaked and she was tugged unceremoniously back inside Abra's chamber. "Quick, help me with the ties," Abra hissed.

"Where the devil is Pasha?" Geneva hissed back. She stared at the frock Abra had slipped on.

"I told her to get something to eat. She hasn't returned," she whispered. "Hurry."

"Lady Westbridge will never let you out of her sight now."

"Don't you think I know that? What did she say?" Abra straightened her spine, but the buttons were a cumbersome bunch.

"Hush, I can't concentrate."

"Ha." Abra's feet shifted, knocking Geneva's fingers loose from their rhythm. "Can't you go any quicker?"

"I'm trying, blast it. Stay still." Geneva kept steady progress on her task while weighing the words in her head. But she and Abra had shared everything since their days at Miss Greensley's. If she couldn't share this, then… She drew in a deep breath. "Your horrid stepmother accused me and Mr. Oshea of something nefarious, of course."

"She's the devil's own, for certain. Which reminds me, what in heaven's name was he doing in your bedchamber?" Abra shook out her skirts and spun around. "I'm waiting."

"He offered to assist me…"

Abra's brows rose.

"In locating my locket," she huffed out in an overly defensive breath.

"That libertine. I just saw him sneaking from your chamber." Abra clutched Geneva's hands. "Don't do it, darling. Men don't offer to assist a woman from the good of their heart. He will expect something in return."

That wasn't anything Geneva had thought. He'd been so… so sincere. "What are you talking about?" Then again, there was that blasted kiss.

"Much as I hate offering Miss Hale any credit, I fear she's right. He wishes to force you into becoming his mistress for his help. There's no other explanation."

Geneva scowled. "You just said any man would be lucky to have me."

"He's crossed a line. I take back everything nice I said about him." Abra squeezed her hands. "Darling, it's common knowledge that men from titled families are referred to as gentlemen, but many are definitely not."

Geneva yanked her hands away, impatient, frightened, every insecurity she possessed assaulting her. "I never said that I went to him for help. He came to me." She poked her thumb in her chest, then rubbed the spot. "He asked my reasons for coming to Stonemare and I decided to tell him the truth." She scrunched her nose. "Most of it, anyway." She hadn't told anyone about the man in the greatcoat and her mother begging him to "take her too." That would require too much explanation she couldn't explain, even to herself.

That rendered her friend silent… For half a second. "Oh. I suppose that's good. Are you finished? I'm stunned my stepmother hasn't yet stormed my bedchamber."

"Yes, yes. I'm finished." Geneva stood back and looked her over. "Almost perfect. Straighten your hair."

Unfortunately, their good fortune ran out. The door flew back.

Lady Westbridge's willowy frame filled the arch. "What are you doing here?" she demanded of Geneva. Her gaze surveyed the lovely room with its bright blue hue and touches of pink. "I insist you locate to another chamber immediately."

Abra's mouth dropped and Geneva was sure her own expression mirrored her friend's. "That is quite impossible, Mother," Abra said through a clenched jaw.

Geneva took her hand and squeezed a warning.

"She had a *man* in her chamber, Abra. *You* have a reputation to maintain. If we are to secure a match with Martinda—your *baron*—" she quickly corrected. "Then make no mistake Lord Ruskin will not tolerate scandal."

Abra's face paled. "If you are angling for a match between me and Lord Martindale—" She sucked in a harsh breath. "You are sadly off course, Mother. I will *never* marry that degenerate."

The marchioness lifted her hand, an open palm prepared to strike, but Geneva pushed Abra back and stepped in her place.

The sting went deep, the slap wringing her ears through.

Shocked silence blared against the wall before Lady Westbridge donned her cloak of haughty superiority. She aimed a particularly scathing sneer at Geneva, then lifted her chin, addressing Abra. "This is what comes from mingling with your lessors." She turned on her heel and stalked out.

Geneva covered her hot cheek with her hand and slowly faced Abra. "How often does she hit you?" she demanded softly.

Tears filled Abra's hazel eyes. "I'm so sorry you had to witness that."

She lowered her hand. "How often?"

"Not often. Not any longer."

"I take it Lord Westbridge is unaware of this—of *her*... mistreatment?" Allowing Abra to suffer Lady Westbridge's abuse was unconscionable. "Perhaps she's right, Abra," Geneva said gently. "This is a castle. There must be an available chamber somewhere in this monstrosity." Her impulsive nature was bad enough, but her pride was her downfall. Her temper as well, but she managed to hold on to that.

Unable to bear the hurt in her friend's eye, Geneva turned and stole through the sitting room of their shared suite, where no sign of Mr. Oshea remained and into the corridor.

Lady Westbridge was a reprehensible woman, but Geneva had promised Abra she wouldn't cause a scandal. If Abra's stepmother was attempting to usurp Lord Ruskin for the Marquess of Martindale, then it was imperative Geneva honor her word. Under no circumstance should Abra be forced into a union with a man who had never shown her friend the respect she deserved. And, if push came to shove, Geneva would go to Lord Westbridge, whatever the cost, to save her friend from a fate no better than residing in Newgate for the rest of her days.

GENEVA FOUND A stairwell close to the Morpho Suite and climbed the stairs to an upper level. She didn't stop there, continuing up another two flights. There were no lit sconces, but the windows near the stairs let in enough natural light to expose dusty, unbeaten rugs. All the doors were closed and the first two she opened turned out to be storage. Odd pieces of furniture covered with tarps. Trunks, paintings against the walls and such.

The third would suffice, she decided, but it was quite chilly. It appeared to be an old servants' room that included a washstand, a chamber pot beneath the bed, and a pile of linens atop the mattress. There was even a bedside table with an oil lamp. Unlit, of course, but Geneva could manage. She'd suffered worse than Lady Westbridge's attitude.

Geneva set about making the bed. There was no canopy or curtained area to stave off the cold. She would have to search out coal or fuel for later or, at the least, a few more blankets. The one advantage was its location to Abra. She hurried back down the stairs for her belongings and a candle to light the lamp.

Pasha had always been an ally for Abra and Geneva's friendship, so Geneva didn't anticipate any problems from that quarter.

Geneva entered the sitting room. "I located a small chamber—"

But Abra interrupted her, waving a note gripped between her fingers. She paced, her steps furious. "Papa has sent for us."

Fear touched with a sense of wariness oozed through Geneva. "You mean you," she said slowly. But she knew another bill had arrived, and this one would prove considerably more costly.

"No. Us. And I intend to inform him of the truth. My stepmother shall not get away with her actions. We're to meet him in the morning room. He says it is more conducive to privacy. In other words, he's arranged this little rendezvous with no chance of interruption."

Geneva nodded, but she had no intention of allowing Abra to sacrifice her future over Geneva. Geneva could take care of herself. Her potential losses were not nearly as consequential as her friends'. Any one of her friends.

With no delicate way out of their predicament, hands clutching, they made their way down the hall and the stairs. Upon reaching the ground floor and with the butler's direction, they soon found the designated 'torture' chamber.

Geneva and Abra entered a sanctuary of refined elegance.

The walls, painted a delicate cream and adorned with gilded moldings, provided a subtle backdrop to the room's understated opulence. Above the marble fireplace was a portrait of a woman whom Geneva thought might be the Oshea brothers' mother. It was in the fullness of her lips and the softness of her expression. She'd seen a similar expression on Noah Oshea's face when he interacted with Miss Isabelle.

At the center of the room, a round table held a vase of freshly cut flowers from the estate gardens. Their fragrance mingled with the faint scent of a lemon polish. Geneva had the most absurd urge to curl up on a pillow in the corner near a small bookshelf overflowing with volumes of poetry and botanical studies. Despite its grandeur, the room exuded an inviting coziness where a fire crackled in the hearth and cast flickering shadows across the walls.

Beneath tall, arched windows, a cushioned seat upholstered in damask fabric offered a tranquil spot to gaze out at the rolling moors beyond. The windows were framed by sage-green velvet drapes and dominated one wall. Sheer, white linings allowed for little light to filter into the space due to the gloomy day that matched Geneva's day thus far.

Lord Westbridge stood before the windows with his hands clasped at his lower back, looking out at the mist-shrouded gardens. The Persian rug had muted her and Abra's footsteps.

"Papa?"

He didn't turn from the view. "You lied to me, Abra. I'm very disappointed in you."

His words broke Geneva's heart. "It wasn't her, my lord. The fault lies entirely with me."

Abra gasped. "No! It's not true."

Geneva squeezed her hand and spoke over her. "It *is* true, Lord Westbridge. I found a letter from my mother addressed to the late Lord Pender. I was determined to confront him. I asked— begged—Abra to accompany me. But when we arrived, we learned… we learned he'd expired," she finished on a cracked whisper as more tears welled. She blinked them back.

He turned then, peering down his hawkish nose, his gaze moving Geneva to Abra and back. "I see." He let out a pained sigh, and Geneva knew grief from the depths of her soul.

"After the service, we shall be returning to London and you shall be returning with your mother and me, Abra."

This was worse than losing Mama.

"But, Papa…" Abra whispered. "I couldn't possibly allow Geneva—"

All the sternness Geneva imagined him leveling on his opponents in Parliament or any who dared treat Abra less than was her due showed in his face—brackets about his mouth, the creases in his forehead, the set of his shoulders. "That is all. And I'll hear no further say on the matter." He then turned that fierceness on Geneva. His countenance gentled. "I'm very sorry, my dear. But these are the consequences. I shall provide your fare back to London. As long as there is no more scandal, of course."

Abra opened her mouth, but he put out a palm, staying any refute.

"Your mother is determined you marry Martindale, but you wish to marry Ruskin. Am I right on this?"

"Yes, Papa." Her tone was barely audible.

"Ruskin has approached me, Abra. If you were to back out, I will have no other choice than to accept Martindale's suit for you. Ruskin has yet to ask you for your hand, correct?"

She nodded, silent this time.

"Good. Then you see the predicament we face, my dear."

Tears rolled down Abra's cheeks with another, short, nod. Geneva squeezed her hand again, her own vision re-blurring.

Lord Westbridge abhorred making Abra cry, Geneva knew. He turned back to the windows. "That is all, then. You are excused."

As so often, as one, they fled.

Once they'd reached their suite, Geneva shoved her tears aside. "I found a small chamber."

"Absolutely not. I mean it, Geneva. I won't hear of it."

"But—"

The tracks of Abra's tears had dried on her cheeks, but her fierceness matched her father's. "I'll not allow my stepmother to chase you out. You're staying and that's that."

"All right," she agreed, thinking of that shrew being able to walk in at will. "I'll stay." With Geneva about, Lady Westbridge would think twice of raising her hand against Abra.

Another thread rippled through Geneva. Finding those empty chambers had flooded her with ideas and renewed enthusiasm for locating her locket.

And also because Abra had made an excellent point—why *should* Mr. Oshea wish to help her? He didn't even know her.

"I'm still going to tell Papa," Abra promised softly.

Geneva hugged her. "Remember this, darling. If Ruskin doesn't come through, you'll always have No. 26 Berwick Street at your disposal."

A short burst of unified tearful laughs spilled through the chamber.

CHAPTER FOURTEEN

THE BALLROOM HADN'T been utilized for anything outside of Isabelle's pianoforte playing since the Middle Ages. And, while Aunt Verda had modernized the huge room by replacing the flooring and adding more lighting, Noah couldn't help feeling it would have been warmer with old-fashioned rushes tossed about. There were tables strewn around for seating, and long tables at one end were laden with lamb, pheasant, beef, and a wide variety of vegetables and fruit. Even single servings of custard were displayed on a smaller table for the taking.

As predicted, many of London's elite had taken the North-eastern track. Still, Noah was stunned by the number of people milling about. He'd no idea Father had been so well known, which seemed a silly notion, considering how often he'd up and disappeared to London for weeks on end. He'd sat on the House of Lords, so of course he'd been well known. The peerage was always well-known and his father had been unmarried for so long. The true shocking thing was that since losing their mother, Father hadn't trotted home with some green debutante to foist upon them; instead, had died a widower.

It was Noah who didn't frequent London. Not like Lucius.

He shook off his maudlin thoughts, fearing they would drag him to the doldrums and remind him he was also unattached. But the image of the elfin features of Miss Wimbley filtered through him, leaving him with a longing so fierce, he had to stop himself from rushing out and dragging her into his arms for more of those tantalizing lips of hers. With a low growl threatening to erupt from his chest, Noah busied himself elsewhere in surveying the throng.

Despite the reason for the gathering, the crowd was lively.

Lady Abra entered on the arm of Baron Ruskin with her parents right behind her.

Lucius and Docia were talking, their heads together in a corner far from Rathbourne. Sander mingled with a confidence afforded the titled, despite being untitled, though he did maintain a firm grip on Aunt Verda. Isabelle had taken dinner in her chamber.

Inhaling deeply, Noah made the rounds too. One person he did not happen upon—he covertly surveyed the ballroom—Miss Wimbley.

And then she walked in. As proud as the queen herself.

The gown she wore—*thank you, Docia*—was so dark, it appeared black. The sight stole his breath. From the corner of Noah's eye, Rathbourne frowned and took a step in Miss Wimbley's direction. Noah moved quickly to intercept him. "Good evening, Your Grace. I take it your accommodations are to your satisfaction."

"Yes, yes. Pardon me, Oshea. There's someone I must speak with."

Noah clasped his hands at his lower back. "Is your valet comfortable? You must let me know immediately if all is not well."

"I said—"

"I'm sure we can find anything you need. It may take a while"—Noah let out a self-deprecating laugh—"Alnmouth is no London, after all." He cut his gaze to Miss Wimbley. She stood near the Washington table, her blank expression telling, but Julius, his favorite younger brother, appeared next to her, offering her his arm.

She accepted gracefully and allowed him to lead her to the food.

"I told you, we're fine," Rathbourne ground out.

"Of course, Your Grace. If you will excuse me, I see my brother, the new earl. I must let him know that you are quite content with the chamber he graciously held off inhabiting in light of your appearance." With a shallow bow and pulse erratically pounding, Noah worked his way in Julius's direction, as Noah had no intention of speaking with Lucius about Rathbourne. Lucius had no care for how comfortable the man was.

By the time Noah reached Julius—thirty minutes later due to the overwhelming throng—he and Miss Wimbley were giggling like schoolchildren, speaking in low tones.

"You both realize this is a *solemn* occasion?" Noah said, taking an empty chair at the table, sounding like the curmudgeon he was. The orange blossom fragrance returned full force and he fought to keep his eyes open and maintain his posture. People were sure to notice if he gave in to impulse and lay his head on her shoulder.

Miss Wimbley's face cleared. All but the sparkle in her eyes. "Apologies, sir. Mister Julius was just telling me—"

"That Father hated me and was hardly ever home," Julius smoothly interrupted. "He rarely called any of us by name."

Miss Wimbley frowned. "Why is that?"

Noah shifted, suddenly uncomfortable, but said lightly, "I've no idea. I just knew when he referred to *me* by name, either I was in for an ear-boxing, or he wanted some unfathomable task accomplished." *Hence, Julius.*

"I don't look too kindly on fathers myself," Miss Wimbley said—somewhat darkly.

"Never say so, Geneva," Julius said. The sardonic tone his brother's voice took on hurt. Despite the ten-year age difference, Noah had acted as practically the only father Julius had ever known. And, to use her given name without her consent was wholly improper.

Noah's gaze shot to his brother. "Jul—"

"I've been granted leave, Noah. I'm not breaching etiquette. I know you raised me, but you are not Father."

Curiosity lit Miss Wimbley's pert features. "You raised Mister Julius, not your uncle or elder brother?"

"Lucius was already at school when Julius ca—er, was born."

"What of your mother?"

"She died in childbirth. She's buried at the chapel." Julius turned somber. "I never knew her."

Miss Wimbley set her hand atop Julius's and squeezed gently. "I'm sorry. I don't know what I would have done had I not known my mother. She was sickly from the time I was five, but I was fortunate to have her another decade."

"You were indeed," Noah murmured. "Julius, perhaps you wouldn't mind fetching Miss Wimbley and me each a glass of wine?"

"Certainly." He pushed from the table.

There was no time to waste. Noah leaned in and lowered his voice. "Why does the duke appear to disdain you so much? Miss Wimbley," he added on the off chance she would give him the same leave in calling her by her given name as well.

"I was friends with his daughter at school," she said with the hint of teasing in her voice. "And, we, er, were caught in a couple of scrapes."

Noah's lips twitched. "Of which you were not the instigator, I take it?"

She didn't speak for a long moment, eyes lowered. "Of course I was. You couldn't possibly believe the daughter of a duke would be caught writing suggestive text on a chalkboard, could you?"

"Like what?" he challenged.

"Hmm." She cleared her throat. "*'If she be black, and thereto have a wit / She'll find a white that shall her blackness fit.'*"

Noah was hit with a violent fit of coughing. "She didn't."

"She didn't, it was I." Her adorable nose wrinkled. "Surely, it's not difficult to imagine what occurred after that, is it? Abra came after me like a feral cat. A fight ensued." She lifted a delicate shoulder. "It was quite hateful of me. I was full of anger. Young girls are quite vicious, you know."

Good God, she'd had no idea what that passage actually meant. Still didn't, he'd wager.

Julius returned with their wine and took his seat, his mouth gaping. "A fight? Between ladies?"

She grinned at him. "Indeed. Alas, the instructress walked into a classroom of chaos. Our punishment was the three of us sharing a dorm room and taking all our meals together for the remainder of the term. As it turned out, we had much in common."

Noah looked across the room where Lady Abra sat with her parents and the baron, then turned back to Miss Wimbley and angled his head. "Oh?"

"Abra and I were both outcasts of a sort. Her mother being of foreign ancestry, of course. Her father does not discount her; in fact, he absolutely dotes on her. But there are those who are petty and vindictive." Again, her nose wrinkled. Self-disgust? "I happened to have been one of them at the time, even though my own background was blatantly more questionable." She paused and Noah was struck by the contemplation in her dark eyes. "Our punishment created the bonds of a friendship that can't be severed with mere words."

Gripped by curiosity, Noah asked her, "What did Rathbourne's daughter have to do with the situation?"

"Does it matter? Meredith, er, Lady Pender," she modified quickly, "was in the room when the fight broke out. She was actually friends with both me and Abra. Her attempts of intervention lauded her a blackened eye."

Julius gasped and Noah barely held back his own.

"Needless to say," she went on, "when the duke learned of the incident, he was not pleased. She begged him not to take her out of school. She very nearly hadn't escaped that fate."

With that bit of context, Rathbourne's reaction to Miss Wimbley made sense.

"But why is your background questionable?" Julius asked her.

"Obviously, you belonged. Such a school would not be free, would it?"

Miss Wimbley's head snapped to him as if the thought had never occurred to her. "How true. And very logical of you," she said softly.

GENEVA COULDN'T BELIEVE she'd never questioned how she'd been able to attend Miss Greensley's School of Comportment for Young Women of Quality before. She'd grown up in a flat on Berwick Street. But Mama had talked endlessly of her own school days at Miss Greensley's and how Geneva would follow in her very footsteps. Her mother's diligence in teaching her to speak properly, to mind her manners, to carry herself with grace… well, it had never been in question. Not to her, at any rate.

But *who* had funded her education? And, more importantly… why? Other vague occurrences whispered about her mind—how Mama had grown up in a grand home, then quickly saying, speaking of such around Papa upset him. *"So, only speak about it when your father is at sea, darling. It makes him feel as if his providing for us is inadequate…"*

Her head hurt, spun with questions and the lack of answers. She pushed away from the table. "If you'll excuse me, Mr. Oshea, Mister Julius. I require a-a moment." On trembling legs, she willed herself upright, to walk, not run or collapse, as she made her way across the huge ballroom, quite aware that not only were Mr. Oshea's, Abra's and Lady Westbridge's eyes on her, but Miss Hale's, Lord Chaston's, and the Duke of Rathbourne's were as well.

She escaped into the hall but found no solace. There were people everywhere. She snatched a candle from a nearby table and managed to maintain her composure until she reached the privacy of the stairwell to the secret room she'd decided to claim. The perfect isolated sanctuary where no one would witness her crushing humiliation. By the time she'd reached the small chamber, the silent tears coursing down her face were rampant.

She went straight to the sideboard and lifted a pitcher.

Empty.

Despair of some fifteen stone weighed on her shoulders. She'd cried more in the last two days than the last six years—since her mother's death. "Oh, Mama," she whispered to the room at large. "Where *did* you get the blunt to send me to Miss Greensley's?"

Drawing in a deep, unsteady breath, she plunked the pitcher back on the sidebar and took up the candle. Minutes later, she entered her chamber in the Blue Suite. She set the candle on the escritoire and dug out the case with her mother's letter to the previous Lord Pender and read it again. Unnecessary, since every word was indelibly imprinted on her brain.

> *Lord Pender,*
>
> *I beg of you, please. Things have turned most dire. My husband... is a violent man. You must do something to save my Gen... All that is precious to me is in your hands. Everything in my posse—*

Who had funded her education? The only name she'd come across was Pender's, so it seemed the most plausible explanation, except for the question of why. It would behoove Geneva to remember that the note she held hadn't been sent. Perhaps her mother had entertained others. But a picture of Mama having taken to her bed—*the great, swirling, black greatcoat*—from the year since in bouts of darkness left her doubting that notion.

Everything eddied and churned in Geneva's head. Around that time she'd been five years of age and the imposing figure wearing that bellowing, black greatcoat. How the memories dominated her in this grand castle with its secrets and gothic undertones.

She went to slip out of the lovely, dark-blue gown but groaned, realizing she required assistance.

There had been no other men in Mama's life but Geneva's own bastard drunkard of a father who, in retrospect, had spent most of the life she had been home at sea. Gone for a year or two at times. She shuddered at the memory of their last encounter.

Grabbing one of her old frocks, she went to Pasha's small chamber for assistance.

CHAPTER FIFTEEN

THE MORNING OF the previous Earl of Pender's service dawned with a bright sun. Surprising. It also followed a protocol that Geneva had never seen before. Certainly, not if one grew up on Berwick Street. Some of the nearby and more questionable neighborhoods to which she'd carried the Sapphire Society pamphlets had exposed her to scenes her friends would shudder at. One couldn't avoid such things when it came to getting the necessary messages out. But even with her brush against the upper crust, this beat all. It began with a procession of the family—the new earl, all three Mr. Osheas—and a slew of servants and townspeople walking the mile to the church. Mrs. Verda Oshea and Miss Isabelle took a carriage, obviously due to Miss Isabelle's inability make such an arduous trek.

In good conscience, Geneva couldn't evade the event altogether and was forced, er, *invited*, to accompany Miss Hale in her rig.

"You looked quite fetching last night," Miss Hale told her. She raked a critical eye over Geneva until Geneva shifted on her feet. "I don't believe that gown ever did me the justice it does you. It even matches the circles beneath your eyes."

The one reason Geneva could come up with was that it wasn't some variation of yellow. "Thank you," she murmured, proud of how she was managing to hold her tongue, if not her thoughts. She glanced down. Today, she wore the same gown, but with a dark shawl Abra had loaned her. "You chose not to walk with the family?"

"Of course not," Miss Hale huffed. "I'm not family." The "yet" was clearly implied.

The ride was tedious. Since Miss Hale's carriage followed the family's equipage, there was quite the wait at Alnmouth's one church, St. John the Baptist. After a lengthy service, another ride ensued to the family's chapel on Stonemare land.

The Pender family mausoleum loomed at the edge of the graveyard, a gray, weathered edifice with intricate carvings of the family crest and ancient symbols of mortality. Ivy clung to its sides, and an iron gate leading to its interior stood open, creaking faintly in the wind.

The mourners clustered close with their heads bowed. The late earl's name seemed to echo among the tombstones, sending a shiver over her skin. From the back of the large crowd, Geneva found herself conflicted by all the praise lauded on the late earl. His reputation hadn't seemed to be a worry for anyone, save his brother, Mr. Lysander Oshea. The London broadsheets had held innumerable counts of his exploits with women and at the most notorious gaming hells. So many, that Geneva had long ago quit reading them.

The wind kicked up as if agreeing with or disputing her musings—she couldn't discern which—and she clamped her hand on the useless hat she wore. Still, the gusts whipped the pins from the loose chignon she wore at her nape. She couldn't make herself care.

Being from Berwick Street offered advantages. One in particular, was that it rendered her practically invisible. Perhaps not around the duke, but outside that pompous ass, not many thought her important enough for a second look.

The crowd shifted, jolting Geneva to her surroundings. The clergyman had finished his ramblings and she took refuge behind a large oak as the throng made their way to the various carriages lining the graveled road. She had no desire to suffer the short distance to Stonemare while dodging Miss Hale's lobbing insults.

"Geneva?"

Hearing her own name startled her—her given name, too, against all etiquette. Reminded her that she wasn't actually unseen. "Oh, hello, Mr. Julius."

"Docia is looking for you."

"Is she? I would prefer she didn't find me."

He grinned and held out his arm. "Then allow me to escort you back to Stonemare."

Unable to resist his infectiousness, she returned his grin, dipped a quick curtsey, and accepted his arm. "I'd be honored, sir. And grateful, truth be told. I vow, dinner last eve was more than enough 'lord' this and 'lady' that to last me a lifetime. That is, if you don't mind risking your reputation. Is there an alternate path that will keep me from sight?"

"Indeed, there is." Again, that quick, cheerful smile. Which seemed incongruous since he'd just lost his father. *The vast, swirling greatcoat…*

It was his smile… the smile reminded her of someone near and dear to her. Geneva came to a halt, put a hand to her forehead, and faced him, taking in the strong jaw, the dark eyes, blue like hers, though their shape was all Oshea. It was his mouth that struck her as different. Fuller lips, like hers.

Like… Mama's.

His head tilted to one side, lines creasing his forehead. "Is something wrong?"

"I'm not sure," she whispered. She glanced about the path he'd guided her down. It followed the cliffs to the edge of a forest.

"You must sit. You're as pale as chalk," he said, leading her into the shade of the forest to a fallen log. "You should have taken Docia's carriage."

Geneva couldn't breathe. The tightness of her corset mana-cled her ribs until spots blinded her. "No. No, I'll be fine. Just… give me a moment." Her usually emboldened voice came out wheezing.

Another gust of wind blew from the cliffs, bringing with it a whiff of dampness. Dark clouds moved across the sky, muting the brighter sun from earlier. It put a sudden chill in the air, punctuating it with an ominous foreboding.

Julius. If he was who she thought he was, they indeed deserved to use one another's given names. He lowered beside her, and his brows furrowing in a concerned frown. "Tell me."

"Who—" She cleared her throat, faced him fully, clutched her hands tightly in her lap, and tried again. "Who is your… mother?"

His frown smoothed away. "The previous Lady Pender, of course. She died giving birth to me. I-I never knew her."

The vast, swirling greatcoat…

Geneva's gaze fell to the ground. She unclenched her fists, wrinkling her borrowed dark skirts and flexed her fingers. She took his hand. "Julius…" She lifted her eyes. "I-I think you may—I think… It's possible—" She swallowed.

"What?" The concern in his eyes had her faltering.

"Oh, Julius, I have this memory. I was only five. But I think… I think you may be my… my *brother.*"

He jumped to his feet, his lips parted in disbelief, hurt or… or was it outrage searing his expression? "That's impossible. I look like my brothers," he bit out. "I'm an Oshea."

"You have every right to be angry, but—" She held his gaze and refused to let go. "But you also look remarkably like my… *my* mother."

The world seemed to stop. Frozen in a different reality. Julius had turned to marble. Not a single peep from a bird, nor chirp from a cricket touched her ear. The wind stilled, leaving the sky darkened by the hidden sun. No leaves rustled. No dust stirred. Only the waves of the ocean crashing against the rocks penetrated the thick, damp atmosphere.

"We shall see about that." The thick fog of his anger was impenetrable. He spun on the path and darted through the trees.

"Wait…" Her voice trailed, watching helplessly as he disappeared in the foliage. She stumbled to her feet with tears blurring her vision, only to trip again, felled to her knees and coming face to face with one of Stonemare's footmen whose name escaped her. Just the night before, he'd served drinks to the guests. Now, he lay on his back, staring up into the trees.

But it was the large, red stain over his heart that had her whispering, "Dear God."

NOAH KNEW HE should be in the ballroom with guests. But to his irritation, Lucius had departed Stonemare straight from Father's graveside. Noah had entered the vestibule, only to find the new Earl of Pender carrying his own bag down the stairs.

"I have something to take care of."

Mirth rippled over Noah. "Cornwall?"

Grimacing, Lucius ground out, "Yes. Let Isabelle and Julius know, would you?"

Lucius hadn't waited for a response. Rathbourne's news of his daughter's condition had truly rattled his brother.

Noah was tired and conflicted and something else that he lay entirely at the dainty feet of Geneva Wimbley. He entered the study and went to the desk, plucked his spectacles from his pocket, and slipped them on. Looking up at the painting of his father staring down with that familiar smirk, Noah contemplated on the complication and complexities that had so troubled his father. A great sadness filled him at the waste, the loss that would remain forever out of reach, leaving behind questions that now would always linger as mysteries. He drew in a long, slow breath and, closing his eyes, murmured a wistful prayer for Father's eternal peace.

Alas, his father had never been much of a father to Lucius, Julius, and him. It was Sander who'd filled that void for as long as Noah could remember.

Shaking off the morbid memories, Noah pulled the painting away from the wall, exposing the safe behind. As far as he knew, no one but Father had ever utilized it. Perhaps Sander had on occasion, but considering the dust and the difficulty of turning the key in the lock, it had been quite some time since anyone had thought to look inside. He juggled with it until the inner mechanisms caught and allowed the key to turn. He tugged at the opening until it creaked under the pressure he applied.

Inside, he found stacks of vowels and ledgers and coins and jewels. He pulled out the top ledger with one goal in mind: to see if Miss Wimbley happened to have been a beneficiary of Father's rare generosity. Of which Noah had his doubts. Father had not been renowned for handing out gifts. In fact, the only gift Noah had ever received hadn't been a puppy or a kitten, but an actual baby. Noah flipped through the pages, noting that most of the entries were applied to the massive gambling debts Father had accrued. There was nothing to indicate tuition for Julius, but then Uncle Sander took care of those matters as man of business of the titles and estates holdings.

It took ten minutes before Noah's insides tightened with an apprehension he couldn't explain. The notation was toward the back of the book. One entry scribbled almost ineligibly, *Greensley Fucking School.* Next to that was an exorbitant amount, which meant his father had likely paid the entire amount upfront.

From behind him, the study door burst wide, hitting the wall. Julius flew in, his hair disheveled and his eyes wild as a raging storm.

Noah tossed the ledger inside, slammed the safe shut, and pushed the painting in place. He pulled off his spectacles and tossed them on the desk before hurrying to the door. "Julius, what the devil?" He closed the door and locked it.

His younger brother's hands squeezed into fists then flexed out his fingers. Over and over, he did this. He couldn't seem to speak.

Noah shook him by the upper arms. "Damn it, *Julius.*"

"Is it true?" he croaked out.

"Is *what* true?" But that was all Noah could get out of him before a scream threatened the stone walls with the same force as his failed experiment. "Dear God, now what?"

Both he and Julius dashed for the door, but Noah had locked it. He grappled with the key before getting it turned and yanked the door back. In the entry hall, numerous guests spilled from every direction. All witness to Miss Wimbley's slight, violently trembling body. The dark gown she'd worn the night before and to today's service for his father was covered in dirt and bits of grass and leaves. Most striking was her pasty-white face. Her black gloves were saturated and her lily-white chest...

Covered in blood.

Her horrified gaze met his.

Noah strode forward and wrapped an arm around her shoulders. He surveyed the crowd and found the source of the scream based on Lady Westbridge being lifted from the floor by Baron Ruskin. The older woman's eyes fluttered open. "You," she hissed, pointing a finger at Miss Wimbley, "are a menace." She turned to her husband. "We are departing, Westbridge. Right this instant. Come along, Abra." The woman marched up the stairs like a general. The surrounding spectators stirred, as if troops preparing for battle, and fell into line.

Lord Westbridge, to his credit, sent Miss Wimbley a telling glance perhaps touched with sympathy. But with too many curious bystanders, he offered nothing more and followed his wife. Notably, Noah was mollified to see, the marquess growled something at his wife, who stiffened with obvious outrage.

Halfway up, Westbridge turned back. "Abra." The stern control was unmistakable and marked with a dark undertone. Miss Wimbley made a concerted effort to brace her spine, but Noah refused to release her. The only thing holding her up seemed to be her pride. And his support.

Abra had dashed over. She kissed her friend on her pale cheek. "I'm sorry, darling. I'll find a way to leave Pasha behind for you," she whispered. She glanced at Noah then back to Miss Wimbley. "So you won't be alone."

Miss Wimbley's lips took on a blue hue. Noah worried she

would expire on the spot. "What happened?" he asked her.

"The footman. I-I can't remember… His name escapes me." The brittle rod of her spine threatened to crumble beneath his hold as aftershocks began overtaking her resolve. As a scientist, he knew of the earthquake phenomenon. He'd even visited the sight of the Comrie quake in Scotland that had usurped a dam near Stirling to breach. He'd been twenty-one at the time.

"Come." He led her to the study. "You, too, Julius," he called over his shoulder.

Sander followed as well.

Noah led her to the settee and Sander brought her a glass with two fingers of brandy.

Miss Wimbley shook her head. "No."

"Drink it." Sander spoke gently but quite firmly. "I'm afraid you have a long day ahead of you, Miss Wimbley."

She raised her hand to take the glass, but it shook too violently.

Noah wrapped his fingers around hers and set the glass to her lips.

She sputtered and coughed, but the color slowly returned to her face.

"Now, tell us why you're covered in blood." Again, it was Sander who kept things matter-of-fact and on point.

The door opened quietly and Verda entered. She took one look at the situation and barked at Uncle Sander to quit hovering over Miss Wimbley.

Miss Wimbley glanced at Julius, who met her gaze with his chin raised. "I was in the forest alone and something frightened me. I ran and t-tripped." Once more, the color drained from her face. "I fell on the footman. He was already… already… gone."

Verda gasped and, Noah knew, all but Julius were taken back to that moment nineteen years ago when the wandering lunatic, Cracked Calvin, had been found dead. Bashed on the head with a rock.

"What are you saying, Miss Wimbley?" Sander spoke softly

but sharp as a knife's point that slid silently into its unsuspecting quarry.

Her head moved back and forth. Clearly stunned. Her lips moved, but nothing emerged.

"Where?" Sander bit out.

"In the forest. Near where I w-was s-sitting." The words burst out on a sob.

"At the far end, before you reach the cliffs," Julius clarified.

"Dear God. I'll inform Baldric." Sander strode to the door, but the ancient stableman entered at that moment. A minute later, Baldric was gone, the door banging shut with Sander's shove.

Miss Wimbley flinched.

Noah glared at his uncle before turning back to her. "Tell us what happened," he said gently.

It was Julius who answered. "I accompanied Geneva back to Stonemare. I—" He shot her a helpless look. "I'm sorry. I-I shouldn't have deserted her," he stuttered out.

Noah frowned at his brother. Frankly, he shouldn't have been alone with her in the first place, but that was a scolding for a later time. "What the devil, Julius? I've never known you to abandon a lady before."

A fiery light in Julius's eyes met Miss Wimbley's. "She asked who my mother was." The belligerence distracted Noah from his actual words—

A chill weaved through Noah's spine and spread to his fingertips. "Pardon?" *This couldn't be.*

Miss Wimbley closed her eyes with her head thrown back. "I-I used to have this dream." Her eyes opened and she focused on Julius. "I've since figured out it wasn't a dream, but a memory. Until two weeks ago when I found a note from"—again, her gaze found Julius's—"from my mother." Her bloodless fingers gripped her empty glass.

Noah could feel his life spinning out of control. "A dream?"

"Not a dream," she reiterated. "A huge man visited my

mother. He wore a…" She took a deep breath, her gaze surveying the surrounding faces. "A black, swirling greatcoat."

Noah was struck by Uncle Sander's intensity and the fist clenched at his side. "Was there anything else significant about this memory?" Sander asked her.

"He just seemed so big." Her shoulders hunched where she huddled in on herself. "I suppose it was because I was so small."

"How small?"

"Five. I was five years old."

"How old are you now, may I ask?"

"Twenty-four."

Panic infused Noah. He had to stop this but had no idea how.

The tendons in Julius's neck looked about to snap. "I-I was born when you were five."

Sander leaned forward. "It wasn't a dream, was it, Miss Wimbley?"

"No. I distinctly remember my mother being ill. I was staying with our neighbor below, Mrs. Cornett." Tears spiked her lashes. "She said my mother was on her deathbed. I was so frightened, I had to see for myself. I ran into the hall and up the stairs, but the man in the greatcoat nearly ran me down. He barged into Mama's and my flat and slammed the door in my face. She offered to give him—" She glanced at Julius. "Something. But I couldn't make out what. Oh, it was all so long ago."

Julius's eyes flashed. "She said I look like her mother. But I don't. It's not possible, is it? I-I look like my brothers." He sounded so desperate, Noah's heart ached for him.

The study door opened again and Docia strode in. "Everyone is leaving—" She stopped, took in Miss Wimbley's ruined frock, and her mouth gaped. "Good heavens, Miss Wimbley. What did you do to my gown?"

"Stow it, Docia," Noah snapped. "Hicks is dead. Miss Wimbley stumbled over him in the forest."

Her eyes flew to Verda. "Oh, no." Her wail was just as it had been all those years ago. "It's just like… like last time."

Miss Wimbley, frowning, didn't appear to hear. "I never knew someone could die with their eyes open," she whispered. "It's like the person's life just ends and they turn to stone." She shuddered and Noah wanted to take her hands. Reassure her all would be right. But for the audience present, he would have.

She shook her head, then tilted it, seemingly unaware one of her tears had escaped and trekked slowly down her cheek. "Last time?"

Docia collapsed in a dead faint.

CHAPTER SIXTEEN

GENEVA ESCAPED TO her chamber. Away from the horror of stumbling upon a dead body and the accusing stares, the whispered murmurings, Lady Westbridge's screams and her devastating words—*"You are a menace"*—before leading the gossipmongers from the vestibule as if Geneva had contracted cholera and dared to breathe their sainted air.

She slowly circled. Something was different. And wrong, noting less clutter than usual—her belongings. All her belongings had been dispensed of.

Disappointment nearly drowned her beneath the weight of despair. A piercing anguish sliced through her. Hurt, then… rage.

She tore through the chamber, ripped the linens from the bed, pounded the wall with her fists, kicked the chamber pot with her thin slipper, and fell. Her big toe throbbed. That proved too much and she slid to the floor, sobs wracking her yet washing away the macabre notions of this horrid castle. The frightening Sander Oshea's mien.

Not that she was angry with Noah Oshea. The fury roaring through her was directed at herself. She loathed that deep down, she had been fool enough to harbor illusory hopes. Fanciful dreams that did *not* include being anyone's mistress.

That blasted Noah Oshea. He had no right to treat her like a grand lady then dash her hopes by having her bags packed for her. Likely, they were stashed in a cart readied to whisk her to the train depot.

Geneva swiped her arm across her nose and forced herself to think.

Julius detested her now. Yes, it had to have been he who'd had her things removed. He'd been angry enough to spew fire. Just over one tiny question that had popped out of her uncontrollable mouth. The tears made a turbulent resurgence and streamed down her face. How desolate her life had become. She covered her face with her hands. Oh, to be back in her tiny flat in Berwick…

The door opened and Pasha entered. Her eyes swept the disaster Geneva had wrought. "Oh, my," she breathed.

"They confiscated everything." Geneva hiccupped.

"No. No, miss," Pasha said quickly. "I moved them myself. To my lady's previous chamber."

Geneva looked up at her and wiped her eyes. "You did?"

Pasha nodded. "You deserved grander, miss."

"That was very nice of you, Pasha. I-I suppose I'm so overset, I can hardly think." Geneva gave her a grim smile. "Abra is gone, then?"

"Yes, miss. She made me play sick so I could remain with you."

Geneva shook her head, the tears welling again. It was very possible, Lady Westbridge had been granted one of her most fervent wishes: Geneva wiped from Abra's life. The tears refused to stem. "I'm so sorry, Pasha. Help me up, would you?"

Pasha obliged then pulled a strip of linen from her apron pocket and held it out. "Never you mind, miss. I can barely abide her ladyship, er, if you don't mind me saying."

"Of course I don't. I happen to share your feelings on the matter."

Once Geneva was balanced, Pasha stood back and her eyes widened. Her hands flew to her mouth in an almost comical expression of horror.

In fact, if things hadn't turned so dire, Geneva might have been inclined to laugh. As it was, she looked down at Miss Hale's lovely frock and grimaced. "I do believe I require a bath."

"Yes, miss, I fear so. Please, let's hurry so no one sees you."

"I don't think there's any reason for worry on that score.

"I've discovered a unique ability I possess of clearing a castle of guests—wanted and unwanted. It matters not."

Geneva followed Pasha from the small bedchamber into the sitting room and pulled up abruptly.

Julius stood near the hearth.

She stiffened her spine, donning the shield that had served her so well in her early days at Miss Greensley's—a cloak of impenetrable silent resilience. "I'm not up for a confrontation, sir. As you can see, I am in desperate need of cleaning up," Geneva said flatly. She'd never needed anyone before, and she certainly didn't now.

His mouth opened slightly, then closed, as though trying to form words, but he couldn't quite find the right ones. His gaze dropped briefly to the floor then rose back up to hers, searching her face as if hoping for a sign of forgiveness. But she was not in a forgiving mood. His shoulders, normally squared with a confident air, slumped.

"I came to apologize, Geneva. I'm truly sorry. I should never have deserted you in the woods like that. Noah is right. I was just so… so startled." The lines at the corners of his mouth deepened, and for a brief moment, his expression softened—an echo of the boy she imagined he'd once been. The moment passed as quickly as it had appeared, replaced by a strained resolve. His jaw tightened. "I was hoping you might spare me time to talk. After you're rested, of course."

She pressed the heel of her hand to her forehead with her eyes closed. "I suppose a discussion is inevitable. Tomorrow, perhaps."

"All right." His dejection cut through her weariness.

"I'll meet with you," she relented less sourly. "In the morning? If you don't mind waiting. I truly must discard this horrible gown."

His lips lifted in that familiar smile so wistful, like Mama's. "Of course. I shall be happy to burn it for you, right in front of Docia, too."

She smiled back, hope filling her for the first time. "That won't be necessary, but I appreciate the sentiment."

"Do you think she did it?" Sander asked Noah.

"Absolutely not." But what did Noah really know of Miss Wimbley, except for the forthrightness that matched the bold stroke of her handwriting? Had Hicks attacked her? No, that didn't feel right. The man had been with them for over twenty years. A grim smile touched him. "She did do us one favor."

"What is that?"

"With all the unwanted guests hastening away, Stonemare can now return to normal." Noah's somber jest fell short, watching as his uncle strolled, unsmiling, to the windows and looked out with his hands clasped at his lower back.

"Except for the matter of another dead body," Sander said.

There was that. Noah rubbed his chest, unable to ease the ache there. *Hicks, dead.* Noah couldn't believe it. As with Sander, Noah and his brothers had been closer to Hicks than Father. There was no wife or children to inform. The man had been a loner. Yet that didn't alleviate the loss.

Baldric ambled in. "Parish constable's here for Hicks," he growled in his gravelly timbre.

The parish constable moved into the library. At once, Noah was comforted by the sturdy presence of the man. He was shaped by years of outdoor work and his no-nonsense approach to life. His face, weathered and ruddy, bore the marks of a lifetime spent in damp winds and harsh elements, with a nose slightly reddened by the chill and a beard perpetually flecked with raindrops or mud.

Sander shook his hand. "Thank you for coming so quickly, Constable."

Nodding, the man tugged off his broad-brimmed hat, clutching it in hand. His eyes, sharp and observant, carried a glint of keen intelligence despite his otherwise-plain appearance. They appeared to miss little as they swept the room. "Another one, eh? Getting to be a regular thing around here. Won't be able t' keep this 'un quiet."

Noah winced. "No."

With the constable's help, they'd been able to quell the details of Father's death from broad knowledge. Hicks's death, however, would be all over London by nightfall. Hell, nearly half the *ton* had been in residence. Witness to Lady Westbridge's hysterics. And the fact that Geneva Wimbley had been covered in his blood… It didn't bear thinking about. The unkind, persecuting rumors that would unfold with brisk and undue efficiency—how was Noah to mitigate the damage with a group of gossipmongers who thrived on such abhorrence?

And when had Noah decided it was up to him to take up the cause? But cause of what? Finding who'd murdered his father or saving Miss Wimbley's beautiful neck?

Not to mention… there was a killer in their midst. "Do you think the murderer could have been a guest?" Noah asked.

The constable's feet shifted. "It's possible—"

"Doubt it," Baldric interrupted. "He was stabbed. In the heart."

The words stalled at the blood rushing Noah's ears. "What?"

Sander shoved a hand through his hair. "Jesus. Same as Damien," he breathed. "It's as if the family's cursed."

A knot coiled deep in Noah's gut. The sense that things had taken a sinister turn erupted gooseflesh that traversed the surface of his skin, despite the fire in the grate and the brandy he'd sipped. "What the hell is going on?"

CHAPTER SEVENTEEN

THE NEXT MORNING, Geneva woke to the tantalizing fragrance of coffee after a hard and not-so-restful sleep. Her body ached from head to toe. She wriggled her toes. Yes, definitely sore.

"Oh, good, you're awake," Pasha said from across the chamber. She held up one of Abra's day dresses in soft peach.

Geneva frowned. "Tell me Abra did not leave half her wardrobe behind."

"Just a few things she thought you could use," was the pert reply.

Shaking her head, Geneva struggled to sitting, feeling each and every taut muscle. She crawled out of the huge bed. Her neck cracked, her shoulders, her spine. She wobbled on unstable knees that also cracked. "Did I miss something?"

"Not yet. But you did promise Mister Julius an audience."

Geneva put a hand to her head and let out a low growl. Or groan. Both seemed right.

"Breakfast just arrived for you. Along with his note. How do you take your coffee?" Pasha asked her.

"Rarely. How do most take it?"

"Lady Westbridge takes a dash of milk, no sugar."

"I'll have cream and two sugars, then."

Grinning, Pasha set the peach frock aside, went to a table near the windows, and poured out a cup for her.

The fragrance of fresh scones had Geneva nearly melting to

the floor. She almost tripped hurrying over—she was ravenous. She plopped a spoonful of currents then drizzled clotted cream on the largest one and took a huge bite. "You best have one of these," she said around a mouthful. "They are delicious."

"Thank you, I will. The note is on the tray."

Geneva took it up and skimmed through it, wrinkling her nose. "I think I may need something sturdier than that peach silk. He wishes a walk. Feels the wind has restorative properties."

"It likely does, miss. 'Tis your great luck my mistress left one of her sturdy walking dresses too. Perfect for a sturdy breeze."

"Hmm," she said around another mouthful. She swallowed then took a tentative sip of the coffee. It was strong enough to clear out any lingering cobwebs. "Goodness." After a second sip, she decided coffee was most invigorating.

"Where is Miss Hale's black gown?"

Pasha gave a delicate yet disdainful sniff. "I sent it back with the maid who brought your breakfast."

A shudder rippled over Geneva. "Brilliant. My thanks."

An hour later, Geneva descended the main staircase in a castle that seemed eerily quiet after all the hubbub of the last three days.

Julius strolled into sight from somewhere, meeting her in the large foyer. Neither said a word. He just opened the heavy, oak door and ushered her out into a brisk, cool wind. The Northumberland weather was as volatile as Parliament's reaction to allowing women financial independence. She lifted her face to the cool breeze. It felt wonderful after the horrible day before. "Aren't you concerned there is a killer about?"

He pulled up, frowning, then led her back inside.

She wished she'd kept her mouth shut. But to her surprise, he wound them quietly through the vestibule and down another couple of corridors and out an obscure entrance. "Will this suffice?"

"Yes," she breathed. Apparently, he'd needed the air as much as she.

The path they took was a different one than she'd traipsed with his brother upon her arrival. This one was much closer to the sea. "You aren't going to toss me over the cliffs, are you?" She was half-jesting.

He scowled. "That's not funny."

"Apologies. Inappropriate words tend to spring forth of their own volition when I'm beset with trepidation." She let out a breath. "Actually, they tend to emerge regardless. I'm not known for my reticence."

He grunted. At least she thought he grunted.

"Are you always so gregarious to women you've invited on a stroll?" she said in an attempt to keep things on a lighter note.

"Usually more so." He slowed his steps. There was a long hesitation before the tension seemed to ease from his shoulders. "I hope you'll forgive me. I suppose I'm treating you as I would a sister with whom I'm vastly annoyed." He glanced at her. Assessing her reaction?

Geneva allowed a small, peace-offering smile and shrugged. "I've no siblings to speak of…" She cut her gaze to him. "That I know of," she amended. "I've no idea how siblings behave toward one another."

"Don't you have friends who have brothers or sisters?"

"Yes, but I've rarely been invited to their homes. I grew up on Berwick Street in Soho. Some of my neighbors are of, er, questionable character." She let out a sigh. "Let's just say I try to reserve judgement, as I feel there are just as many good people about. Despite our humble beginnings."

"What of your father? You've never spoken of him."

And for very good reason. "Dead." *Almost certainly.*

"Oh."

There was nothing to say to that.

"Will you tell me about your mother?" He sounded tentative. Almost shy.

Geneva's insides softened. "She was the gentlest person who ever lived." Wistfulness infiltrated her. Something she always seemed to experience when she thought of her mother. "There was a fragility about her for as long as I could remember."

He guided her past the fallen turret. "What makes you believe I…" His voice trailed away.

The question was an excellent one. One she wasn't certain she could answer, but she understood his curiosity. "There are subtle nuances I've noticed that remind me inherently of her. The way you tilt your head, perhaps. Mostly, I sense the same sweetness about you. Your consideration and thoughtfulness."

He turned a sneer on her, which did nothing to dispel her of the notion. She returned it with a smile sweeter than the coffee she'd drunk.

Turning her attention away, she squinted up at the hazy sun that had muted every morning since she'd arrived in Northumberland and breathed in the briny air that tasted of rain. She stared out at the distance, where dark clouds stirred. "I think what I recall most is that swirling greatcoat. As I said, it seemed a dream. But there are details that are just so… so clear. I was standing outside our flat. I heard Mama say, 'Take me too.' He didn't, obviously. And then there was Mrs. Cornett—"

"Mrs. Cornett?" His voice was colored by an inquisitiveness, not censure or doubt.

"The neighbor residing beneath us. She's quite elderly now. She said something most curious. That I would soon have my own playmate."

"I still fail to understand," he said, shaking his head. "I mean, how do you know the figure in the coat was my father?"

"Ah. I found a missive she'd started, but, sadly, it was unfinished. I found it only recently," she hurried to say. "It was addressed to the previous earl." A fleeting thought of the ruby locket went through her mind, but she doubted Julius knew anything about that. Why complicate an already complicated situation? It would serve no purpose. Besides, Noah Oshea had already offered to assist her with that little issue.

Julius shook his head. "It all seems so impossible." He stood at the edge of the cliff looking out to the open sea.

"Would you mind stepping back?" She shivered. "Even if it turns out we are not related, I don't relish another gruesome event. One was enough, thank you."

He turned an impish grin on her but did as she asked. "I grew up here, you know. I know these cliffs inside out."

"Really? This is my first trek out of London. Besides Miss Greensley's school, of course."

"It really is spectacular." He took her hand and tugged her after him to a trail she hadn't noticed before that led down to the water. "The ocean is an amazing natural phenomenon," he told her, waving out an arm. "I'd take you down to the beach, but the tide is rising."

Curiosity gripped her. "How can you tell?"

He indicated a set of jagged rocks that pointed to the stormy sky and the foamy waves crashing against them. She half expected Poseidon himself to lurch from the depths to snatch them both from their perch on the trail. "When the tide is low, you can see the base of the closer rocks where they disappear in the sand."

The power of the waves left her in awe. "Goodness, it's quite mesmerizing, isn't it?"

"Quite." He turned and led her back up the path toward more stable ground. "So, you're all alone now?"

Though bristling, she concentrated on her footing for the steep climb. "I have very dear friends." The words came out defensive. *Reminiscent*, she thought wryly, *of the sneer he just attempted.* "You've met Lady Abra, but there are others." They reached the top and she bent over to catch her breath.

"I sense a loyalty about you."

She came slowly to her full height. "I would do anything for my friends." She spoke so fiercely, he stopped and looked at her. She lifted her chin and refused to be the first to break eye contact.

A long moment passed, then he turned that impish smile on her again. "I can see that," he said. "You appeared to be much revered by Lady Abra."

"Yes." Her stepmother, not so much. "Lord Westbridge has always treated me—the friendship his daughter and I share—respectfully."

"How do you—" His face turned red. He started walking again.

His thoughts were not so difficult to discern. "Pay my rent? Buy my food? Keep myself in clothes?"

"Well, er, yes, to be blunt."

Well, this should be fun, she decided. "I, um, occasionally write articles for the scandal sheets," she said lightly.

"Never say so!" Genuine surprise had him gaping.

"I can see I've shocked your delicate sensibilities," she teased. "I also write pamphlets for *The Chartist Movement* and other activist groups. I'm paid for most, but some I do gratuitously. There is a grave injustice in how women are treated. Even for men who are not of significant means and I don't know where to start when it comes to the children. So many." The regular biases rippled through her. "I cannot and will not be silenced."

"I've never heard the like," he said slowly. "How does that work, exactly?"

"Like you mentioned, I must have a way to provide for myself. I do enjoy eating. Frocks and petticoats, while mandatory, are not my priority. I'm teasing, of course. The fact of the matter is, someone must stand up and be heard. And, I warn you," she said, smiling. "If you are faint of heart, I suggest we table the conversation."

He returned her smile. "I don't doubt it." They walked on in silence for a time until he broke it. "Your passion makes me almost wish to believe our relation familial."

She stopped. "I do believe that's the nicest thing anyone has ever said to me," she said before a rustle from the trees alerted her instincts. Instincts she'd honed that had served her well in some of the most dire of London neighborhoods.

The glint of a shiny dagger sailed through the air with sharp precision—aiming straight for Julius's heart.

NOAH ENTERED THE morning room, where a fire blazed in the large hearth, tamping the chill. Even should a heatwave send the temperature to twenty-seven Celsius beyond the castle walls, inside the temperature would likely register at four—in the height of summer.

Winfield entered and oversaw the pouring of strong coffee by a maid he didn't recognize, reminding him of the loss of Hicks. "Where is Julius?" Noah asked.

"On a walk with Miss Wimbley."

Panic shot through him, sending his pulse in an erratic fury. "Surely not." He spun back for the door. "There is a killer about. Have they forgotten and lost their bloody minds?"

"They immediately returned inside," Winfield said in that stoic manner. "Then meandered through the halls and left by way of the door that faced the cliffs." He finished mildly with, "I also sent Fletcher to follow. At a distance, of course."

Noah stopped, his pulse immediately slowing. "Oh. Well, yes, er, my thanks." He took his seat at the table and drummed his fingers on the heavy oak. "Um, how long have they been gone?"

"Fifteen minutes, perhaps."

Noah hadn't slept well through the night. Julius's normally good-natured features, haunting Noah's dreams with shock and hurt. There was an imperative need to talk. Confess, actually. Noah had difficult truths with which to enlighten his brother. Now that Father was gone, there was no one who knew the complete story of Julius's beginnings. But he, Miss Wimbley, Mrs. Knagg, and perhaps Uncle Sander could piece the events together.

There was one thing in particular, however, that still required addressing: that small package that had fallen when Father had laid Julius in Noah's lap. He preferred knowing exactly what secrets he was up against. One thing of which he was certain, whatever had been in that parcel was surely the ruby locket Miss

Wimbley sought.

Unfortunately, he hadn't seen it since the night Julius had entered their lives. He could only think of two places his father would have stashed it: the master chamber or the safe in the study.

It had been so long ago, Noah could hardly recall any details. His only glimpse had been the chain itself. He didn't doubt her claim that she wanted it for its sentimentality. Gold was scarcely valued at four pounds per troy ounce on the open market.

He downed the entirety of his coffee. It burned down his throat. He pushed from the table and strode to the door. "Winfield, I'll return to break my fast."

This was likely his only opportunity to search the safe undisturbed. Fewer questions. Noah stalked to the study, straight to the portrait of his father and, ignoring the familiar smirk eyeing him, unlatched the painting from the wall. He took the key from the desk and, with much less struggle than before, opened the safe and pulled out all the contents, dropped them on the desk, then slipped on his spectacles.

Noah set aside the ledgers and the stacks of vowels then rifled through a few stacks of private correspondence. It was what he found beneath the sheaf of papers that stopped his breath. With light fingers, he lifted the wrapping he barely recognized from so long ago. A piece of a *London Times* broadsheet. He smoothed out the yellowed paper and read: *23 January 1828 – Duke of Wellington Forms New Tory Government.* Noah had been too young at the time to understand the political implications. Three years later, when he'd finally left for Eton—trepidation notwithstanding, in having to leave Julius behind—there was little he recalled on discussions beyond those of cursed Latin lessons, cricket games, and horrid meals.

He glanced inside the wrapped paper and his shoulders fell.

Empty.

It was certainly the original paper. He'd never told a soul what he'd witnessed that night. Hell, the minute Father had set

Julius across his knees and told him to name his brother, his focus had become single-minded. Julius had been the pet he'd always wanted.

What a little terror he'd been. A wry smile touched him at the thought. The times he'd badgered the wet nurse who'd turned out to be a sot, then terrifying the nursemaid until Verda had stepped in and put a stop to his juvenile bullying.

Father had never taken to Julius. But then, he'd never taken to any of them. His sporadic visits home had left Noah as both mama and papa to an infant and he would not have given up a single moment.

Noah dropped into the chair and pulled off his spectacles. He rubbed his eyes, then drummed his fingers on the desk. What could have happened to the contents? And… when had they disappeared?

The logical answer was Father. Noah needed to search the master bedchamber.

The sound of uneven steps penetrated and Noah stood as the door crashed back, hitting the wall, rattling the nearest framed artwork.

Tears streamed down Isabelle's face. "Oh, Noah, it's horrible."

Noah strode to her and picked her up. "What is, darling?"

She buried her face in his shoulder, sobbing, but there was no need for her answer.

Fletcher strode into sight with Julius slung over his shoulder and a frantic Miss Wimbley right on Fletcher's heels. They pounded up the stairs.

"What the devil?" Noah breathed.

Isabelle raised her head and swiped at her face. "Julius has been stabbed."

CHAPTER EIGHTEEN

Noah lowered Isabelle to her feet. "Find your father, darling. And have Mrs. Knagg send fresh water to Julius's chamber."

"Of course." She moved quickly, her noticeable limp not slowing her one iota.

Chaos followed Fletcher and Julius into Julius's untidy chamber with Noah trailing the group. Miss Wimbley still wore her cloak and there was blood on one hand.

"Put me down, you big oaf." Julius's growl of pride was a good sign and Noah let out a relieved breath.

"Calm yourself, stripling," Fletcher growled.

"*Stripling*? I'm nineteen."

"Right now, you're a pain." Fletcher dumped Julius on the bed, where he landed with a thump.

Miss Wimbley rushed forward, disheveled hair askew, eyes widened in terror—and fury.

This was the second time in two days—Noah's blood froze into an ice pool of slush—*no*…

He forced himself to slow even as red-hot rage should have dealt with the ice surging through him. Father had been stabbed in the heart. That made three incidents.

Miss Wimbley turned her fury on Fletcher. "Are you mad? He could be dying." She raced to the basin of water on the sideboard and snatched up a clean towel, dropped it in the water, then wrung it out, slinging droplets. "Take off your coat," she demanded of Julius.

The entire scene played out like a badly acted Shakespearean stage production that Noah couldn't drag his eyes from.

Julius scowled at her. Fletcher stepped forward and did the deed himself.

"It's just a scratch," Julius bit out. But the slash on his coat and the gushing wound told a different story.

Miss Wimbley laid the damp cloth directly on the cut with trembling hands.

"Ow." Julius's less-than-masculine whimper startled Noah out of his stupor.

"How are you with a needle?" he asked Miss Wimbley.

"Not so good."

"As good with a dagger, I'd wager," he shot back.

"Oh, I'm much better with a…" Her voice trailed and slowly, she straightened to face him. "If you are implying something particular, sir, perhaps you would be so good as to spell it out in plain words. I am, after all, a resident of one of the more lacking London neighborhoods." Her voice didn't raise so much as a decibel.

Noah frowned. "What do you mean?"

"A knife flew from a copse of trees and hit my arm. If Miss Wimbley hadn't shoved me, the nasty thing would have hit me square in the chest. Burns like the dickens," Julius grated out. The room filled with a thick silence. His head tilted to one side and he narrowed his eyes on Noah.

Noah willed away a flinch. *You're* my *brother*, he wanted to shout.

"Surely, you are not saying you believe Geneva tried to kill me, Noah," Julius said softly. "Fletcher said she didn't. He was there."

But Noah was frightened out of his wits. The belief she was there to whisk Julius from him nearly choked him. He was angry at himself for not protecting Julius from nearly being killed. Guilt that he hadn't delved closer into Father's demise crawled over his skin like one of Isabelle's nasty, little bugs, letting loose the havoc he'd lost control of. All that fury and culpability and self-hatred congealed into a furling ball of fire, and he turned it on *her*. "I don't know. Could it be she lured you out there so you could be attacked?" he said softly, leveling a stare and refusing to take his eyes from hers.

If possible, her already pale face went positively bloodless.

Sander and Verda chose that instant to enter with Isabelle dragging her foot behind.

"We've sent for the doctor, but it will likely be a while, Noah," Isabelle said. "I have the needle and thread. Mrs. Knagg is on her way with fresh water."

She worked her way through the fray and went almost nose to arm with Julius. "Cor, Jules. Can I sew you up? Mama's been making me work on my embroidery. I can do an almost perfect straight line of stitches now."

Julius, despite his horrified expression, couldn't suppress a grin—no one could when it came to Isabelle. "Since when?"

"Yesterday." Her answer was hedged and everyone about him, save Geneva Wimbley, laughed, albeit softly.

And Noah. He had no desire to laugh at the moment.

"Of course, you may sew him up, poppet," Verda said lightly.

Using his good arm, Julius scrambled back on the bed as far from Isabelle as he could get without falling on his arse on the far side. "Absolutely not."

The housekeeper entered and that was the end of that conversation. She took on the task herself, unfortunately, requesting Noah's assistance, trapping him while Miss Wimbley made a hasty escape before he could apologize. He didn't truly believe she had enticed Julius to his doom… but the fleeting sensation that her presence had something to do with the tragedies refused to abate.

Biting back an oath of frustration, Noah told himself it didn't matter. He knew where she was staying. There was plenty of time to speak to her.

He put his head down to deal with the matter at hand.

"OH, DEAR. SOMETHING'S wrong, isn't it?" Pasha's concern nearly tipped Geneva over the edge of the cliff of sanity. She wanted to crawl into a hole like a frightened mouse.

"I should say so. Pack our things. We are bound for the next train south. I don't even care where it goes."

"There's blood on your hand…"

Geneva waved out her hand. "Oh, that? Apparently, Mr. Oshea believes I just attempted to have his brother murdered, who, incidentally, is also *my* half-brother."

Pasha didn't bat a lash.

"Aren't you shocked? That Lady Westbridge was right about me all along?"

She smiled then, something that resembled a mischievous cheekiness. "Oh, miss. There is more to you than what Lady Westbridge believes. If you were intent on murder, I expect you would never be caught."

The tension in Geneva fled, though her eyes itched from holding back the desire to sink to the floor and sob until there was nothing left.

"Furthermore, if you were inclined to go after someone, I suspect you would have a very good reason." Pasha came across the chamber and patted her hand. "All will be well, miss. You'll see. Now, shall I commence packing?"

Geneva was still so stunned, and angry, and *hurt* by Mr. Oshea's implication, she could hardly draw air into her constricted lungs. According to Miss Hale, she was only suitable enough as a mistress. Independence was her life's goal, she reminded herself, firming her resolve. Still, her dry eyes burned. She owed him *nothing.* "Yes, but just make it an overnight bag. I think we shall pay Miss Hale a visit." There was still the matter of her lost locket, and abandoning her quest now would be giving up a piece of herself. She would hold Mr. Oshea and his lofty promises to count. Once she convinced him of her innocence, of course.

"Very good, miss. Why don't you wash up and rest a bit? I shall handle any intruders on your behalf."

That sounded like an ideal proposition Geneva did not have the energy to refute.

CHAPTER NINETEEN

ISABELLE LEANED CLOSE to examine the messy process of stitching up human skin. She was a bloodthirsty little thing, reminding Noah he was to blame for such interests, as she'd spent much of her young life in his laboratory with him. Not that he'd regretted dedicating a corner for her own studies, with her stacks of books and board of pinned insects. Though he was usually able to avoid looking at those morbid, little corpses of hers.

Uncle Sander moved forward and took his daughter by the shoulders. "Come away, poppet. This is inappropriate for a young lady to observe."

But Isabelle shook him off and looked askance at her mother.

Verda cleared her throat. "Er, Sander, if Isabelle wishes to watch, then she should be allowed to do so. How else is she to become the first successful woman physician otherwise?"

"Thank you, Mama," she said with an impish grin.

Noah suppressed a grin of his own. His aunt's mild words were reminiscent to Noah's own youth when she'd produced a book of essays by the scientist Elizabeth Fulhame. At the time, Noah had been stunned, perhaps understandably since he'd only been ten at the time, that women could be scientists. Back then, Verda had blithely informed him that women did indeed have brains. Noah had taken the words to heart and had included Isabelle in his studies from the time she'd been able to walk, to engage and encourage her interests.

Her parents were extremely watchful over her. They trusted

him implicitly due to him having raised Julius from infancy. But he didn't trust himself. Not completely. He'd been the one on the moors with her when the adder had bitten her on the ankle. The wound had grown infected and deformed the bone so that it hadn't developed properly. Sometimes the debilitating guilt was more than he could bear.

This was one of the many lighter moments that clogged his throat with a joy so great, he couldn't talk.

A scowl turned his uncle's lips and Sander dropped his arms to his sides, stepping back—but not too far. "What happened, Julius?"

"As I told Noah, a dagger flew from the trees headed straight for me. Geneva reacted instinctively, pushing me down so that it only grazed my arm."

"'Tis a tad more than a graze, Mister Julius." Mrs. Knagg finished cleaning the wound. "Hold the gash together, boy," she instructed Noah.

He rolled his eyes but did as she demanded.

Julius winced, and that was before the needle touched his skin. "Blast," he gritted out.

"Language, son," Sander said.

Julius clamped his lips tightly.

Sander looked at Noah. He didn't see him, but Noah felt the sear of his intensity. "Do you have reason to believe Miss Wimbley had something to do with the attack on Julius?"

The chamber stilled as it had when Noah had addressed his accusations directly to Miss Wimbley. His lips tightened to a painful line. *No.* He just didn't know how to deal with the sheer depth of emotion she evoked in him. Things he couldn't— refused—to label.

Julius huffed out his frustration. "Not this again."

From over his shoulder, Noah caught Isabelle's frown on him, then her father. "Miss Wimbley couldn't possibly have tried to murder Julius, Papa. She's a woman. Women don't kill people. And certainly not Miss Wimbley. It's unseemly, and she's much too nice." She shifted her attention back to the stitching process, squeezing her hands at her sides. It wasn't because she was squeamish, Noah knew. She was doing her best not to reach out and touch the puckered skin.

"As your mother has always pointed out, *strongly*, to the men in this family," his uncle said, "women have brains." Neither did Sander, Noah noticed, mention Cracked Colbert's murder of almost twenty years ago that had been committed by Docia's maid, Olive Townsend, who'd also killed Docia's sister, Eleanor. Father had delivered her to a lunatic asylum near Colchester to live out her days.

Olive, as it had been discovered, was a product of one of his father's many affairs throughout the years. Just as Julius was.

There. He admitted it. Julius belonged to his father, not his mother.

But of course, Noah'd had an inkling all along. But he'd shut it away because he loved his younger brother so much. Father had given Julius to Noah to look after, to guard every day of his life. And in his estimation, he'd done a capital job of it... until Geneva Wimbley had shown up ready to pry Julius away from him and his family. These were the thoughts that escalated his pulse in a dangerous, heart-pumping rage. The sort that blinded him with anger. Compound that with an attraction he couldn't explain, and the anger swiftly catapulted to outrage.

"If she didn't set up the attack, who did?" Noah gritted aloud without thought. "There have been three—" His gaze fell on Isabelle. She watched him with her bright eyes, not missing a thing. "We'll table this discussion for later."

Her hands went to her slim hips, her eyes glittering with a suspicious sheen, then flashing their own kind of dagger. She moved to Noah and poked him in the upper arm with her finger. "You're wrong." She spun so quickly, Sander had to reach out and steady her. "I'm going to ask Miss Wimbley," she said hotly, pushing past her parents to the door. "And I'm going to prove to you she couldn't have carried out such a nefarious endeavor."

Sander winced. A direct contrast to Verda's grin. Pride beamed warmer than the sun from her. "Isn't she the brightest thing?"

But minutes later, the uneven gait echoed and Isabelle stood in the arch, tears on her face. "She's gone."

MISS HALE SWEPT into the drawing room, her eyes going from Geneva to Pasha. "My, my, what did I do to earn this unexpected visit?" She was all that was gracious… and grating.

Geneva glanced about. "Is your cousin still in residence?"

"No. After that dramatic entrance you made at Stonemare, covered in blood no less, Henry wasted no time in spiriting himself away. With strict orders I hire a proper housekeeper, else he would turn me out. Papa's will would allow no such thing. As usual, he's full of bluster."

Letting out a held breath, Geneva saw no reason in not laying it all out. "I'm being accused of murder," she said glumly.

Surprise flickered in Miss Hale's widened eyes, but then she laughed. *Laughed.* A tinkling sound that floated like bubbles in a flute of champagne Geneva had once shared with Meredith, Hannah, and Abra after Abra's disastrous come-out ball. "Oh, how absolutely delicious. And who were you supposed to have offed?"

"Take your pick: the footman and now an attempt on Julius."

"Oh, dear. Noah is most protective of the lad."

"Lad? He's nineteen, as he shouted so eloquently."

"You wouldn't know it by the way Noah treats him. It's a wonder he allowed him to attend Eton." Miss Hale rang for tea then took Geneva's arm and led her to the seating area before the hearth. "Tell me everything."

So Geneva did. From the dagger coming for Julius to Noah Oshea's insinuation that she'd been the culprit. "I couldn't bear to stay there another minute.”

“Are you returning to London, then?”

Not until I locate my locket. “Um, no. We thought to stay the night with you, let the infuriating man get himself under control. If you don’t mind, of course.”

“You absolutely must,” she said with great enthusiasm that felt a little disorienting. “You’ll stay in your old chamber.” Miss Hale spoke as if Geneva hadn’t stayed over but once and only two nights prior. She glanced at Pasha. “There is even a small room for your maid.”

“Thank you. It’s all been quite disconcerting.” Geneva rubbed her forehead with the heel of her hand. “Because someone did throw a knife at him from the trees. I just can’t make sense of who would wish harm to such a sweet, young man.”

An older woman Geneva didn’t recognize entered with a tray.

“Thank you, Cook.”

The older woman left without a word and Miss Hale poured out cups, and to Geneva’s surprise, offered one to Pasha. “The previous earl had many enemies,” Miss Hale confided. “He was not discreet in his handling of women, nor was his father,” she muttered. “He cared not if they were wed. And a good number of the *ton* did attend his memorial service. Any one of them could have remained behind.”

Geneva drummed her fingers on her knee. “I hadn’t thought of that.”

The look in Miss Hale’s eyes turned speculative. “Your concern for Julius is most curious.”

“I…” Geneva took in a deep breath. “You are correct in your assertions regarding the former Lord Pender. I believe he seduced my mother and Julius is the result.”

Miss Hale’s mouth dropped then snapped shut, dropped again and so forth. If Geneva hadn’t been so upset herself, she might have enjoyed the sight.

Geneva smoothed her hands over her skirts. “I can see I’ve

rendered you speechless."

Miss Hale blinked and appeared to gather her bearings. "A rare feat, I assure you," she said on a breathless huff, almost sounding as a laugh.

"Yes, well. I'm not certain, of course, but there are... things. Little things that prick at my skin and refuse to abate."

"I rather thought you were about to tell me that it was you and I who were related," Miss Hale said softly. "Ah, but that would have been a shock, no?" She stood quickly. "Come. Let's get you and your maid—"

"Pasha."

Miss Hale inclined her head. "Pasha, then. You must get settled. But I feel a need for air. This has all been quite astonishing."

Thirty minutes later, Geneva followed her hostess into the late-afternoon sun. The temperature was cool, but the wind had eased, making the walk pleasant. She led her down a path at the back of the manor, where the ocean waves pounding against rocks drowned out nearly all sound.

"We're going to the ocean?" Geneva shouted over the force of nature.

"Do you mind terribly? There's something calming about the water's ebb and flow, the damp air—" Miss Hale waved out her hand. "Indeed, my blood seems to absorb its very power."

"You know, I saw the ocean for the first time just a few days ago. It's quite impressive." The hike down left Geneva breathless but exhilarated. Further conversation was impossible until they reached a surprisingly sandy beach. "Do you come down here often?"

"Not for some time, really." There was a sense of loss about Miss Hale's tone that drew Geneva's quick glance.

"As I recall, you never answered when I asked about your parents."

Miss Hale was so quiet, Geneva didn't believe she'd heard the question, or if she had... "My mother died of a contagion." She inhaled deeply.

"Oh, Miss Hale—Docia, if that is all right with you—I'm so sorry." Geneva lifted her hand but hesitated to touch her. She looked brittle enough to shatter. She dropped her hand to her side. "What of your father? Were you and he close after…"

"After Mama's passing, Papa spent most of his time away from Chaston." The bitterness etching her voice rendered sentiments similar to those that swirled through Geneva regarding her own odious sire. "Then, one day, he just up and left."

Geneva's mouth dropped. "What? I don't understand. What do you mean? That he… he *never* returned?" She gasped a quick breath, too astonished to snap her mouth shut.

Miss Hale looked out at the open sea with an indiscernible expression, her distant gaze unseeing. She shook her head. Without answering, she turned and walked along the pebbled sand, leaving Geneva to stay where she was or to follow.

She followed. "Where are we going?"

"There are some interesting areas about. I must have been a child the last time I came down here. My maid at the time refused to allow me to come along, and she had a fear of dark places. She murdered Cracked Colbert."

She hurried to keep up, and not just physically. It was all too much. "Cracked Col—I don't understand."

"Oh, he was a mad old man. Bound for Bedlam if he hadn't been done in."

"What? No! Your *maid* killed a mad man?" Mercy, how many other revelations could there be?

Miss Hale went on. "I almost believe she pushed my sister down those stairs, and I wouldn't be surprised to learn she'd poisoned my mother. There's no proof of either after all this time." She let out a melancholy sigh. "It's just a feeling."

"Good heavens," Geneva breathed. A sense of impending doom clamored in, around, and up her spine. She eyed the waves ebbing over the sand then pulling back with each pass. Apprehension added to her mounting anxiety. "Do you think the tide is rising?"

Miss Hale stopped and glanced at Geneva, flicked her gaze to the sea and back, then turned. "We should be fine." The confidence with which she spoke did little to reassure Geneva. Miss Hale resumed walking, but her steps picked up and now appeared purposeful.

Geneva glanced over her shoulder for her own assessment of the water. It seemed to be moving faster. Of course, that could have been Geneva's own lack of understanding how the ocean actually worked adding to her mounting anxiety. In any event, she hastened after Miss Hale. "What is our hurry?"

"I said we should be fine," she snapped with a glimpse of her usual surliness. "But that's only if we limit our time."

"Then what the devil *are* we doing?" Geneva demanded. She could not swim and had no desire to learn. Certainly not wearing heavy skirts and a snug corset where she'd never be able to retrieve a breath long enough to survive seconds if she sunk under.

Miss Hale's stride increased and Geneva dashed after her. Just ahead, a rocky path led up an incline where Geneva spied an opening in the hillside. "There are caves?"

"Of course."

Her terseness set Geneva's teeth on edge. The woman was a conundrum. And she hadn't slowed her steps. If anything, the closer they drew to the macabre opening, the faster her hostess moved. Uneasiness crept over Geneva. London had its share of dark, confined spaces and Geneva typically avoided them at all costs. "Is there something unique about this cave?"

They reached the opening and Miss Hale came to a sudden stop at the threshold. "I-I used to play here as a child. My father used to bring me. He told me harrowing tales of piracy and smuggling that happened during the Peninsula War." Her voice had taken on a childlike quality, as if she'd slipped into the past. "Sometimes I lie awake at night feeling as if he hadn't left at all."

Bumps raised over Geneva's skin. A chilling gale lifted the hair at her nape and a spray of salt water moistened her face. She glanced over her shoulder to the beach, empty but for all the ebbing and flowing of the sea on the sand. The flowing had definitely expanded in its velocity. She took Miss Hale's arm. "Perhaps we should head back."

"Not yet." Miss Hale took a tentative step deeper within, but instead of releasing Geneva's hand, her grip tightened.

Something unsettling permeated the cave. Geneva swallowed hard, not about to let go. *There are no such things as ghosts.* Again, the incline angled up to drier ground, as if the sea never reached this level.

Miss Hale gasped and her quick stop had Geneva crashing into her.

"What—" Geneva's hand flew over her mouth. "Oh, no. Not again."

CHAPTER TWENTY

"THEY WENT *WHERE*?" Noah had left Julius sleeping in his chamber with Isabelle looking after him.

"Hitched up the 'orse 'erself, 'er an' that maid o' 'ers. Tho' I reckon the maid did most o' the work." Rory, a wiry young man with a lean, hard-earned frame and a sun-bronzed complexion that gave testament to the satisfaction of his working outdoors, hung a rake on the wall and faced Noah. "'Ad to 'elp 'er, sir, but they both seemed sharp as tacks, they did."

"Rory! An answer, if you please."

"Aye, sir. Chaston House. Seemed in a bit o' a 'urry, they did."

"Saddle my mount," Noah ordered.

With the clear weather, Noah made it to Chaston in twenty minutes, taking the shorter route over the moors. There was an apology to make. But something deeper drove him. Fear. Fear that she'd disappear and he'd never see her again? His attraction, for the length of time he'd known her, seemed too intense. Hell, they'd met just days before.

Of course she was interesting, her intelligence obvious, her passion equally so. But it was more. He wanted her. And he *hated* that he wanted her.

It. Made. No. Sense.

And Noah was nothing if not sensible. He was a bloody scientist: logical, pragmatic, analytical.

He pulled to a stop, dropped to the ground and, without even bothering to secure his horse, stalked up to the house. Taking a page from Julius's book—though he did give two sharp raps—Noah entered without waiting for someone to answer.

Cook, practically Docia's only servant, entered the hall wiping her hands on a towel. The fifty-ish woman was unusually thin for a cook in his opinion. "Oh, 'tis you, sir. The mistress an' 'er friend took the trail to the beach."

"The beach. What the, er, what for?"

"Said they needed air." Her brow furrowed, adding additional creases to her already wrinkled forehead. "Been gone awhile, tho'."

"Thank you. I'll find them."

Noah took a side door out of the manor and found the closest path that led to the water. Urgency tore through him, but he forced himself to slow. He couldn't very well find Miss Wimbley and Docia with a broken leg, or worse, neck. There was no sign of the women once he'd reached the ground, but he spotted an unusual brush in the sand he suspected as the result of the hems of their skirts. The longer he followed the markings, the higher inexplicable panic tore through him. *The caves.*

His gaze shot to the sea. The tide was still out, thank God. He let out a small, pursed breath, but it did little to absolve the sense of urgency. A vision of Miss Wimbley's limp, unconscious body flashed before him and he took off in a run. He raced along the trail, his alacrity growing with precipitous speed.

Fear, so thick in his veins, it was tangible—and spreading from his toes up. The blood rushed his ears, drowning out the pounding waves. His breath came in short, rapid pants. He stopped and shaded his eyes toward the cave's entrance up the hill.

A flash of bright green disappeared inside and he took off again. There was no chance of that cave being affected by an incoming tide, but there would be no other way up to the house if Docia and Miss Wimbley lingered too long. They would be stranded overnight.

Noah reached the entrance and his insides plummeted...

There was a sharp inhale, from whom, he couldn't tell, then Miss Wimbley's low wail bounding against the stone walls. "Oh, no. Not again."

"Who's hurt?" he demanded, rushing forward.

Docia was on her knees next to a pile of moth-eaten clothing—except for pieces of ivory lying at odd angles.

"Oh, shit," he breathed.

Docia's face was in her hands, her body trembling with silent sobs.

To Miss Wimbley's credit, she lowered herself beside Docia and placed an arm about her shoulders. "Who is it?" she asked softly.

Noah darted forward and attempted to check the pockets of a greatcoat to no avail, as it disintegrated from the slightest touch. The silk waistcoat beneath had fared better—so he'd been a gentleman—and Noah found a fob watch. There was an inscription, but it didn't matter—he couldn't have read it for the lack of clear lighting.

"It's Papa," Docia said. Her voice was numbly calm. "He never made it to London. And no one ever realized."

While most of the fabric had deteriorated, there was a clear slash that went through the layers. Most disturbing was the dark spread over the heart of a yellowed lawn shirt. Noah pocketed the fob then came to his feet and assisted Docia and Miss Wimbley to theirs.

"Come. The tide's rising. We don't wish to be stranded." He spoke gently but firmly nudged them along. "Docia, I'll notify the parish constable so they may retrieve his... him." Noah wanted to check old Chaston's skeleton, but now was not the time for obvious reasons.

In stark hindsight, he was eternally grateful that Miss Wimbley had been angry with him and chose to stay with Docia. As difficult as she could be, Docia and his family had long ties. Finding her father's remains in this manner was abhorrent. No one deserved such answers as these in so great a dramatic fashion.

"I OWE YOU an apology."

He did. Geneva stood by the hearth in Miss Hale's prim, old-fashioned drawing room and rubbed her arms, staring into a blazing fire Mr. Oshea had so kindly brought to life. "I suppose a stabbing having taken place so many years ago was worth noting," she said dryly, glancing over her shoulder at him.

He grimaced.

She turned back to the fire. "When do you suppose it happened?"

"Twenty years ago is my guess. And for the record, my entire purpose for coming here was to make my apologies. I had no notion Docia's father—" He let out a small cough. "Everyone believed he'd taken off for London that year. And with the rumors of his extensive travel, well, it was thought he'd taken off for America or Australia. I was a child at the time, so I suppose my memories are somewhat faulty."

Geneva shivered. "At least there wasn't blood involved this time." Wincing, she cut her gaze to Mr. Oshea where he stood by the windows.

Those keen eyes were on her face—correction, on her... lips.

She opened her mouth to express her own regrets, but the words stuck in her throat.

He prowled toward her. Stalking her. Like the big, black cats of the Amazon jungle of which she couldn't recall the name. Her fingers tingled. Perspiration gathered between her breasts. She was rooted to the floor and could do nothing but stand there. Waiting... because her lips burned to feel his. Weighted lead settled in her feet, rendering her lethargic, unmovable. An Elgin Marble. Her thought processes seemed functional, but her mobility, no. He was a male Medusa and she'd caught the eye and was frozen in time.

"You," he said with a harsh bite, "drive me wild. In a way I can't explain. God, that I could. To myself, leastways."

His words cracked the encasement that held her spellbound and she grabbed him by the lapels and sealed her mouth to his. The moist heat mirrored other things happening to her body she couldn't describe.

A whirling fire blazed through her core to her heart. She was where she belonged in that moment, with this man. Her own impulsive nature, which she so despised, struck with a vengeance.

His tongue swept between her lips and into her mouth, officially taking command of *her* kiss, *her* body. Her reaction. Nothing belonged to her anymore. The sensations roaring through her stole even her ability to breathe on her own. As if he were the one breathing life into her blood, knowing she would expire on the spot if his tongue stopped stroking hers. Would freeze if he set her from the warmth she now embraced.

The world as she knew it ceased to exist. What *would* an affair of the heart hurt? The traitorous words whispered through her. *As long as they were discreet—*

She jerked her head back and fought the arms holding her. Her feet weren't even touching the floor. "Set me down, you blackguard," she ground out, disgust swamping her. To become his mistress stood against everything she believed of herself. The loss of her friends' respect would crack her soul into a million pieces. She couldn't do it.

Men may rule the world, but they did not rule her.

Confusion darkened his gray eyes to molten iron and she spun away. "I best check on Miss Hale." Her words emerged more breathless than cool as she'd intended. "I'm sure you know the way out." She turned for the door, anxious for escape before she either capitulated and ran back into his arms or burst into tears. Neither being an acceptable outcome to the tumult thundering through her.

"I came by for one other reason." His words, calm as the

ocean breeze, cut through the thinness of her frock, and she glanced over her shoulder. "Isabelle wishes to play for you. A musicale, if you will. And Julius…" He heaved in a breath and passed a palm over a face that looked as tired and haggard as she felt. His hand fell away and he speared her with a directness to rival her own. "I expect you'll be returning to Stonemare. We've still to locate your ruby," he said softly.

Yes. But not for that reason, she wanted to rail, *but for you…*

"Of course. I'll return tomorrow. With Miss Hale," she added harshly. "I don't think she should be left alone."

"Certainly not. As I said, I shall notify the parish constable regarding Chaston."

Her insides softened. "I'm sure she'll be grateful for your help."

"Grateful?" For the first time since Mr. Oshea had arrived, a small smile tipped his lips. And the sight devastated her. Threatened the lifelong self-assured opinions she held herself to.

Oh, Mr. Oshea was a dangerous, dangerous man.

She strode to the door. "Until tomorrow, then." Once outside the drawing room, she put her fingers to her sensitive lips and closed her eyes.

"Then I shall return for you in the morning, Miss Wimbley." Soft yet steely determination sounded through the door. The words sent her scurrying up the stairs and to the safety of Miss Hale's sharp, uncompromising rebukes.

Geneva deserved every lashing dished out for her own stupidity.

GENEVA LEANED BACK against the closed door in Miss Hale's elegant chamber. "You should get out of that gown. I'm no lady's maid. I dress myself, as I suspect you do." She heaved a sigh. "But I'll assist you if I must. Unless you'd like Pasha to assist you?"

"Don't bother. I don't wish to go back to Stonemare." Miss Hale was curled in a ball of grievance upon her massive bed, her eyes and nose red from a treacherous bout of sobs.

The only way to handle a disaster of this magnitude was with a stern hand. It would be no different than dealing with an unwelcome situation on Berwick Street. "You do not have to go tonight. It's much too late. We shall leave first thing tomorrow."

Miss Hale shot to sitting and pointed at Geneva. Her normally perfect coiffure stuck out in various places. "I won't, and you can't force me."

With narrowed eyes, Geneva drew on her Berwick Street firmness. "Oh, I can, and I will." She stalked to the bed and grabbed Miss Hale by that finger. "You listen to me, Docia Hale. *Miss—*" she said at the same instant Miss Hale did. Geneva inhaled a deep, steadying breath, wishing she possessed a modicum of Abra's placid composure. "I will not allow you to remain here alone." She let go of Miss Hale's finger, went to the vanity, and poked around until she found a lace handkerchief. She stalked back to the bed where Miss Hale had lain back down, curled up in the ball again.

Geneva lay on the bed facing her and pressed the scrap in Miss Hale's hand. "I'm sorry about your father," she said gently. "But he's been gone nigh on twenty years. If you force me to stay here with you, I shall make your life hell. Do not test me on this, Docia. I know what I'm about. Berwick Street is not Mayfair."

"You don't understand," she mumbled into the hankie and, to Geneva's surprise, the pretentious miss hadn't corrected her name.

Geneva firmed her voice. "Everyone understands. The new earl and Mr. Oshea, er, Noah just lost their own father in a grisly manner. *My* father is dead too. Not so long ago as yours, perhaps. But..."

Docia rolled to her back and blew her nose. "How did he die? Your father, I mean."

Obviously, bringing up that night and the knife would open

Pandora's Box. Geneva was already teetering on the sharp edge of that blade. "He was a sailor. Gone for months on end."

"Do you miss him?"

"Gads, no. He was a horrid father. The times he was home, he lived in a tavern in Seven Dials, or so I'd heard."

"I don't wish to return to Stonemare. You can stay here. With me."

How generous she was. "No. Mr. Oshea will be returning for us in the morning. Miss Isabelle wishes to host a musicale. We cannot possibly disappoint her."

Docia rolled back to her side facing Geneva, her reddened eyes flashing. "I want my blue chamber back," she said, sounding like a petulant child rather than a woman who'd reached her advancement at the age of thirty. In other words—more like herself.

"Bah. You'll do fine in the Brimstone. It's yellow. You *like* yellow." She waved out her hand at the pale-gold curtains, the yellow chintz counterpane, the dress Docia had been wearing the morning Abra and Geneva had arrived at Stonemare that was now draped over the settee. "It's everywhere."

"I'm not going, I tell you."

Geneva smiled, and it did not feel pleasant on her face. "Yes, you will. Let me tell you why. You are a bold woman, Docia. We are alike in that way, I think."

"I am nothing like you."

"Not in all ways," Geneva conceded, considering her words. "It's true you haven't bested drunkards calling out the most appalling epithets, or boys with nimble fingers *attempting* to relieve you of your purse, or been subjected to bawdy remarks from corner-street prostitutes when you happen by."

Docia bolted upright. "You haven't!"

"I have *and* I survived. And, my dear, so shall you."

Docia flopped back down, slamming her hands and kicking her feet on the mattress with a screech worthy of one of those prostitutes. "You're a horrible person, Miss Wimbley."

"Perhaps so. By the way, I give you leave to call me 'Geneva,'" she said, grinning and laying her hand atop Docia's. She squeezed her fingers. "As we are about to sleep together."

Docia growled. "Dear heavens."

A good sign. "Now, get some sleep. You look terrible. Note that I'm only telling you that out of the goodness of my heart."

"What heart?" Docia muttered, her fingers squeezing back.

Interestingly, she didn't retrieve her hand, drawing a smile from Geneva.

❖ ✦ ❖

CHAPTER TWENTY-ONE

"GOOD MORNING, NOAH," Isabelle called from the door of Noah's laboratory.

He glanced up and saw her arms full of boxes, nearly giving him an apoplexy. He hurried over. "Tell me you did not come down those stairs so burdened," he demanded crossly, relieving her of the load.

"I didn't realize you were working. I thought you were to Chaston for Miss Wimbley." She followed him to the far corner he'd allotted her for her entomology studies.

"I sent your parents after them."

"Them?"

Noah bit back an oath. Isabelle's curiosity could drive a man to a lunatic asylum. The news that the former viscount's body had been discovered in the caves had not yet reached his young cousin and he hoped to keep the information from her a bit longer. "How many times have I told you not to carry things down those stairs? One misstep and you'll break that stubborn skull of yours."

She clasped her hands in front of her, the perfection of a Michelangelo angelic pictorial—a *false* pictorial for anyone who knew the true Isabelle. "Apologies, Noah." Her contriteness wouldn't fool a flea. But berating her after the fact... well, if anything did happen to Isabelle, Verda would drag Noah to a makeshift guillotine and cut loose the blade herself. *With* Sander's blessing and help, of course.

"Will Docia be accompanying Miss Wimbley, then?"

"You are the epitome of the terrier with a rat. You being the terrier."

She turned that impish grin on him. The one that no one could resist. "I suppose that makes you the rat."

"I suppose it does," he grunted out. "What's in the box—"

"Why?"

He let out a sigh and set the boxes in a clearing on the table, keeping his back to her. "Why what?"

"Why is Docia coming? You aren't going to marry her, are you? She's not right for you. I think you should marry—"

No. This is *not* the conversation he would have with his fourteen-year-old, romantic-minded cousin. Still, memories of heat and fire of Miss Wimbley's—*Geneva's*, though she'd yet to give him leave in using her Christian name—lips the night before hitting him with the force of combining potassium permanganate and glycerin. It was a combination that mimicked his insides: a vigorous exothermic reaction that typically resulted in flames and smoke. Spontaneous ignition in which it was referred in the scientific community. Flames and smoke? Yes. That aptly described the portents surging through him.

"Noah?" Isabelle's voice jarred him.

A rush of blazing heat raced up his neck. "What's in these boxes, poppet?"

"Oh, insects for my board. I picked them up in various locales on the Continent."

Noah lifted the top of one and peered in—with great caution, of course.

"They're dead." Her amusement poured over him.

He pulled off the lid and retrieved a paper written in her neat hand, and read: *Euscorpius italicus, Valle Maggia, Tico, Switz.* "Good God, Belle. Where on earth…"

"It says right there."

Noah shivered. The scorpion was large, a good inch or two from tail to pinchers. The bluish tinge was unique. "I pray you don't name another chamber after this monster. It's enough to instill nightmares."

She let out a giggle that did injustice to her youth and intelligence. "I could rename the Brimstone for Docia," she said slyly.

He shot her a warning glance. "Just don't show this… this"—he indicated the scorpion, feeling a little green—"to her first."

"Did Miss Wimbley say she wouldn't return without Docia? I think you hurt Miss Wimbley's feelings when you accused her of trying to kill Julius."

"I did not accuse her of trying to kill Julius." He had no intention of informing the little matchmaker he suspected Miss Wimbley of having an accomplice.

"Yes, you did. And it hurt her feelings. I like her."

So do I. "I didn't intend to hurt her feelings. In any event, I told her you were hosting a musicale."

"What?!"

He masked a grin and selected another box, carefully opening that one as well.

"There's nothing to fear, Noah," she said. "They're *all* dead."

He shot her a scowl. He couldn't think of another thing he despised more than bugs. Perhaps adders. Yes, he despised adders more.

She laughed. "Papa refused to allow me to bring home live species. He thought the captain might succumb to a bout of hysteria and sink the ship. When?"

"When what?"

Her growl of frustration was most satisfying. "*When* is my musicale?"

"Ah. Rather soon, I suppose. But that's up to you, of course," he said.

"Goodness," she said on a breathless huff, dragging her foot in her haste to the door. "I must practice. I wish Lady Abra had been able to remain. Sadly, I think that mean old stepmother of hers would not have departed if Lady Abra had stayed, though." She disappeared, her uneven steps echoing up the stairs.

Chuckling, Noah looked down at that blue scorpion and, shuddering again, replaced the top on its current home before its final destination of immortalization with a pin stuck thick through its ugly body upon its soon-to-be permanent home. Isabelle's Bug Board.

"I TOLD MISS Wimbley I prefer my blue chamber," Docia announced once they were on the road bound for Stonemare.

"It's the Morpho," Geneva murmured. She glanced at her 'lady's' maid. "I thought it might be nice for Pasha."

Pasha's eyes widened and flew about the carriage.

"Just for a change," Geneva went on. "She's worked really hard over the past few days." She bit her lip to keep from laughing. From the corner of her eye, Geneva caught the mirth in sparkling in Mrs. Oshea's green eyes.

The maid's eyes blinked furiously and Geneva took pity on her. "I'm teasing, of course." She looked at Docia. "You are certainly welcome to share our suite," she said sweetly.

Docia's irritation erupted in a huff of air.

"Docia, Miss Wimbley and her maid are already installed," Mrs. Oshea said, her eyes still glinting with humor. More impressively, she spoke without an ounce of censure or guile. Geneva envied such composure. While she could hold her temper, it was the boldly blurting out her thoughts at will with which she struggled.

She studied Mrs. Oshea from her corner in the carriage. The woman's hair was bright enough to light the interior. There might have been a streak or two of silver. But her green eyes were sharp and Geneva doubted she missed much.

"And, you are quite right, Miss Wimbley. Isabelle is forever assigning fanciful names to the chambers."

"There are certainly enough of them," Sander Oshea said.

"She began talking at the age of three and she still hasn't named all of them."

"You shall stay in the Yellow room, Docia, until Miss Wimbley's departure. I refuse to hear another word about it," Mrs. Oshea said.

Docia's head dropped. "Brimstone."

Again, Geneva had to bite her lips.

"Ah, yes. I'd forgotten that," Mrs. Oshea returned, her green eyes twinkling like brilliant twin emeralds.

Silence ensued for a moment before Geneva could no longer stand it. "How is Julius?"

A speculative contemplation from Mr. Oshea speared Geneva and she lifted her chin. "He was downing a hearty breakfast upon our departure," he finally said.

His wife's hand lightly squeezed the hand resting on his thigh. The sight sent a touch of bittersweetness through Geneva. Mrs. Oshea turned a genuine smile on her. "I think he shall live to plague us all."

From the corner of her eye—something she seemed to be doing quite often of late—Geneva watched Docia study her fashionable kid-leather-gloved hands. "Why would someone wish to kill him? He was just an infant when all this business of offing everyone came about."

Mr. Oshea's mouth tightened, but it was fear clouding Mrs. Oshea's eyes.

Geneva slid her gaze to the gently blowing grasses out the carriage window. Did they, like Noah Oshea, blame her for Julius's near demise too? Despair as heavy as a leaded pipe seeped into her veins. Could she have been the one who'd brought violence to Stonemare? For the life of her, she couldn't see how. No one but Abra knew she was even in Northumberland—she swallowed a groan, suddenly realizing the inaccuracy of that thought. All of Mayfair and beyond Christendom had to know she was in Northumberland by now. Perhaps not *why* she was there. Lud. Nothing made the least bit of sense.

Mr. Oshea let out a short *oof* that startled Geneva. She whipped her head around. He cleared his throat. "I believe I owe you, not only my—our—apologies, but our thanks for your quick reaction in saving Julius yesterday, Miss Wimbley."

To Geneva's shock and mortification, tears misted her vision. Quickly turning her gaze back to the window and willing the tears back, she said, "Thank you, sir." Someone—Docia's, she suspected—hand tightened on hers, but she feared facing that person would be her undoing. Instead, she returned the gesture. This had to be the longest drive of her entire life.

"Miss Wimbley." Mrs. Oshea's voice had gentled and Geneva tried to blot it out—without success. "Geneva. I hope you don't mind if I call you 'Geneva.'"

Geneva shook her head and—*blast it*, the tears fell after all.

"Oh, my dear, I didn't wish to drive you to tears." She reached across and squeezed Geneva's hand as she'd seen her do her husband's. And you shall call us 'Verda' and 'Sander.' We are far less stuck on propriety in these parts. So, I'll hear no more about it."

"Take this," Docia demanded, shoving a lace handkerchief into her own gloved hand.

"Thank you," Geneva hiccupped to Docia, to Verda, to Mr. Sander Oshea, though she knew she could never envision addressing Mr. Oshea as 'Sander.'

"We don't know the circumstances surrounding Julius's birth," Verda went on. "So, you can imagine our surprise when Julius informed us you believed him your brother."

"I truly did not come here to upset anyone. I..." Geneva shook her head again, knocking more tears loose. "It was as I said"—*mostly*—"I came to speak with the previous Lord Pender about a dream or... or recollection that refused to allow me peace. I'd no notion, hadn't realized he'd... he'd..."

"Don't think about it," Verda told her. "You are most welcome at Stonemare. It's just that the news that Julius..." Her voice fell away.

Mr. Oshea grew thoughtful. "You know, looking back—" He turned to his wife. "Remember how insistent Noah had been about having to take care of Julius?"

"Yes." Verda looked at Geneva. "That was the year my husband and I met."

"My brother, Damien, er, Pender had been in London." His eyes squinted toward the ceiling of the carriage. "Damien said he had an issue to deal with before returning to Stonemare."

The hair at the base of Geneva's scalp lifted and a ghostly whisper brushed her skin. "And you believe that Julius may have been that 'issue'?"

"It's possible," he allowed. "What strikes me most, if my memories are not failing me, is how Noah kept saying Damien had given Julius to him."

Geneva gasped. She thought Docia did too.

"There was also the fact that Noah was the one who'd named Julius. It hadn't sounded all that odd at the time. Lady Pender had indeed died in childbirth. But I do believe we are missing a large piece of this intrigue."

The shock that flitted across Verda's face was quickly masked. "You believe there was another child?"

"Why else would there have been a wet nurse in house?" Mr. Oshea said.

"There had to have been a midwife as well," Geneva said softly. "Would Mrs. Knagg know anything?"

"We had few servants at the time," Mr. Oshea told her. "But it wouldn't hurt to ask. It was certainly during her bout of employment."

"Do you think there was another child who… didn't…" She couldn't complete the sentence.

Mr. Oshea's eyes narrowed, and tension deepened around his mouth. "How else could my brother have pulled off this nearly-twenty-year fabrication?"

"Do you think Noah knew all of this?" Docia asked.

Mr. Oshea turned his gaze out the window. "I'll be putting

that very question to him."

As would Geneva. Right now, she didn't trust anyone in Stonemare for the truth but Pasha.

CHAPTER TWENTY-TWO

NOAH PULLED HIS watch from his pocket. He likely wouldn't have another opportunity to search Father's chamber. With Isabelle preoccupied with her upcoming performance and his aunt and uncle accompanying Docia and Miss Wimbley from Chaston, this was the perfect moment for decisive action. He doused the candles and locked the door to his laboratory then quickly made his way up to the master chamber. At the door, he gripped the cold, circular, iron handle. He leaned his forehead and flattened his other palm on the heavy, cool oak, letting memories roil through him.

His father crashing into the vestibule that chilling, stormy night with the basket on his arm. The wind whipping his greatcoat about his powerful legs, rain saturating the floor. His searing gaze through the crack of the door, pinning Noah in place, too afraid to move away once he'd been spotted. Father entrusting him, for that first and only time Noah could recall, with a secret that now threatened all he held dear. Noah drew in a shaking breath through his nose, let it out, and turned the handle.

The bed was made, leaving no sign that Rathbourne had been in residence for Father's services. An ache hit his chest at the loss. Loss for a man who'd been incapable of letting those closest to him in his heart. Still, Noah had loved his father because Father had given him Julius. And Julius had been worth any wrath Father had dealt out.

Noah moved to the vanity. The tabletop was devoid of shaving instruments. It appeared Winfield had already seen to his sire's things being packed away. He tugged open a drawer, and again, empty. There was no use going through the remainder. There would be nothing to find. Still, just in case…

The wardrobe was the same. No frockcoats, waistcoats, lawn shirts, or cravats. No stockings, garters, hessians, pumps. Nothing.

The dark-green drapes were open and Noah went to the windows, then took it a step farther and unlatched the doors to the balcony. He stepped out. At the Julienne-styled rail, he set his forearms against the stone, allowing the cool breeze to whip his hair about. The briny sea air stung his eyes, causing his eyes to tear, and if anyone said different, he'd wallop them.

Bone-deep heartbreak thudded against his ribs that hurt through to his soul. He could only pray Lucius wasn't headed for the same destiny.

The sound of clopping horses jolted him from his unsteady tranquility, and the pounding against his ribs heightened, his pulse stirring with erratic thumps. *She was back.*

GENEVA STRODE INTO Stonemare, head held high. She couldn't believe she'd let that bully Noah Oshea chase her away with his ridiculous insinuations. Pasha was right. If Geneva had been the one to throw that knife, it would have hit its mark. Noah had been looking for ways to get under her skin, and he'd landed two. A flush of heat rushed her at the carnal desire that had made off with her brain for that second stratagem. She'd capitulated to his kisses as freely as a Covent Garden doxy. It was exceedingly vexing.

Enough. She turned her irksome thoughts from Noah Oshea to her night at Docia's. Her hand squeezing Geneva's had opened her eyes. Such reluctant vulnerability really stole into Geneva's heart. Yes, yes. The woman was as pretentious and self-centered as ever. Geneva could not only see beyond the surface, but, ironically, could relate to an absurd degree, despite the wide chasms separating their stations in life. One thing was clear: Docia could use lessons in developing friendships with other women. And she could scarcely do better than starting with Geneva.

Right now, however, it was past time to see for herself how Julius fared. She followed Pasha into the Morpho Suite—the name was growing on her—and changed into another of Abra's lovely castoffs. A day dress of bright apple green that swished with elegant grace against her legs. She slipped from the sitting room and took the stairs one level up to where Julius's chamber was located and wound her way through the corridors.

She tapped at his door.

In an instant, it flew back. Miss Isabelle stood there. Her dress suited her wickedly playful personality with its eye-catching pattern of wide stripes in gold and cream, setting off the delicate chain around her neck. She was a lovely sight and Geneva's heart burst with joy. Miss Isabelle's mouth dropped and a second later, she threw her arms around Geneva's waist, banishing all other thoughts. "Oh, Miss Wimbley. I was afraid you may have changed your mind about returning."

"Please. Call me 'Geneva.' Might I call you 'Isabelle'?"

The girl nodded. "Certainly." She spoke as if Geneva were relaying something long ago settled.

"I couldn't possibly leave without saying goodbye to you."

"Geneva?" Julius called from the bed.

"He's quite cross," Isabelle informed her in a stage whisper. She glanced over her shoulder then back. "I do believe he requires a rest. Just like a fussy infant."

Geneva grinned. "Perhaps I can help calm his overly sensitive constitution."

An enchanting giggle erupted from Isabelle and she stepped back, inviting Geneva in.

Geneva strolled to the bed. "How are you faring?"

"Like a cosseted fool," he growled out. "My arm hurts like the devil."

Isabelle gasped.

"If you don't wish to hear my blasphemy, poppet, you may retire to your laboratory and loving collection of bugs." Julius struggled to sitting.

In true enviable affection, Isabelle stuck her tongue out at her cousin. She turned back to Geneva. "I study bugs. I brought some interesting species from the Continent. Would you like to see?" she finished eagerly.

Julius snorted. "I warn you, many of her collected species are not for the faint-hearted."

Geneva didn't have the heart to inform the two of them she'd already been introduced to Isabelle's "corner." "I've never met anyone who studied bugs," she said. "Is that a… thing?"

"Yes," she said so matter-of-factly, it momentarily stunned Geneva.

The child was so fascinating, it boggled one's mind. "Why?"

"I wish to be a doctor. But I can hardly operate on humans." Isabelle's nose wrinkled. "They wouldn't even allow me to stitch up Julius's arm."

Julius snorted. "You had your nose close enough—there was blood on the tip."

Again, she stuck her tongue out at her cousin. The camaraderie between them had Geneva rubbing a hand over her heart.

"Go play with your scorpions, scamp," Julius told her.

Geneva stopped. Her hand moved against her neck, which had grown damp, and she took a step back. "Um, did you say… *scorpion?*"

Isabelle's impish grin flashed. "Almost blue. The hue is not as calming as the morpho butterfly's, mind, but still, it's very impressive." The grin took on a mischievous tint. "I don't think Noah appreciated my find."

"He didn't?" It was difficult, but Geneva managed to swallow a whimper that would surely give way to the mirth tickling inside her.

"Didn't you know? But how could you? He's not so freeing of information."

While that was likely true, Geneva had no comprehension of the topic in question.

"He's afraid of spiders and snakes. In general, most insects. To my credit, I tried explaining how vital they are to the ecologic system."

Geneva gasped. "No," she breathed. "Noah—er, I mean, Mr. Oshea afraid? But…" The man was the epitome of brute strength.

A choked cough of raucous laughter spilled from Julius across the chamber. "Belle, I could use some fresh water."

"Oh, yes. All right. I'll return soon." She hurried out.

Geneva moved to Julius's bedside, where a full pitcher of water stood. She lifted a brow at him, then poured out a glass and handed it to him. "Truly? Mr. Oshea is afraid of spiders? Snakes, I understand." She dropped into the chair next to the bed. "Still, it's difficult to imagine the man fearing anything."

"He does. It's comical, actually. There aren't many species of spiders of the poisonous variety about this far north. Too cold, I expect." He shrugged, then winced, having obviously forgotten his wound. "Nothing truly harmful. But what do I know? Isabelle is the resident expert." He laughed softly then stopped. "Except snakes. Adders are prevalent in Northumberland, especially as the weather grows warmer. They are dangerous, so mind where you walk."

His words startled her and she sensed something quite per-sonal about them. She opened her mouth, fully intending to inquire regarding that very thing, but something stopped her.

Julius didn't appear to notice and went on with a short laugh. "I can just imagine Noah's reaction to seeing that blue scorpion of Isabelle's. Just the thought of such a creature gives me the willies."

Geneva laughed too. "You?"

His stunned expression was priceless, brows disappearing under the untidy hair covering his forehead. "You don't fear spiders?"

"I grew up in a near slum, sir," she said with a wry smile. "Disturbing creatures are a normal part of life outside the confines of Mayfair. Though the snakes I typically encounter are of the human variety."

A contemplative look entered his eyes. "What, then, is it you fear?"

Geneva's gaze dropped. No one had ever asked her such. "I'm not sure I could even articulate an answer." A wry smile touched her. "My loss of independence, I suppose. But that does not appear to be in jeopardy."

"What else?"

She shrugged. "Being forgotten." The words came out a mere whisper.

"I doubt anyone could forget you. *I* certainly won't."

His words snapped her out of the odd doldrum and her gaze fell to his bandaged arm. "Are you truly all right?"

"Yes, blast it. Thanks to you."

She didn't rise to his baiting tone. "Then why are you still in bed?"

He went to cross his arms—flinched—then grinned. "Because I'm being waited upon hand and foot, of course," he said. "And the family has threatened my life if I so much as step outside this room."

She didn't return the smile, tilting her head to one side. "Who do you suppose would do such a thing?"

"I've no notion. I've been on the Grand Tour the last few months. I haven't made anyone angry in years."

"Well, there's me," she informed him blithely.

"What?"

"You ran off and left me in a forest!" she accused him. "Alone! Where I tripped over a dead body. I vow, I would have preferred facing an adder!"

"Yes, well, I apologized for that." There wasn't an ounce of repentance in his voice. "Besides, most brothers would have done the same. As a jest." He tipped another grin. "You would know that if you'd grown up with your sibling around or visited your friends who have siblings." He let out a mocking sigh. "It's quite fortunate that you've found me. Otherwise, you would be a hopeless case."

She narrowed her eyes on him. "Hopeless case?"

"Well." He picked at the sling holding his arm then speared her with a pointed look. "I think we can safely assume now that you shall never be forgotten... *sister.*"

Stunned, touched, floored, Geneva stumbled to her feet, unable to speak for the sudden tears constricting her airway. Then, shaking her head, she ran from the chamber. More accurately, she ran from the sudden and unfamiliar emotions drowning her.

CHAPTER TWENTY-THREE

Geneva rushed into the Morpho Suite and dashed straight for her bedchamber, silently latching the door behind her. She couldn't face anyone. Not even Pasha. Blue was reputed to be a calming color, but the seething emotion inside Geneva was anything but calm. It was a red so deep, she feared it resembled black. She fell against the shut door with her fist at her mouth. *Brother.* She swallowed back a harsh cry, swiping the tears from her eyes that did nothing to stem the flow.

She went to the window and stared out at the sea crashing against the rocks. Nature had a way of displaying the fervent unrest that swirled within her. Fast-moving clouds grew dark, preparing for one gale of a storm—much like that churning sea that replicated the jumbled thoughts in her brain. She had a brother. She was no longer... alone.

Unless another attempt on his life wrenched him away.

Unyielding determination started in the toes of her uncomfortable slippers. How dare someone attempt to hurt Julius? Her spine was so rigid, if she breathed too deeply, she was certain it would fracture. The tears dried on her hot face. She reached back in her memory, trying to recall how the earl had met his demise. Nothing. No one had said a word regarding his cause of death. It was the oddest thing. If his heart had failed, someone would have said as much, right? Perhaps. But she'd avoided the crowds. And why mention anything to her? Had he died of anything other than natural causes, the guests would have acted entirely differently. One thing about the *Beau Monde*, they thrived on scandal. The more salacious, the better.

Still, it was quite curious. But whom was she supposed to ask? Certainly not the family.

Pasha! She took her meals with the servants. Servants talked. Abra, Hannah, and Meredith had all said so. The stories they'd shared when the four of them had been in school, to Geneva, had sounded too fantastic to believe. But, no, they'd assured her, getting away with anything within the confines of their gilded cages was near impossible.

But Pasha wasn't prone to gossip that Geneva could see. Still…

She slipped back out of her bedchamber and found Pasha tending to the wreckage Geneva had wrought in the second bedroom. "Oh, dear," she murmured.

From over her shoulder, Pasha grinned. "You needn't fret, miss. I've seen worse."

"You have? Not from Abra, surely."

"No. Lady Westbridge—" Her face turned a bright shade of scarlet. "I shouldn't—"

"She has the devil of a temper," Geneva said.

"Yes."

"Pasha, I shouldn't ask, I suppose, but I was wondering if the servants mentioned how the late earl…" Geneva's own face heated.

Pasha stilled. "One of the maids…" Her voice was barely audible and Geneva went to her.

Dread unfurled within Geneva's chest like a dark bloom. "The maid said what?"

"Nothing. Not really. Something about there being blood, before Mrs. Knagg, stopped her. But—"

"But what?" Geneva whispered, her throat tightening.

"Mrs. Knagg grabbed her arm and squeezed. I saw the bruise." She whispered too.

"And no one said anything else?"

Pasha slowly shook her head. "Do you think someone…?" She swallowed.

"It's certainly mysterious." Had the earl been murdered and they'd somehow kept it quiet? The footman had. A matter Geneva had witnessed. Intimately so.

Was the family being targeted? Had it even occurred to any of them? Was it possible she somehow brought menacing forces to this stark land? Panic like she'd never known iced her blood. The sudden urge to speak with Mr. Oshea—Mr. *Noah* Oshea—on the topic of who had thrown that dagger at Julius tore through her with the sharp end of a spear. The grounds required searching.

"I'll be back later," Geneva told the maid. She marched to the door and grabbed the handle… then stopped.

The man was liable to rush headfirst into danger without a thought to himself, thus getting himself killed. To never feel his lips again? To breathe in that unique essence that seemed to have seeped beneath her skin? That couldn't be borne. She'd rather die. His family could not do without him. Her family… she couldn't think of that now. Of Julius. She hurried back to the windows and looked out at the heavy clouds.

Could she beat the oncoming storm?

It was imperative she try. Rain would wash away signs left by the intruder. Her difficulty would be escaping the castle without notice. Geneva placed her sweat-dampened palm on the pane. The glass was cool, not cold, to the touch. She could survive a little rain.

Bypassing the main stairs, Geneva also avoided the main servants' stairwell, stealing into the one that led to the floor she'd previously found. This time, however, she remembered to carry a candle. She peered into the old chamber. Everything appeared as it had before. It would have made a great hiding place.

Hiding place! That reminded her. She'd had made no progress in the search for her mother's ruby locket. But those thoughts would distract her and she shoved them aside.

Geneva strode through the myriad winding halls, opening

doors, looking out windows. All in an effort to maintain her bearings. Two sides of the castle backed to the water. But the corridors were a maze of confusion. Some views left one unsure there was even land between the castle and the cliff's drop. Common sense would indicate some distance from the edge. She could actually envision the blasted pile of stones collapsing into the sea with but one minute earthquake.

Geneva shivered, stepping back, and continued along her path until she located a dust-filled set of stone stairs that in places were crumbling. The treacherous trek slowed her progress down the four or however many flights—she'd lost track. That was all she would need—to trip and break her neck. Lord knew, by the time anyone located her, she would be a pile of bones like Docia's poor unfortunate father.

Once she'd reached the ground level, she pushed cautiously on the door and peered about. The hallway was dark, and to her right was another set of stairs that appeared as if they led down to Mr. Oshea's laboratory. Meaning she was very close to the door that exited to the exact area of the castle she hoped to investigate.

An ominous shiver pebbled her skin, but she couldn't afford to let that stop her. There might never be another opportunity.

She slipped out the door.

In the short amount of time it took from the four flights above, she was hit with a battering, chilled wind. Her hair was whipped free of its confinement and sent pins flying. A black, roiling mass of clouds looked close enough to touch and gave a feel of early evening despite the noon hour. She glanced down at the apple-green frock and scowled. It was a blasted beacon. She hadn't even sense enough to snatch a wrap to ward off the ocean's cold, damp assault.

Geneva glanced up and grimaced. She hadn't much time before hell's wrath let loose from the violent swarms overhead. She stepped off the small, concrete stoop and ran for the edge of the trees, hoping her memory wouldn't fail her and that she was gauging correctly where the dagger had flown from the trees.

Just inside the tree line, she found a clear sign of her suspicions and gasped. Large, visible footprints obviously belonging to a man, at least through her inexperienced eyes. She was not a tracker. She was a Londoner. A woman born and bred in one of the world's largest cities. She lowered to her knees, Abra's beautiful frock forgotten.

The footprints were deep and fresh. She followed them where they led toward the cliff. Another few neared the path down to the water—

"Well, well, well."

Geneva spun around. *"You."* She pointed at the man with a trembling hand that mirrored the tremors in her knees.

He took a step toward her.

She stepped back.

They both moved in a dance that left her perilously aware of the drop behind her.

NOAH ENTERED SANDER'S and Verda's comfortable sitting room, heading to the fire and rubbing his cold, bloodless hands together. "Here I am, properly summoned," he said by way of greeting.

Neither returned his smile.

"We need to talk," Sander said.

Noah's abdomen tightened at the ominous words. And Uncle Sander not even suggesting Aunt Verda leave them be did not bode well. Stilling, he faced his uncle, his body quivering with a surge of indignation. "I'm no longer a child of ten, sir."

Sander sauntered over and held out a tumbler of brandy. "No. You're not. I would never offer a ten-year-old the best of Pender's spirits."

The tension from his neck subsided and Noah accepted the offer. He sipped despite the early hour of the day, giving him half a minute to organize his thoughts. "I take it this inquisition is not out of concern of another turret failing," he said, going for a lightness that belied his inner turmoil.

"Only if you have need to warn us of such," Sander shot back.

"Mmm." He strolled to one of the wing-backed chairs and dropped down. "I'm listening."

Verda stirred from the settee where she was sitting. "We require the truth behind Julius's birth, Noah. How did he come to be in your care?" The gentleness of her voice sliced through his heart with the point of a fire-forged dagger and there was nothing gentle about a thrust to one's chest.

He threw back the rest of the brandy and willed it to burn away the pain... the *fear*. "Mama had been confined to her chambers, but not her screams," he said softly. "I didn't know what was wrong. Just that I wasn't allowed to see her."

Silence filled the room in which Noah had always taken refuge, a room that no longer felt safe. Glass clinked and he looked down to see that Sander had refilled it.

"'*It was a dark and stormy night.*'" Inside, he wanted to laugh at the irony of Edward Bulwer-Lytton's overdramatic opening of *Paul Clifford*, but a jaw encased in stone—porous stone—could shatter with enough pressure. "I heard the pandemonium in the vestibule and peeked through a crack in the door." The frigid air from that night seemed to pierce his skin. "There was a basket on Father's arm. I didn't notice it at first. I started to back away, but he called me 'Noah.'" He stopped and caught the unspoken question on Verda's face. "He typically referred to me as 'boy.' Frankly, I would have said he didn't know my name."

"The basket?" Sander asked.

"I thought he'd brought me a puppy."

"Instead, he gave you an infant," she said in bitter disgust.

"Yes. And, of course, the babe was nameless." Noah decided it was best not to mention anything about Father giving Noah leave to drop Julius in the pond. Such a revelation would serve no purpose and would only hurt Julius if he ever learned of it. "Father handed Julius to me and said Mama was having a baby and he wanted everyone to believe that baby and Julius were born at the same time."

"Good God," Sander breathed.

"The last thing I remember is that he said was that this was to be *our* secret." Noah let out a long stream of air. "He'd never trusted me with anything before. And, well, that was a stunner."

"Then it's a possibility." Verda's chin fell to her chest. "That Julius is a product of your father and Miss Wimbley's mother."

"There is something…" Sander said slowly. "Years ago." He turned to his wife and took her hand. "It was the night we met, actually."

"The Lyon's Den?" she whispered back.

"Yes. Damien and I had argued. He was most agitated. To a degree that I suggested he, er…" He speared his wife a quick look, red flags dotting the high points of his cheekbones Noah was certain had nothing to do with the heat from the fire.

Aunt Verda squeezed his hand. "Do go on, darling. I also remember informing you that very night the libertine of which your brother was reputed."

With his free hand, Sander covered his mouth in a choked cough. "Yes, well, I told him he should visit his, er, mistress. His response was that he had, and her husband had returned from the sea, and that he'd had to climb out the window like a common housebreaker." He cut his eyes to Noah. "He was quite aggrieved. Later, when he suggested I hire Verda as your governess, Damien said he would be heading back to Stonemare after handling a small matter before departing."

Noah let out another long-held breath, his heart threatening to leap from his chest. "But that doesn't mean…"

Sander lifted a brow at Noah. "That your father sired a child with Miss Wimbley's mother? Lower your hackles, son."

"No," Verda said. "But we must ask ourselves how Miss Wimbley happened upon Damien as the result of her reasoning in the first place."

But Noah already knew the answer. It had been spelled out in the note from her mother. *You must do something to save my Gen... All that is precious to me is in your hands. Everything in my possession...* Some of the words had been marred by tears or fingers, but the note had clearly been addressed to Father. Chest hurting, Noah was quite aware he was attempting to fool himself. All to no avail.

"And Miss Wimbley?" Verda asked.

Noah's insides rebelled and his teeth gnashed. He stood and moved to the windows. "What about her?"

"Don't be daft, son. We've seen how you look at her. You can hardly manage a complete sentence when she is about."

"Isabelle adores her," Verda added. "She's always possessed an uncanny intuition. Don't you agree?"

Sander smiled. "Assuredly, my dear." He turned back to Noah. "If you wish to discuss your intentions toward her..."

While Sander usually offered sound advice, Noah couldn't quite make the leap in confessing the chaotic emotions that surged through him where Geneva Wimbley was concerned. They were too volatile. Too fluctuating. A disastrous outcome when it came to chemistry experiments. *She's not an experiment.* He wanted her in a way that frightened him. From this position, the second of his largest failures loomed in full view. The collapsed turret he'd destroyed with his stubborn arrogance at following safety protocols being the second.

The first had been his inability to save Isabelle's ankle from the infection of the adder's bite. It had stolen her rightful life from her and it was Noah's fault.

"Gads, you are strung tight as a viola string." Sander's goad drew Noah's glance over his shoulder. "You're not thinking of that damned snake again, are you?"

Noah's lips tightened.

"Oh, Noah. When will you realize that such a thing could have happened to anyone?" Verda said softly. "You were not to blame."

Sander grinned. "You need a wife, Noah. I think Miss

Wimbley would suit you admirably."

His suggestion did not fall by the wayside. Quite the opposite. Because Noah's thoughts bombarded his every waking moment with the exact same words.

"You should bed her and be done with the business," Sander went on.

Verda gasped. "Sander!"

A red haze blinded Noah temporarily. His hands clenched into fists. "Is that what you did to Aunt Verda?" he bit out.

A quick hiss showed his mark had hit its target. The charged silence didn't ease for almost half a minute. "My apologies, son. My remark was uncalled for."

"Indeed." Noah turned his gaze back out the window to the churning, dark clouds. A flash of bright green caught his eyes. "What the devil?"

"Where is Geneva?" Docia's crossness cut across the sitting room. "I've been looking for her. I vow, she is hiding from me."

Noah didn't blame her for her irritability; Geneva had a way of vexing those of the most calming of natures, and Docia was hardly that. "Hiding from you?" he suggested, watching said woman edge her way around the pile of stones. "If she is, then she took drastic measures." The hair at his nape lifted with a sense of foreboding.

Docia strolled up beside him, her French perfume forcing him to bite back a sneeze. "What do you mean?" She let out an indignant huff. "Well, that isn't very sporting of her."

Miss Wimbley hadn't donned so much as a shawl, and with the clouds turning dark, she had no hope of beating the oncoming storm. Noah didn't hesitate, dashing from the sitting room for the nearest stairwell. He skidded down the three flights and out the laboratory door, where the gales nearly knocked him off his feet, and raced for the cliffs—

A grizzled-faced man he didn't recognize towered over her slight frame. His stringy hair billowed in the demon-gusts. He stepped forward and she stepped back. He took another, edging her closer to an imminent end. His massive hand came up, palm out—

"*Geneva!*" Propriety forgotten, her given name escaped from him on a full-throated cry. Using all the strength he could muster into his voice, he prayed she heard over the powerful surf below.

The man's hand stopped midair. His unshaven face swiveled to Noah. Hate emanated from him in powerful waves. But the man didn't run. He spun back to Geneva, planted his palm on her chest, and pushed.

"*No,*" Noah roared as she disappeared from sight.

CHAPTER TWENTY-FOUR

THERE WAS NO going after the bastard, he'd disappeared through the trees. Noah reached the cliff, terrified he'd find Geneva's body, broken and bloodied. To his relief, she'd landed half on the path below. She lay on her back, one arm and one leg hung over the edge. *God help her.* One deep breath could send her over, tumbling to an inevitable fate. The blustery force seemed colder than it had the night Father had set Julius in Noah's lap. A raindrop landed on his nose. Her time was expiring.

Noah raced down the path and knelt at her side. *Unconscious.* The fall hadn't been as far as he'd feared. He did a quick check of her limbs and neck. Nothing appeared fractured, but spinal injuries were known to render a person paralyzed.

"What happened?"

Noah's gaze shot to the voice shouting from the top of the cliff.

Baldric stared down at him and yelled, "She need a trolly?"

"I don't know yet." Noah cleared his mind of everything that could go wrong to concentrate like the scientist he was, though inside, dread was its own monster threatening to suck him into a vortex of black horror. He swiped more rain from his face.

Gently, he rolled her like a log doing his best to keep her neck as straight as possible and did a cursory check along her spine. Nothing seemed out of alignment, but he feared causing further damage if he lifted her.

But the sky opened up, drenching the two of them, and there

was no other option. With extreme care, he carried her up the winding path. She weighed hardly a feather, but gusty winds and blinding rain did their damnedest to fight him on the trek up, Noah reached the top and it was a wonder he could stand.

Baldric met them with a cloak and threw it over her. A small attempt to protect her from the worst of the elements. But the flimsy coat was no match for the malevolent wind ravishing them and it sailed away.

Noah aimed for the closest door. The one that led to his laboratory. He turned to Baldric. "Fetch the constable… and the doctor. Just to be safe."

"Reckon they'll want t' be moving in at the rate things are happenin' 'round here," he muttered, striding away faster than Noah had ever seen him move before.

Noah stepped inside, nearly plowing into Sander. "Someone pushed her. I-I couldn't reach her in time." Guilt cut the air to his lungs and they burned.

"I saw. Come, let's get her warm and dry." Sander held the door open to the ground floor. "Take her up the main staircase. It's warmer and safer."

Noah didn't hesitate, with a surge of new energy and sheer will, he took the stairs by two then ran for the main staircase.

Isabelle met them at the base.

"Tell Pasha Miss Wimbley fell. She requires dry clothes," Noah barked.

Verda appeared at the top of the stairs with her quick, assessing gaze. "Winfield, have Mrs. Knagg send the servants up with hot water," she said. "Quickly."

Noah hadn't even noticed the old man. Winfield disappeared as silently as he'd appeared. Regardless, Noah couldn't have choked out another word if someone held a musket to his head. He reached the Blue Suite and found Pasha inside Geneva's bedchamber, holding a worn, cotton night rail. The coverlets had already been folded back.

"You'll need help with the sodden clothes," he said with a low growl.

"But—"

Verda brushed past him. "I'll assist Pasha," she told him. "Go to the kitchens and bring tea in the event she comes to. And brandy for yourself," she added.

"Wrong. I'll be searching the woods for the culprit."

HOURS LATER—CORRECTION—HOURS AND hours later, Noah pushed the damp hair from his forehead and entered the Blue Suite. The color, according to Isabelle, represented calmness, but he was anything but. The oppressive and heavy atmosphere nearly suffocated him, as if he'd entered the family's mausoleum and the door had clanged shut behind him.

The blood in his veins pulsed with a frenzy pushing out any notion of rest.

He glanced at the clock on the mantel. It was late. Too late, really, nearly eleven, after having spent hours with the parish constable and a team of volunteers from Alnmouth in search of the man who'd shoved Geneva off the cliff with coldblooded intent. It had to be the same man who'd aimed a dagger at Julius's heart. And killed Hicks and Father? Nothing else made sense. He was one and the same, Noah knew it through to his bones.

Noah's description of the man could have fit any number of men in and around the area, as there had been nothing specific he could point to that would differentiate him from one of the locals.

He'd left Verda, Isabelle, and Julius in charge of Geneva. But only Julius remained at her bedside. On silent feet, Noah moved to the side of the bed and set a hand on Julius's shoulder. His brother jumped at the contact.

"Noah. Any luck finding the bastard?" he demanded softly.

"None. Whoever he is, he's likely insinuated himself deep within the community. For all I know, he's joined the search." *A horrifying notion.*

"What did the doctor say?

"To keep her comfortable. What else could he say?" Julius's voice trembled.

What indeed? A spiked coil twisted deep in Noah's abdomen. "Has she wakened at all?"

"No," Julius whispered. "The doctor confirmed what you'd already determined. She's suffered no broken bones. But there's one hell of a lump on her head."

Noah's hand squeezed into a fist at his side. "And the scratches on her face?"

"Minor. Mrs. Knagg applied a tincture. A few pebbles had to be dug out of her arms. But she didn't even stir during the process. Gads, it had to have hurt. Perhaps not as much as a slash from a knife," he added on a lighter note. A failing effort.

Noah couldn't muster a smile.

"What do you suppose possessed her to leave the castle without proper covering? She had to have realized the weather was about to drastically change."

Noah brought up his hand and touched hers. "I don't know. I couldn't see her expression. All I could see... was that bastard deliberately putting his hand out and shoving her to her death." He shook his head, attempting to dispel the waking nightmare. But it was a sight that would remain with him for the remainder of his life, he suspected.

"I'm frightened for her," Julius said in a choked voice. "She *is* my sister. I know it. She's so pale and looks so... so fragile in such a huge bed..." His trailing whispers echoed through Noah and the band about his chest tightened.

With a light squeeze on Julius's shoulder, he said gently, "Get some rest. I'll remain by her side—"

"I can't."

"You can, and you will. If there is any change, I'll let you know immediately. Go."

For a minute, Noah thought Julius would unequivocally

refuse, but then he nodded and stood. At the door, he turned and looked over his shoulder. The pain on his face, raw and nearly unbearable to witness, nearly felled Noah to his knees. His red-rimmed eyes glistened with unshed tears.

"I'll look after her," he promised again. *And pray she wakes.*

With a sharp incline of his head, Julius left.

Noah went about the chamber stirring the fire, checking the candles, tucking the covers about Geneva before taking up Julius's vacated chair and vigil. He leaned forward, setting his elbows on the mattress, and studied her elfin face. What he saw filled him with haunting dread.

The boldness she readily displayed was now concealed behind closed eyes. The glow of the candles smoothed her pale countenance to a soft gold. He would light every candle in the castle to keep it so. His gaze moved over her exposed hands and he reached for one. It felt so alive, yet she hadn't moved so much as a fingertip. He couldn't even detect the pulse in her neck.

Fear constricted his throat. He grazed her hand with the pad of his index finger, back and forth. The rhythmic motion soothed him, leastways. Her skin was cool to the touch, not clammy or feverish. The muscular tone was prominent, allowing him to release his held intake of air.

A sting pierced the back of his eyes until he couldn't breathe. For so many reasons: not reaching her in time; for not finding the bastard who'd dared attempt to kill her; for not being a physician; for not being God to possess the power to make her wake...

Noah laid his forehead against her cool skin, willing his warmth into her. Willing life into her. She emitted a small groan and his eyes burned.

"Mr. Oshea?" Her voice cracked the harsh tension in which he'd been encased as the words penetrated. Her words.

"Geneva?"

"I-I don't remember giving you leave..." She seemed to run out of air to complete her chastisement of him. Something he greatly welcomed at this moment.

"Quite right, Miss Wimbley." His own voice was hoarse with emotion.

"I'm terribly thirsty, sir." Her attempts to rise failed.

He shot to his feet, toppling the chair behind, quickly moving to assist her. "Careful now."

"My head feels as if trampled beneath a runaway carriage, dragging my entire body along." She pressed the back of her hand to her head. "What happened?"

"Don't talk just yet." He poured out a small glass of water and went to hand it to her, but her hand was shaking too violently. He set it to her lips. "Slowly, love."

She drank furiously. "More."

He did as she… demanded… with joy touching his heart. Her hands appeared steadier and he allowed her to manage the glass on her own. "Are you hungry?"

"A little." She handed the glass back.

"I've some bread here, if that will suffice. I'll ring for broth. I don't think you should have more than that just yet."

"Why? What do you mean?"

"Do you remember what happened?"

She started to shake her head then, wincing, stopped. "No."

"You've been unconscious for almost twelve hours."

Her luminescent eyes widened, bathed by the low glow of flickering candlelight. "I-I don't understand."

Pasha rushed in. "I heard something fall."

"It was my chair," Noah told her. "I'm thrilled to report Miss Wimbley is back among the living." His jest fell flat in his ears.

"Oh, thank the heavens." Pasha hurried over and righted the chair.

"Do you think you could chase down some broth? Nothing heavier," he cautioned.

"Of course." She rushed back out.

"I demand to know what happened, sir." Geneva's bold impatience relieved him to no end. Also reminded him of her somewhat reckless nature.

"First of all, my name is Noah. You will henceforth address me as such."

"All right," she said meekly and completely uncharacteristically. "Will you enlighten me now?"

"You fell off the cliff."

"Do not toy with me, Mr.—er, Noah. As I appear to be alive, I couldn't have possibly fallen off the cliff. That jest is most inappropriate, sir."

"I wish I *were* joking. Thankfully, you landed on the path below." Shuddering, he fell back in his chair, unable to bring himself to tell her how close she'd been to actually tumbling to the beach below.

"Oh, dear. You've gone quite pale. Perhaps we should call for your vinaigrette?"

"You don't remember?"

She started to shake her head again but stopped—again. "Nothing comes to mind. Other than the cold." Her eyes snapped to his. "I remember being cold."

As if punctuating her words, a clap of thunder rattled the windows. Rain pounded hard against the pains until Noah thought the glass would break.

Irritation flooded him. "You hadn't even worn a cloak." He grabbed her hand. It had warmed. Fit so perfectly within his. "God, you could have been killed. And it would have been all my fault."

CHAPTER TWENTY-FIVE

T HE THROBBING IN Geneva's head really did feel as if she'd taken a dive off the cliffs. But what the devil had she been doing outside the castle? Her mind was a blank slate. Mr. Oshea—Noah—was white as alabaster. She peered at the large hand enfolding hers, and a sense of utter safety seeped through her.

Oddly, she remembered threatening Docia if she didn't return with Geneva to Stonemare. She remembered Abra, Pasha, and her taking the train to Alnmouth. Lord Pender's funeral services. Running after Julius and tripping over—

Wait... "*Your* fault?" She smiled at that. "I take it you pushed me?" But the pounding in her head increased, attempting representation of crashing cymbals at a concerto.

He withdrew his hand and the warmth along with it and scrubbed a palm over his face. "Miss Wimbley."

"Geneva," she whispered with closed eyes, willing away the pulsating throb. "I give you leave to call me 'Geneva.'" She opened her eyes and lifted her hand to touch his hair...

He raised his head, meeting her gaze with his haunted one. A small smile curved his lips, turning her insides to mush.

She lowered her hand to the coverlet.

"Geneva. I like that. It seems to roll off my tongue."

"You're in my bedchamber. You're willing me back to life. Seems only fitting..." She spoke softly, sinking into the notion of how right it felt.

He smiled too. Then he frowned. "I couldn't reach you in

time. I nearly got you killed."

"What utter rot. That's ridiculous," she snapped. "Whatever I was doing out there was through no fault of yours. Such asinine chivalry is quite irritating." But her fingers gripped and twisted within the coverlet as each question in her head pounded with the force of a hammer. Why couldn't she recall going outside or being there? What *had* driven her to such stupidity? And why did fear grip her throat with the impact of a ballista?

Pasha reentered the chamber in a breathless rush.

Noah turned quickly to relieve her of the tray she carried.

"I'm sorry it took so long. Everyone was asleep. But one of the scullery maids helped me pull together a pot of tea."

Steam rising from the bowl and teapot hit Geneva's nose and dove straight for her stomach, which sent a noisy message. Noah set the tray on the bed and poured out a cup of tea, dropping in more sugar than she'd consumed in her lifetime. "Please, that's enough."

"It will help with the aching head." He held it out then pulled back. "Are you certain you can hold it?"

It was on the tip of her tongue to lash out regarding her abilities to do that much, but the concern in his eye stopped her, and instead, she held up her hands to see if they still shook as badly. "I think I shall manage." A husky tonality seeped out of her she didn't recognize.

He set the cup in her hands. The touch of his fingers brushing hers sparked through her. Her hands jerked, but he averted disaster, making things worse by cupping his fingers about hers. The slosh of the hot tea braised his fingers, not hers. "All right now?" The gravel, gritted sound raised bumps over her skin.

She wanted to rail at him to move back. He was too close, the sandalwood scent going up her nose. The utter masculine essence that stole the oxygen from the suffocating room. She closed her eyes, avoiding his penetrating perception. She guided the cup to her lips, her hands steadying, while inside, her body was all chaos.

A long moment went by before Noah released her hands and

leaned back, finally allowing her to breathe.

He folded his arms over his chest with his head tilted to one side. She tried not to watch him, but of course, it was an impossible feat, his every move caught by the corner of her eye. "Don't forget your broth. Though don't overdo it. You don't wish to cast up your accounts. Very messy."

"This is an entirely inappropriate conversation when one is attempting to enjoy a bracing cup of tea."

"Perhaps I should take over, sir," Pasha said.

Noah glanced over his shoulder. "No need. Pasha." He turned back to Geneva, meeting her eyes, yet still addressed the maid. "I shall remain with Miss Wimbley." A devilish smile crooked his lip. "Back to bed, Pasha. You shall likely need your strength on the morrow. I bid you good night."

To the maid's credit, she didn't immediately leave. "Miss?"

"It's all right, Pasha. I'm confident enough Mr. Oshea will not ravish me, as I'm so infirm."

Pasha's eyes narrowed and her lips firmed. "If you're sure…"

Geneva nodded because what else could she do? Then she watched, helplessly from the bed, Pasha depart, the woman determinedly leaving the door open.

Another long pause ensued. Pasha's footfalls could not be heard for the thick carpet. Nor the sound of her door latching, which drew a quick grin from Geneva she hid behind her cup.

Noah met her eyes and smiled too. The moment was poignant and drowned the pounding from her head with another sort of rush. One of heat, and an overwhelming desire to move over and invite him to join her.

She struggled for something, anything, to say to sever the hold he had on her. She cleared her throat. "Um, how old were you when Julius came to Stonemare?"

"I was ten. My father showed up on one stormy night—so commonplace, I know—handed him to me and said I could keep him."

"Where was your mother?" she asked softly.

"Having another baby. Father told me he wanted people to believe she bore Julius and the other at the same time." He shook his head. "As children, we are told little of the process."

"True. I remember my mother being so ill, yet no one explained her 'symptoms' were normal. Our neighbor who lived below us told me she was on her deathbed."

"Good God," he breathed.

"Yes. I was five. That's when I saw that man… saw… your father."

A hush infiltrated the space that was… peaceful. "What of the other child?" she asked, breaking the silence.

"I don't know. As I said, Father wished all to believe she'd had twins. I suppose the midwife would have known. But a high percentage of children and the mothers never make it past childbirth. I don't even know if the child she had was male or female. It was never discussed."

She shuddered. Such a dire thought had one wondering whether the purpose of going through such an ordeal was worth one's life.

"Have your broth, Geneva. You require nourishment, but mind what I said about too much. There isn't a great deal known about head injuries. But nausea is common."

Geneva didn't respond. She picked up the bowl of broth and dipped a spoon into it. "This was made fairly quickly."

"It's been simmering on the stove in the event you woke hungry," he told her.

Stunned, Geneva stared at him, a suspicious sting that had her dropping her eyes and quickly blinking. "Are you certain?"

"Everyone's been on tenterhooks worrying for you since… well, since you were brought in like a drowned kitten. Even Docia." He gave a grim smile. "The storm broke before I could reach shelter. In fact, you've not been alone for a moment since. Isabelle, then Julius, absolutely refused to leave your side until I returned…"

"Returned?" she said faintly, the spoon poised midair.

The intensity of his gaze pierced her to an uncomfortable degree. "Volunteers have been out combing the woods for the man who tried to kill you."

"A-A man… tried t-to kill me?" A vision of the black, swirling greatcoat surged in her mind and the throb in her head turned into a pointed anvil, sending a swarm of blinding waves through her. The bowl slipped from her fingers, spilling broth over her night rail and the coverlets.

The nausea hit with a vengeance.

IN SECONDS, NOAH had Geneva from the bed and was holding silken, ebony hair back while the contents of her stomach—which was almost nil—quickly turned into dry heaves. "I have you," he murmured.

"Oh, this is so mortifying," she croaked out.

"I'm going to carry you to the settee. Let me know when you are ready."

"I-I'm ready."

Noah lifted her gently, being especially mindful of sudden moves, and carried her to the fire. He tucked a blanket about her then frowned. Perspiration lined her forehead and her upper lip. He blotted the dampness away with his sleeve, then retrieved a glass of water for her. "I'll return shortly with a maid to change the linens," he said, studying her closely.

Her head dropped in a single palm. "Oh, God."

With nothing more to say, he cupped her head with his hand, hoping to reassure her. It was warm, not feverish, to the touch. "I'll be quick." He dropped a kiss to her forehead then reluctantly released her and strode through the sitting room to Pasha's chamber. She hadn't taken to bed yet and was pacing, likely believing—worrying—he would ravish her charge to ruin. "Miss Wimbley is ill. She requires assistance in changing her… her…"

Heat crawled up his neck.

"Of course."

"I'm going for Mrs. Knagg. I'll be back momentarily." He didn't bother ringing. The late hour assured everyone was abed. He took the closest stairwell below stairs and found Mrs. Knagg reading by lamplight. "She's awake, I take it."

"Yes, and, er, she's ill. We must change the linens, I fear."

"All right. I'll be right there with a couple o' the maids."

"Thank you, Mrs. Knagg." Noah hurried back to the Blue Suite, where a crowd had gathered in their nightclothes. Isabelle, Julius, and Verda all huddled outside Geneva's door. "What the devil?"

"Noah, please," Verda chastised him with a pointed look.

"Apologies, Aunt. What are all of you doing here?"

"We were worried," Isabelle said.

Julius's fists clenched, even the one in the sling, and that must have hurt. "You promised to wake me the moment she came to."

"It's barely been twenty minutes—"

Mrs. Knagg's entrance with two maids also in their night-clothes carrying a stack of clean linen interrupted his slightly less-than-fiery defense. She marched her troops through without pause, disappearing into Geneva's chamber. The door slammed pointedly in their faces.

"What happened?" Julius demanded.

"She's ill."

"Has she taken a chill? A fever?"

"A fever? Um, I don't believe so."

"It's the concussion. I've read about such things," Isabelle said. "There's often nausea and vomiting involved." Her gaze moved to the closed door of the chamber. "That's what happened, isn't it?"

"Yes," Noah confirmed. "It was quite sudden."

"You shouldn't have let her eat anything," she returned. "She should be kept under close observation. Did you ask her if she was seeing stars? Or if she was experiencing dizziness?" Isabelle sounded nothing of her fourteen years. Her diatribe gave him the time he needed to gather his wit.

"I didn't, my dear. Unfortunately, when I mentioned the man who accosted her… well, events ensued."

"Did she lose consciousness?"

Noah took a minute to mull that over. "I believe she almost did. She dropped the bowl of broth she was holding and swayed."

Isabelle nodded. "She shouldn't be left alone for several days. Did she remember anything?"

"It doesn't appear so. Nothing regarding her fall that I could tell. She remembered other things, from when she was a child."

Isabelle limped over to him and touched his arm. "I think that's quite common for such an injury, Noah. I should like to visit with her. She may require laudanum to sleep."

Noah had his doubts Geneva would consent to dosing herself with an opiate. She would likely rather face the gates of purgatory. He paced the sitting room, stopping just short of storming Geneva's chamber. Instead, he went to the windows, where he couldn't see a blasted thing through the sheets of slashing rain.

"Sit down, Noah. You're making everyone agitated." Verda's pragmatic tone pulled him back to his senses.

Isabelle was right; he should have inquired after her health, or at the least, observed her for signs of danger. Hell, he'd been the one who'd instructed Isabelle on such matters.

Isabelle clutched her wrap at her neck, glancing toward the closed door. "I don't believe she should be left alone. I'd better stay the rest of the night with her."

Verda grinned, casting Noah with a sly look. "An excellent notion, dear."

The chamber door opened and the maids filed out, carrying the pile of soiled linen. Mrs. Knagg trailed. "She needs food. I'll send somethin' up. Gel's thin as a lizard, she is."

"I'll wait with Isabelle," Noah said. "She must be careful eating too much too soon after sustaining a head injury."

"*I'll* stay with Isabelle," Verda said firmly. "You shall retire to your own chamber, my dear."

Noah hesitated.

"I'll make sure Miss Wimbley does not overdo things," Verda insisted. "Take Julius with you."

Julius's spine jolted straight. "But—"

"But nothing, Julius. You'll both do as I say or I shall wake Sander. And he is most exhausted after all that combing through the woods. You know he doesn't bear weariness all that gracefully."

Noah draped an arm over Julius's shoulder and guided his grumbling brother out. "Come on, Jules. We'll pick up our vigil in the morning. I suspect Miss Wimbley will survive Verda's and Isabelle's ministrations." Once in the corridor, though, exhaustion hit him hard.

Julius scowled. "We should be able to stay with her."

Noah's time would come, he vowed. "She needs her rest too. Verda and Isabelle will make certain all is well."

"I suppose."

"Isabelle was right about one thing," Noah said. "She's not out of the woods yet. Very little is known regarding head injuries." Noah had heard horror stories but decided expounding on the subject would lead to unnecessary nightmares. "She shall need lots of care."

"You think the same person who threw the dagger at me pushed Geneva over the cliff?"

"Yes." But another inkling sludged his blood with ice. *What if the man hadn't been after Julius? What if it was Geneva he'd been after all along?*

They reached Julius's chamber in silence and in a moment of impulse, Noah hugged his brother.

"Noah?"

Noah shook his head, finding his throat too obstructed to speak. "We'll find the bastard," he choked out.

Chapter Twenty-Six

"You did the right thing, poppet. But you're not a doctor yet." Noah was quick to reassure his young cousin with a hug two mornings later, giving him full view of Geneva. The gray morning reflected her face, pale still but for red flags dotting her cheeks, which did nothing to make him feel better. Inside, he was frantic. Their patient was feverish, her body chilled.

Isabelle's tears dampened his shoulder. "She won't die, will she?"

Docia strolled in. "Don't be ridiculous, Isabelle. Geneva is much too stubborn to go out with a whimper." Her words, while tough and nonsensical, trembled, betraying her worry.

"She's right." Noah swallowed against the constriction in his throat then cleared it. "You've been here all night, darling. Go eat, then get some rest." He sent a silent plea to his longtime nemesis.

"Come, Isabelle." Docia steadied her voice, adopting her usual pragmatic tone, and held out a hand for Isabelle. "Let Noah stay with her. I expect he'll expire from heartbreak otherwise."

Isabelle stepped back and peered up at him, her face damp. "Heartbreak?" She didn't have to sound so hopeful. "All right. I do feel somewhat faint with hunger. Where's Julius?"

Noah pulled a handkerchief from his pocket and dabbed her face with it. "He's with the others. They are searching for signs of the man responsible before another onslaught of rain pelts us into the sea. Go now."

She wiped her nose and nodded. With his hands on her shoulders, he turned her toward Docia, mouthing *thank you*.

"Eat, then sleep, Isabelle."

The hour was early. Or seemed so, at least. Five, six, he wasn't certain. A glance at the clock told him four-fifteen. He went to the basin and took a clean cloth, dipped it in cool water, and wrung it out. At the bed, he set it on the nearby table. He straightened the coverlets about Geneva then laid the back of his hand against her forehead.

She was burning up. He took the cloth and smoothed it over her cheeks, then, folding it over, pressed it against her forehead. He felt a little ill himself seeing how stark the red spots on each cheek stood out. He hurried back to the basin and hauled it to the bedside table. And with methodic intent, he went through the process of soaking another cloth with which to cool her wrists.

Minute after minute, he continued through. Time marched with Noah having no idea how long he worked. He was grateful for the lack of interruptions and stayed resolute to his mission. With each pass, he took up her clammy, chilled hand in his, squeezed lightly, then pushed on. There may have been an occasional touch of his lips.

Exhaustion fed his fear until he was afraid it would cripple him. He paused, taking a moment to just look at her. That elfin face. The dark lashes, mere shadows against the circles beneath her eyes in an otherwise stark pallor. The full lips chapped and peeling. The scratches were well on their way to healing, barely scabs now. He touched the cloth against one corner of one and prayed.

A second later, her lashes fluttered and opened. The navy hue of her eyes appeared black in the low-lit chamber. Perspiration beaded her hairline and upper lip.

"Thank God," he breathed. Noah poured out a glass of water and lowered to the side of the bed. He brushed a few strands of tangled hair from her face. "How do you feel? Would a spot of tea sit well with you?"

She nodded and snuggled deeper within the covers.

"All right, love. I'll hurry."

Her response was simple—a closing of her eyes and slipping down, finally, thankfully, into a restful slumber.

He rose from the bed and went out to knock on Pasha's door.

The door flew back. Her eyes widened. "Sir?"

"I sent Isabelle to bed. Miss Wimbley requires tea. Could you see to that and have Mrs. Knagg heat water for her? That will help her rest more comfortably."

"Oh, yes. Thank you, sir. I'll be right there."

With a sharp incline of his head, Noah hurried back to Geneva.

She kicked at the coverlets. "It's too hot."

"It's all right, love. Your fever has broken. Pasha has gone for tea." He moved to the bed and helped her to sitting. "Come on, love. Open your eyes."

Geneva groaned, and he nearly sobbed with joy at the ill-fated sound.

GENEVA'S ARMS FELT as if they were ladened with lead. Just opening her eyes hurt. Frustration brought a rush of tears surging. "I can't move, you scoundrel."

"Calm yourself, Geneva. I'll help."

"Calm myself," she repeated in breathless fury. "*Calm myself.*" The last of that phrase was muffled against a broad shoulder as the covers were stripped away. She gasped just as Noah propped her against the pillows as if she weighed no more than a toy doll. "*Sir.*" That squeak surely did not belong to her.

Just as quickly, her night rail was adjusted and the counterpane tucked once more about her waist.

He stood and cast an inscrutable intensity over her that had her checking to make certain the she was really covered. "How do you feel?"

Overheated. "Better. Thirsty," she amended.

In an instant, a glass was in her hand. There was nothing dignified in her haste to slake her thirst. Neither were the snuffles that had an embarrassing rheum running from her nose. "It isn't proper for you to be here." Now she sounded like a petulant child except for the scratchy tone that resembled a frog she'd once encountered at St. James's Park lake.

A glint of humor lit Noah's eyes. He opened his mouth, but she stayed him with an open palm.

"Don't," she croaked, fearing her blurred vision would spill down her cheeks. "I-I need a cloth to wash my-my face." The words ended with a horrid, unfeminine cough.

Without a word, he dipped a cloth into the basin that had somehow appeared on the bedside table rather than its usual place on the sideboard and handed it over. "I believe you've contracted an ague," he said gruffly.

Evidently so. Nodding, she accepted the strip of linen, and with open palms, she ran the cool dampness over her face, clearing her matted eyes. All under that vigilant perusal. She buried her face within it and held her breath for a long, long moment before breathing out. Then, lifting her face, she nearly cried for the sweetness she saw in his eyes.

She squeezed the cloth and water dribbled over her fingers, so he promptly relieved her of the cloth. He set it on the bedside table then dropped into a chair and took her hand. "You don't have to pretend with me, Geneva."

"Pretend what? I'm no good at pretending."

He smiled then, and her eyes, in fact, watered. She'd completely lost control of her faculties. Every one of them. At the top of that horrifying list? Her emotions.

"It's one of your most admirable qualities," he said.

"I didn't give you leave to call me—"

"Ah, but don't you remember? You did indeed, Geneva Wimbley. And I refuse to allow you to retract the invitation."

A vague memory did register. "How long ago was that?"

"A day or so."

She grunted in a way Docia would chastise her for outright. "Where is everyone?"

"I am here for morning duties. Isabelle and Docia spent the night and left only an hour ago. Pasha is assembling tea for you. Something to eat as well, I hope, as I forgot to mention that."

The crossness in Geneva's chest loosened. "Isabelle needs her rest. What is Mrs. Oshea thinking in allowing her in a sickroom?"

Again, that lovely smile embedded itself in Geneva's heart. "There is no keeping her at bay. Verda is helpless against Isabelle's tenacity. The girl has high aspirations. She wishes to be a doctor. I worry for her disappointment."

"Bah." Geneva waved out a hand then quickly covered her mouth in a cough. "Change never occurs without those who do not rush headlong into the fray."

His dark-gray eyes penetrated through to her soul. "You know something of that, don't you?"

She met his eyes then dropped her gaze. "I do, indeed."

"What are you working on now?"

She smiled. "Nothing, for obvious reasons. But I do have an article to complete on the advantages of educating the masses."

"Perhaps you would consider doing one on the importance of women doctors."

She stared at him—speechless—*surely he was jesting*. But his expression clearly showed he was not. "I believe that is an excellent notion," she said slowly. "I'll do anything to help Isabelle."

He leaned forward and took her hand. "There is something I must tell you."

Her stomach dipped. "What?" she asked with an impending sense of dread.

"I don't know where or if this plays into your presence at Stonemare—" His wince was barely discernable, sending the spike of apprehension deeper, but she refrained from speaking.

"There was an entry in my father's records for Miss Greensley's school. I expect it was for your tuition."

Geneva took a deep breath and let it out in a long, even stream. What was she supposed to do with such information? The pain in her head began pounding with visions of that swirling greatcoat when seconds ago, she'd forgotten it altogether.

"What is it? Geneva. Love, I'm sorry. I thought you should know."

His voice penetrated through the black surge that had hit with a vengeance. Eventually, the black ebbed to gray with specks of light. She pressed the heel of her hand to her forehead. "It's all right," she croaked out, the scratch in her throat pulsating. "We suspected, didn't we?"

"Yes, darling, we did."

"Why? Why would he do such a thing?"

He snorted. "It certainly wasn't out of the goodness of his heart."

The pounding in her head intensified. *The black, swirling greatcoat, the gravelly voice. The disdain, the disgust. "Send her to the Black Widow when she's of an age. Hell, I'll even pay the exorbitant fees it'll require."*

These bits of memory teasing her at will were maddening.

She lifted her eyes, meeting his. "Who the devil is the Black Widow?"

"A Mrs. Dove-Lyon," Noah said slowly, rubbing a palm over the back of his neck. A slow flush crawled into his face and Geneva stilled, dread spreading through her like that flush on his face.

"Mrs. Dove-Lyon. The Black Widow of Whitehall. I-I've heard of her. She—" Geneva swallowed. "She…"

He grabbed her hand. "Don't. Whatever it is—if it had anything to do with my father, put it out of your mind. Now. You're here. At Stonemare. With me." He brought her hand to his lips until they rested firmly on her knuckles. "With others who *care* about you."

"But—"

"No! Whatever it is, put it out of your mind. Promise me." His fingers tightened on hers. "Promise."

"I-I promise," she whispered, tears stinging.

$$\cdot\!\!\cdot\!\!\diamond\!\!-\!\!-\!\!-\!\!-\!\!-\!\!\diamond\!\!\cdot\!\!\cdot$$

CHAPTER TWENTY-SEVEN

THE NEXT DAY, Noah and Isabelle had given in to Geneva's demands of leaving her bed, but the sitting room was as far as they allowed her to venture, and she was mightily sick of it, though her confinement had consisted of all of one day. She sat in a comfortable chair that afforded her a nice view out the window. A fat lot of good that did, however, as the clouds were darkening again. One might believe one was under the coal-smoked skies of London. There was one advantage, and that was the freshness of the country. So it didn't smell as putrid.

Docia sat in the other comfortable chair angled toward the cozying fire, studying her perfectly shaped nails. Her eyes flicked to Geneva then dropped again. "What makes you believe Julius is truly your brother?" While her tone was depleted of its biting edge, it sounded almost... accusatory.

"You sound... curious." Concerned, Geneva studied her... rival? Nemesis? Whatever her feelings regarding Docia, they felt *complicated*. The words also sent her hackles rising. She tamped back the defensive urge, inhaling deeply instead. "Did you know that Lord Pender—the *late* Lord Pender—paid my school fees to Miss Greensley's?"

Docia raised her head, meeting Geneva's eyes. "Why would he do that?"

"Quite the conundrum, isn't it?"

Her eyes fell once more. "Still, it's a stretch to believe that Julius is your half-brother. You are nothing alike."

"I disagree." The biting edge Docia had abandoned, Geneva took up proudly.

"As do I," Julius said from the door. He strolled over to Geneva and kissed her cheek. "How are you feeling? You appear much better."

She'd slept the previous day away, only waking for bouts of willow bark, peppermint, and ginger tea doused with honey and lemon, along with broth poured down her by Pasha. However vile the concoctions she'd been forced to consume, they'd worked wonders on the throat irritation. Full recovery was within her grasp. "What of you? Your arm?"

He glanced at the door then slipped his arm from the sling and slowly straightened it. "It distresses Isabelle when I move my arm," he said, grinning. "I say, the stitches itch horribly."

"How does that work, exactly? Do they come out on their own? Will they bleed?"

Docia stood abruptly. "I retract my doubts, Geneva. The two of you are identical peas in a pod," she said with a show of her previous winning personality of disgust. "If you'll excuse me."

Geneva bit her lip to keep from laughing outright until the outer door shut a little harder than necessary. She met the gleam in Julius's eyes, sending the two of them into gales of laughter and the ache in her head back to the far reaches.

He dropped into Docia's abandoned chair.

"Noah said you don't recall the events leading up to your fall."

And just like that, the sharp pain pierced her head. She pressed her fingertips against her temples, black waves swallowing her.

"Geneva! What did you do to her, Jules?"

FEAR CASCADED THROUGH Noah as he charged through the room.

He tossed the letters he held on the low table and knelt beside her, prepared to lift her up. "Water. Quickly. I'll get her to her bed," he barked to his brother. "What did you say to her?"

Julius didn't answer and Noah glanced over his shoulder. His brother's face was stark white. "I-I…"

Geneva's eyes fluttered open amid a groan. "Quit coddling me." She struggled out of his hold. "Stop. Just stop." Her breaths were too rapid. They matched pace with the fluttering pulse in her neck and the furious pounding of his heart. "I'm not a child. I don't understand what's happening, but a bed will not fix it."

"Perhaps that is exactly the remedy," he said, low enough for her ears only.

Her widened gaze shot to his.

"That's right," he whispered. "I wish to take you to bed and drive all your fears away."

"Water?"

"Right here," Julius said. The hard edge in his tone was not encouraging.

Noah glanced over his shoulder and up at his younger brother. And winced.

Julius held out the glass with a steady hand. "If I ever hear you speak again to my sister in such a way, I'll run you through."

Geneva snatched the glass from his hand and gulped down the contents. "That is quite enough from the both of you." She lifted the glass and teetered it side to side for Julius. But he was too busy glaring at Noah to notice. "Take this," she snapped.

Her sharpness jarred Julius and he snatched it from her, scowling and stalking away.

"He's right," Noah said softly, regretting—no, not regretting, exactly. He'd said what he'd meant. What was it about her that had his level head deserting him to the farthest regions of the cosmos? "I should have—"

Her eyes went over his shoulder and came back to his. Her fingers, two, crossed his lips. "I…" Her gazed dropped then raised again. "I understand."

His lips curved slightly. He pressed his fingers over hers and kissed their tips. "No. I don't believe you do. But you will. Soon," he promised. He glanced over his shoulder. Julius was just setting the glass on a table near the window with his back to them. "Now is not the time." He came to his feet. "Are you certain you are well?"

"Yes," she said with a scowl of her own.

"I'm relieved to hear it. Isabelle has set a date for her musicale. A week hence."

"What are these letters, Noah?"

"Gads, I'd nearly forgotten. You received a post from Lady Abra," he said to her.

Her dark-blue eyes lit up for what seemed the first time in days. "I'll come get it."

"No, you won't."

Julius sounded like the man he was fast approaching, Noah thought with a pang, a whole other onslaught of emotion pelting him.

Julius sauntered over and handed her Lady Abra's missive. The other envelope he held out to Noah. "This one appears to be from Lucius."

"I've lost my blasted head," he muttered, grabbing it and moving to the settee. He ripped it open and read.

Well, Noah, my stop in London has proved most enlightening. Your enchanting houseguest, Miss Wimbley, is the talk of the Beau Monde. Or should I say, her bloodied dress is...

Noah pushed a hand through his hair. "Christ."

"Oh, no..." Geneva's low wail echoed through the sitting room.

He cut his glance to her, then flicked his eyes back to the letter he held. "Your dress?"

Geneva groaned. "Lady Westbridge will never allow me to see my friend again."

"What of Lord Westbridge?"

Her features tightened. "At one time, I would have said he would never stand between our friendship. But now..." She glowered with the familiar bold fierceness and his insides contracted with yearning. "There is good news. Baron Ruskin has asked for her hand. They are betrothed now."

From the tone in her voice, Noah couldn't decide if she was relieved or sad. "Don't you like the baron? I thought he was most congenial."

She blew out a pursed breath. "I just hope she is not marrying him for the wrong reasons," she said glumly.

Noah clucked his tongue. "Ton matches are complicated, my dear."

Julius dropped beside him. "Noah couldn't be more right, Gen. The important thing to remember is that Lady Abra not only needs you in her life, but is damn fortunate to have you."

Tears dampened Geneva's lashes and she shook her head. The note from Lady Abra trembled in her fingers.

"I take it she informed you of the latest rampant scandal in which you feature?"

"Oh, yes." She handed him the note.

Gen, I fear you must avoid London for a time. Mother has taken great delight in gossiping with that loose tongue of hers. She has recounted the Incident to any and everyone who would lend an ear. And, believe me, she found no shortage of listeners. Papa will eventually come around. You are, and shall always be, my dearest friend. By the bye, Lord Ruskin has asked for my hand, and I have accepted. But do not fret, my dear. The CSS will live on. You may count on me.

Eternally and unceasingly your friend,
Lady Abra Washington

"'The CSS'?" Noah murmured.

Geneva waved out a hand and did not deign to answer. Someday, he would have answers regarding this CSS mystery.

"I don't understand the issue," Noah said. "Lady Abra seemed quite enamored with Ruskin."

"Ah, but Lady Westbridge is not. She has much higher aspirations than a mere baron for Abra." Geneva's eyes flashed. "There will be much tension until that union is tied."

She struggled to her feet. "I must return to London."

Noah pushed her gently back into her chair. "Not so fast, Miss Wimbley. You are in no condition to travel. Besides, Lord Westbridge is quite capable of handling his wife."

"You don't know her. Lady Westbridge will do everything in her power to undermine Abra's choice," Geneva bit out.

Still, Noah was touched on Geneva's behalf regarding her friend. "I think," he said slowly, handing the note back. "There is as much to be said for what Lady Abra has written as to what she has not."

Geneva frowned. "What do you mean?"

"If Lady Westbridge is as abhorrent as her behavior displayed at Stonemare—"

"She is."

"—then it should suffice to say, this message was written in the event it was intercepted."

"But by all accounts, Abra accuses her of being a gossipmonger."

Julius snorted. "It's true, isn't it?"

Geneva snorted as if he were citing something obtuse.

"Perhaps she was secretly hoping the ungracious woman *would* read it." Julius grinned. "I would if I were her."

Geneva tilted her head, and in that fleeting moment, Noah discerned the minutest of similarities between her and Julius. An instant later, her lips tilted in a smile of understanding. "Yes. I see what you mean," she said, slowly grinning. "Lady Westbridge would hate the line about Lord Westbridge coming around. He really is a good man. I hope he can forgive me." She bit her lip and Noah wanted to kiss her.

"But you did nothing, Gen. Nothing. It wasn't your fault you tripped and got blood on your dress," Julius huffed out in full indignation.

"No, but Lord Westbridge had taken Abra and me aside and spelled out in no uncertain terms that another scandal would not be tolerated."

Noah's brows rose. "*Another* scandal?" He watched as her normally creamy complexion turned an alarming shade of crimson.

"Abra told her father we were going to Cornwall, not Northumberland," she admitted. "To visit Meredith—er, Lady Pender."

"Good God. And he believed you?" Shaking his head, he fell against the settee's back and folded his arms over his chest. "Obviously, the two of you need keepers."

She bristled. "Our plan would have worked if—"

"If my father hadn't died," he finished for her.

Her shoulders fell. "Yes." But she rallied and squared them. "In my defense, I told her we should return to London before anyone found out."

Noah leaned forward, looked into those navy eyes. "And what a tragedy that would have been," he said softly. "We'd have never met otherwise."

Julius plopped down beside him. "Nor would I have learned I had a sister."

CHAPTER TWENTY-EIGHT

I T WAS ANOTHER two days before Geneva finally escaped her rooms and never had anyone been so thrilled. Despite how lovely her Morpho Suite was, she would gladly have slept on the hard ground near the cliffs rather than spend one more moment confined inside. She was exceedingly weary of the whole business of being considered infirm. True, her knees weren't completely steady, but—ha!—that was likely due to lack of use.

Noah held her arm as if he feared she would keel over as he walked her to the music room.

The megrims had eased and the lack of physical activity might have left her feeling lightheaded, but she was restless beyond words and quite looking forward to hearing Isabelle play the pianoforte. The child was a virtuoso. That might have been an exaggeration, as Geneva had never heard a virtuoso before. Abra notwithstanding, she thought, a smile filling her. Oh, how she missed her friend.

Upon entering the music room, she came to a quick stop.

It was plain to recognize the Marquess of Martindale, an abominable man, as the crowd was minimal at best He was much harsher than his late father had been reputed. Sadly, the elder had expired around the time Prime Minister, Lord Liverpool, had in the late twenties.

"No one will bite," Noah told her in a low tone.

But *Noah* hadn't been in the park the day he'd been riding by. "Perhaps I shall do the biting," she whispered back fiercely. She'd never been so grateful to Abra for having the foresight in leaving Geneva a respectable wardrobe. She smoothed her free hand down the cerulean silk skirts.

"Don't be nervous. Come, I'll introduce you."

It was literally too late to back out of the room, as all eyes had turned upon her. Which also stopped her from digging her slipper into the carpet and being seized forward against her will. "I've never been nervous a day in my life." She almost believed her words.

The decorative room was cool due to the high ceilings, but the blazing fire in the hearth reflected by the gilt-framed mirrors staved off the worst of it. This was where Noah led her.

"Miss Wimbley." Sander Oshea inclined his head. "I'm relieved to see you looking so well."

"Thank you, sir."

Noah turned from his uncle to the Marquess of Martindale.

Geneva thought she might be sick. She'd managed to avoid him during the events surrounding the late earl's service, but doing so now was impossible. Only the thought of ruining Isabelle's big night kept her from sliding to the floor in a dead faint.

"May I present the Marquess of Martindale." Noah's words yanked her attention from her coiling stomach. It took everything in her to not take a step back. "His lordship was still in the area visiting with Mr. Asher when the invitation for Isabelle's musicale was issued." Noah spoke without an ounce of emotion. Which said much to Geneva. He seemed to read the marquess as she did, a coxcomb of the first order.

"Miss Wimbley, I believe we've met before. Hyde Park, wasn't it?"

Locking her hands at her lower back, Geneva inclined her head. "Indeed, my lord." She could see the scene as clearly as if it were yesterday. She, Hanna, Meredith, and Abra had been strolling the path along the Serpentine when the marquess had nearly run them down, spouting a snide slur at Abra that didn't bear thinking about. This was the man Lady Westbridge wished to shackle Abra to for the rest of her life.

Geneva blasted him with a bright smile she knew would vex him to no end. Her, an inconsequential cipher. "I see you survived Lord Westbridge's wrath."

Indeed, Abra's father had been quick to lash out in a way that Geneva had tried, running after the man hurling insults. Due to an obscure law on the books that disallowed a lessor from issuing insults to a peer, the incident had nearly had her dragged to gaol but for Lord Westbridge's interference. A scandal of the first order, but Geneva hadn't regretted her actions. The blackguard had deserved it. She abhorred him.

The brittle smile he turned on her, bracketed by deep creases, was frightening, but she refused to be cowed by such a hateful cur and steeled her spine, meeting the coal-black, chilling stare he leveled on her.

Noah touched her arm directing her attention to another man Geneva recognized from the late earl's funeral services. "This is Alnmouth's Rector, Mr. Woodford, and his wife, Mrs. Wood-ford." The erect man with his thinning, white hair and hawkish nose, stood next to the slight woman. There was nothing frivolous about her dark-gray frock. It covered every inch of skin, from neck to, practically, the tips of her fingers.

Geneva dipped a curtsey. "Sir. Ma'am."

Mrs. Woodford took Geneva's gloved hand. But one stern look from her husband and she quickly snatched her hand back as if she had poked a fabled dragon. Ah, yes, the bloodied dress. "My dear, dear, child. We heard of your harrowing ordeal?" she said with a delicate shudder.

Not only did Mrs. Woodford's trailed question leave Geneva with no notion of how to respond—her memories of that day had not yet surfaced, if they ever would—but she wouldn't have answered now to save her own life. "Thank you, ma'am," she said coolly, while inside a seething inferno was set to blow. "As you can see, I'm quite recovered." Her education at Miss

Greensley's had served multiple purposes. She tipped a condescending smile at the woman that included her pious master.

Noah bumped her shoulder with a warning and indicated the next man. He wore a coat that didn't fit so perfectly and his dark hair hung a little too long. "Miss Wimbley, this is Mr. Asher of London." Despite the intensity of the man's dark eyes, Geneva blinked and gauged him with singular fervor. He seemed comfortable in his own skin, something she admired and aspired to.

"Miss Wimbley," he said, taking her hand and brushing her knuckles with his heavy mustache.

"Sir." Her voice cracked.

Beside her, Noah stiffened.

Geneva's gaze shot to him, but his face was unreadable.

"Miss Wimbley. So sorry for your ordeal. Is there any word on the culprit?"

"None," Noah answered quickly for her.

She was insignificant enough for that to be the end of Mr. Asher's attention. He turned to Noah. "I'd heard Miss Hale was staying at Stonemare," Mr. Asher said. "I'd hoped for the opportunity to visit with her."

Curious. Geneva's gaze cut back to Mr. Asher. "Oh?"

A genuine smile eased the intensity of his expression, exposing crinkles at the corners of his eyes. This was a man who went after what he wanted regardless of the obstacles. Another admirable quality. He would be perfect for the haughty and enigmatic Docia Hale. Of course, she didn't know the man; he could be as abhorrent as Martindale, but she didn't believe that was the case.

Frowning, Geneva glanced about the huge room, but there was no sign of the blonde beauty.

But seconds later, Docia strolled in wearing another soft, pale-yellow gown with emerald gloves tied just above her elbows. French, no doubt. "Goodness, we've quite the company tonight, haven't we?" she said in their direction.

The melodic tonality effect was immediate and all attention shifted quickly from Geneva to Docia. The tension in Geneva collapsed so quickly, she swayed. Noah's arm was the lifeline keeping her upright.

"You must sit down," he said, his body vibrating against hers. "I told Isabelle such an event was too soon, but she was absolutely insistent. She felt it would lift your spirits."

With a forced smile, Geneva concentrated on breathing but that made things worse because *he* smelled so delicious, so male, so right, it banded the air in her lungs. "She was quite correct. One more day in that chamber, lovely as it is, I vow I would have leaped from the tower to the sea below."

"She also declared that to be precisely your words." Noah settled her in a chair that was nearest to the fire but still faced the pianoforte that had been placed on a platformed rise. He lifted one hand, signaling a footman she didn't recognize. "What was all that about with Martindale?"

"Just a little incident in Hyde Park that occurred not long after Abra's season debut. It's nothing to concern yourself over." That was all she'd need. To draw Noah into a duel with the malicious marquess.

The footman rescued her, appearing with a tray of wine-filled glasses. She snatched up one and sipped—sherry. Something she'd never quite acquired the taste for. To say so, of course, would be beyond rude, and well, she was trying to tamp back that annoying portion of her personality.

From the corner of her eye, she observed Docia dealing with, simultaneously, Lord Martindale and Mr. Asher. It was a lesson in decorum that should have annoyed Geneva. Instead, she found herself admiring the woman's subtle handling of two clearly eligible men vying for her undivided attention. "Why didn't you marry her?" she asked her companion, her gaze never wavering.

"What?" Noah choked out.

"As I recall, the day Abra and I arrived at Stonemare, you were slated to leave for Scotland that morning to marry Miss

Hale. Why didn't you?" And just like that, the inappropriate question had surged forth, boldness be damned.

HEAT CRAWLED UP Noah's neck along with his irritation. He wanted to rail at Geneva's impudence while also respecting her ability to probe what he hadn't seen so clearly until she'd walked through the door that morning.

The relief that had nearly felled him to his knees. How a brush of her gloved fingers defied a chemical experiment of mixing water with calcium chloride. A method that warmed the skin. Geneva Wimbley was the calcium chloride to his body of water.

The realization had the blood rushing through his ears, as if he'd dropped powder in a beaker and the fuzzing sound churned inside his brain. God, he wanted her with a need that defied logic and, worse, scrambled his common sense. Well, if she could assert her boldness, so could he. He leaned in and whispered, "Why didn't I marry Docia? Because *you* walked through the door." Though his tone remained low, it carried a conviction that went deep.

Geneva had raised the small glass toward her lips, but she stilled, her eyes widening with... surprise? Her mouth moved, but no words emerged. Her cheeks turned a lovely shade of pink that sparked a masculine satisfaction through him.

"Did you believe I was jesting two days ago? I want you," he whispered, "with a craving that refuses to leave me be."

"But... I... But—" She stopped and drew in a deep breath.

All the while, his own intake of air faltered in a state of dreadful apprehension.

A stirring from behind broke the hold she had on his gaze. She blinked and his eyes followed hers to the double open doors.

Verda held Isabelle's arm, leading her through the small

group. His young cousin smiled without an ounce of guile. She stopped and his aunt made introductions before leading Isabelle to the raised platform. Isabelle was all innocence in her pale-blue frock with its white satin bow tied at her back. Her bright-red locks, which matched her mother's, hung down her back in long, wavy tresses adorned with another satin bow fastened at the crown of her head. The delicate, gold chain she wore blended into her skin, only reflecting the candlelight when she turned. She curtsied to the company then took her seat on the bench behind the keyboard.

Many of tonight's attendees would be shocked to learn of her collection of insects—live and pinned—and how determined she was to fulfill her dreams of becoming a doctor. No one knew more so than Noah. It was a difficult path she'd chosen to seek, but Geneva's words returned full force: *Change never occurs without those who do not rush headlong into the fray.* Isabelle was just stubborn and headstrong enough to pull off such a feat.

The fact that his cousin was also an accomplished musician, he was certain, had something to do with her mathematic capabilities. They were prodigious beyond compare. Far surpassing Noah's skills as a child when he'd sat beside Verda in her first few days of invading Stonemare and teaching him how to use the abacus.

Isabelle's gaze found Noah and Geneva beside him. A bright smile lit up her face. He reached over and squeezed Geneva's hand, catching the tender smile she cast his precocious, if somewhat, reckless, little cousin. With a small prim and proper nod, Isabelle looking all the picture of the sweet child she could project at will, when seconds later, she might thrust a vile and disgusting spider in his face.

He'd almost banned her from the laboratory for that outrageous prank.

A dramatic hush settled over the intimate setting. Then... her fingers trilled over the keys with a lightness worthy of Mozart. Perhaps he was just a proud cousin. Yet to him, she played with the ease of a master. The name of the piece escaped him, but it began with a quiet restlessness that stirred the mood and shifted to dark and intense. It was an odd one to start out with.

"How talented she is," Geneva murmured.

"Yes."

The next work Isabelle had chosen to showcase Noah recognized from *The Marriage of Figaro*. Again, with no idea of its title, its elegance came through with Isabelle's light and flighty glide on the keys, bringing a sting to his eyes.

On and on, she played until a light sheen of perspiration shone on her face.

She ended the concert with something new he hadn't heard, and to his astonishment, she added her voice.

He could hardly comprehend the words. It was Geneva shaking beside him, startling him. It took a full minute to realize she was doing her utmost to contain her laughter, as the words penetrated.

> *This Painted Lady, with such grace,*
> *How she bows to her Admiral Red*
> *The sunset's glow, one's swift curtsey*
> *To the Monarch, she bows.*
> *The Cabbage White, and Morpho's celestial show.*
> *Through the verdant wood she sweeps,*
> *Her goal? To find a dainty tail. A Swallowtail, perchance?*
> *Yet 'tis the Brimstone, Green Peacock,*
> *and Mourning Cloak, that advance.*
> *Such splendor merits joy in one's nature*
> *And, lends courage to one's leap.*

Gads! *Painted lady?* He would strangle that child. The closer he listened, however, he realized she was singing of… *butterflies.*

The company jumped to their feet in a round of roaring laughter and applause that filled the chamber to the rafters. All perhaps, but the right and proper Mr. and Mrs. Woodford. Verda stood off to the side with Sander, both beaming with pride. And with Geneva at his own side, cheering enthusiastically, well, it was… right.

Seconds later, Isabelle made her way in his direction with her uneven gait and grand smile. She moved directly past him to Geneva and threw her arms about her waist.

"You were wonderful," Geneva said, hugging her back. "Outrageously clever. Oh, I adored every word."

Isabelle stepped back, clasping her hands together. "Oh, I'm so happy. You truly liked it?"

"It brings joy to my nature and I vow, I have courage to leap!" she said, repeating Isabelle's words back to her. A true compliment, indeed.

Those words, their generosity, the honest candor—he could deny it no longer. *I love her.* The swift and suddenness of the emotion hit him square in the torso, knocking the breath from him. The dancing flickers of the candle flames toyed with his sight, their heat swamping him. He was much too large to faint. Such a fall would leave an imprint in the planks beneath his feet. The chaotic thoughts assailed him in relentless succession. With sheer determination, he blinked away the bewildering reflections.

"I was certain you would perceive my meaning straight away," Isabelle was telling Geneva.

Geneva hugged her again. "Oh, how could I not, you brilliant, brilliant tease. Those of imminent intellect are apt to think in a similar vein, of course," she said in mock seriousness. Then, with an impish grin, she added, "I am honored beyond words." She went on, as if a tear were not trickling down her cheek. "I cannot *wait* to write Abra and tell her that her skills are rivaled only by you."

A blush crawled up his cousin's pale skin, hiding her freckles momentarily. "Truly?"

"Absolutely. I've never heard anything so beautiful and creative in all my life."

Sander strolled up and set a hand on Isabelle's shoulder.

"Come, poppet. It's time to make your grand exit."

"Must I?"

"We'll see you tomorrow," Noah told her. He kissed her cheek.

Sander escorted Isabelle into Verda's care near the door and stopped to speak with Asher and the marquess.

Julius sauntered up. "I vow, her talent grows more phenomenal with every performance."

"It was breathtaking," Geneva said.

"But what the devil was that regarding a *painted lady*? I thought the Woodfords would expire on the spot."

Geneva tapped him on the arm. "A butterfly, silly."

"I had no notion." Julius shook his head. "She's a clever one, I'll hand you."

Noah watched Geneva eyeing Isabelle and her father working their way to the doors with stops here and there along the way. "You were exceptionally late, Jules. What were you up to?" Noah's question drew Geneva's attention away from Isabelle and back to him and Julius.

"This cursed sling is the devil to deal with." He spoke too quickly and his eyes, tellingly, shifted away.

Noah's gaze sharpened. "Julius?"

"Quit interrogating me, Noah. I'm not a child any longer for you to fuss over or manipulate."

Somehow, Noah managed not to clutch his chest and stagger back.

"What a horrid thing to say." The mild remark from Geneva startled not just Noah, but Julius as well.

Julius's expression looked as hurt. And his hand flattened against his chest too. "But—"

She rose to her miniscule height and poked him in the chest. "By all accounts, sir, your brother raised you from infancy because your father put *you* in his care. I've never witnessed anyone more loyal than Mr. Oshea." She rubbed her forehead as if one of those dreadful megrims had begun its attack, but she appeared to will it back. "Let me tell you what you survived, Julius. My father would have sold you to the highest bidder for his next bottle of gin—*no*—not a bottle, but a mere taste of the vile stuff. My mother was not well enough to fend him off. You can't know how decidedly propitious you were to escape such a fate." Her fingers flew up and pressed her temples.

"Geneva," Noah gripped her wrists. "What—"

"The pain." She gasped. "It's excruciating."

Noah caught her before she slid to the floor. "I'll take her out the side door," he told Julius. "Distract the others if you can."

His brother, though, had stiffened in a pose comprised of Italian marble.

"Julius," he snapped.

Jerking at the bark, Julius nodded once and strode to the marquess and Asher, each vying for Docia's attention. The rector and his wife stood about awkwardly, their ears likely still ringing from the "painted lady" reference in Isabelle's innocent lament. Julius effectively stepped past the group, drawing their gazes, leaving Noah an opportunity to usher Geneva through the servants' entrance.

He swept her off her feet and carried her into the Morpho Suite and into her bedchamber, firmly latching the door behind him.

CHAPTER TWENTY-NINE

WITH SUCH GENTLENESS that nearly brought her to tears, Geneva was set to her feet, held on to until she was steady and not in fear of collapsing where she stood. Oh, how she longed to cling to such strength. But it was important to remember and impossible to forget she was that trivial nonentity.

"What was that about, darling?" Noah asked her.

"I-I don't know." Forcing herself from him, she made her way to the settee before a low fire. She did her best to keep her mind clear to stave off any recurrence of that unbearable pain. A glass of brandy was pressed in her hand. She took a sip that burned away the cobwebs, allowing her to breathe again. A small yet encouraging sign.

"Perhaps we should send for the doctor again."

Geneva let out an indelicate snort. "What do you mean 'again'? I've never required a doctor in my life."

"I beg to differ," Noah shot back. "We were most concerned after that fall you sustained. And with the rain…" He shuddered.

Geneva frowned. "I didn't see a doctor."

"Darling, you were unconscious." His lips turned down, and he speared her with furrowed brows. "I think you may have left your bed too soon. Clearly, you were not well enough for tonight's event."

Her palm flew up. "Stop right there. It was *my* decision to attend. Not yours. I wouldn't have missed Isabelle playing had I been on my deathbed or… or dumped in an unmarked grave."

She took in a deep, cautious breath. Thus far, to her relief, the absence of pain remained managed.

His expression softened and he moved quickly and dropped beside her. He framed her face with both hands. Warm, soothing hands. "Yes, you would, wouldn't you?" His husky tonality sent a thrilling shiver weaving through her veins, her bones, her body.

Any words to respond fled in the wake of those warm hands. Her eyes clamped shut as desperate need tore through her. No pickax tore through her head. The only pounding was her heart against her ribs akin to running for her life in Berwick Street. Only this time, she was caught with no desire to escape.

As light as a moonbeam on calm waters, his lips misted hers. Her lips parted, but he dared to tease her with anticipation, allure, urgency. His hands cupped her shoulders, and disappointingly, maintained an almost respectable distance. She flattened her hands on his chest. Molded them to the contours of his body.

She went up on her toes and captured his lips, drew his tongue into her mouth. *Yes.*

His hands slid to her back, pressing her into the hard wall of his chest. Her arms smoothed up and around his neck. Stroke after stroke—his, hers, she couldn't tell and didn't care—their tongues danced. To crawl into his skin would not be enough. He breathed the very life into her.

Right there in that moment, she knew she would perish if…

He broke away, groaning. "We must stop," he said on a harsh exhale.

Geneva covered her mouth with the back of her hand, unable to speak. But of course he was right. If anyone caught them, he would be forced to an unthinkable action—marriage, to her. Worse, she would be run out of Alnmouth, *Stonemare*, ostracized, accused of attempting to trap a man miles above her in class. She broke the contact and tried pushing from him.

But things took a swift change. He grabbed her by the upper arms and shook her. "Oh, no, you don't. Don't you dare get it into your head that I regret you kissing me. I wish to ravish you senseless. But not at the risk of someone walking in on us."

Geneva nodded. It was just as she'd thought.

"I wish to marry you," he said.

"Yes, yes. I understand—w-what?"

"I want to marry you. And I don't want anyone questioning my reasons why."

"But…"

"Don't you want to marry me? I realize I'm nothing but a wearisome scientist."

"You are anything but wearisome," she whispered. "It is I who am unworthy. You are an earl's brother, while I grew up near the slums in London."

"You also have friends in high places. Not that I put stock in such things." He leaned over and brushed her lips again. "I believe we have more to learn of one another, and now we shall have the rest of our lives."

"Oh, Noah." Her arms wrapped around his neck, tears blurring her vision. "I don't know what I did to deserve you, but I'm not giving you back."

The passion erupted with unparalleled ferocity. Once more, his mouth crashed over hers, his tongue lavishing her with untold secrets. Secrets she only wished to explore with him. She pulled away and tugged at his cravat.

"Yes," he breathed, stripping it away.

She shoved at his hands and tugged at the few buttons in sight. One flew and pinged against the ceramic tiling before the fire. The need to feel his skin beneath her fingertips overwhelmed her, but in her frustration, he usurped her hands and stripped off his waistcoat. He tugged the shirt from his breeches and whipped it over his head.

A moan escaped her—he caught it with his lips. One large hand covered her breast in a light squeeze, a move that had her gasping and him smiling against her mouth. She pulled away, her eyes meeting his. Eyes that devoured her, with something she'd never experienced in her life: hunger. For her. No doubt of yearning, not with the palpable craving he exuded.

Heat washed through her.

His hand moved from her breast to her hand. He took it and placed it on the bulge of his breeches. "This is what you do to me. I won't be mending you. Just the opposite." The husky tone stole beneath her skin. "It's *you* who shall be curing me."

Her palm burned through the material. The impulse to enwrap her fingers around the forge-fired rod etched itself into her soul. "I—" She swallowed. She feared that boldness, the bane of her existence, would desert her at a most inopportune moment, but she drew in a sharp breath. "I wish to see."

He smiled with a tenderness that weakened any resolve she could have hoped she possessed. "Of course you do." He planted a kiss on her lips that trembled with... with, not fear, but... exhilaration. "One moment." He rose and went to the door, cracked it ajar, and peered out. He shot her a quick, wicked glance, then pushed until it latched and twisted the key in the lock.

"This is quite perilous," she whispered.

"And exciting."

"Most exciting."

He turned her about and made quick work of Abra's beautiful, blue dress. It sagged and, with haste, her hands splayed across the bodice to hold it in place. Soft but firm lips touched her neck, just under her ear, sending shivers cascading down, swirling and weaving about her spine.

Geneva spun and threw her arms around his neck. "Oh, Noah." The dress slid down her body and she couldn't make herself care. She set her lips to his jaw, touching his skin with the tip of her tongue. His hands, large and warm, smoothed from her back to her bum, molding her to his bare torso, his erection, hot against her abdomen. "We should wait," he said.

"No."

"I want to insist, but..." His hands fell away from her and went to the placket of his breeches. "But I can't."

She fumbled with her stays and corset without success.

His member sprang free—his very large member. She froze, staring. She knew the mechanics. The corner prostitutes cared not for privacy, nor did the men taking them in the shadows of closed door fronts. She raised her eyes to his and swallowed hard. Her fingers tingled for wont of feeling that roused conflagration.

"Go ahead," he growled. "You can't hurt me."

Reaching forward with an unfamiliar tentativeness, she brushed her shaking fingers against velvet-covered fire.

He let out a low-keeling moan and grasped her hand, guiding, showing her how to wrap her hand about him. The heat singed her palm, spread through her from her toes up, settling in a decidedly unmentionable place. The stays dropped in a pool at her feet without her having realized he'd taken over the task of relieving her of them. The corset parted and his breaths grew rapid, sending her stomach into a riot of chaos.

"Beautiful," he murmured, leaning forward and licking her skin, leaving a fiery torrent in its wake. He cupped her breasts and took a nipple in his mouth. The sensation was wickedly obscene. Never had she imagined such sinful decadence existed. A new appreciation for those ladies of the night prickled her.

His mouth moved to the other breast, leaving cool air to pebble the exposed nipple to a hard nub. Large fingers crept their way from her breasts, smoothing over her abdomen, to the curls between her legs. No place anyone had ever touched. The skin there quivered and a shot of warmth touched the inside of her thigh.

Her hand shot to his wrist and she squeezed.

Noah lifted his head, meeting her gaze with heated desire and a touch of amusement. "It's all right, love." He inserted one finger, then a second.

"What…" But the words were pilfered from her like a cut-purse on the run with his goods. Quick as a gale off the sea, she was swept off her stockinged feet, her legs hugging his hips.

His hand stole between their bodies, his breaths harsh rasps.

"I'm sorry, love. I'll attempt to be gentle."

But Geneva didn't want gentle. She clutched his hair in her fists—"I don't need gentle"—and tugged.

His hips surged.

The pain was sharp, but she swallowed her own cry with his mouth over hers.

His hands flexed in the fleshy parts of her bottom. The pain dissipated and, while his impalement filled her, stealing the ability to speak, the warmth blossomed to something insatiable. Perspiration broke out over his skin. It was slick beneath her fingers. Wild yearning soared through her blood. She tightened her legs, reaching for the unreachable. Her heart pounded furiously against her ribs. Groaning, he lifted then lowered her. With each pass, his movements grew more frenzied until their pants united. Until black edged her vision. Until her own body grew intolerable and a burst of stars exploded behind her closed eyes and left her floating adrift.

Noah's hands tightened on her, his neck taut with corded muscles, two grunts, and a shout muffled by her sternum as he was throbbing within her. "God, Geneva. God." His whispered breath was hot against her.

With painstaking care, he lifted her, severing his body from hers and setting her gently to her feet.

The sense of loss was significant. More so, as he stuffed his— oh, heavens, what was she supposed to call that massive piece of flesh after such an event—into his breeches, along with his shirt before buttoning the flap. He strode to the basin and dipped a cloth, cleaned his hands, then took her to the bed and gently cleaned her thighs and her private area. After dropping the cloth back near the basin, he snatched up his waistcoat and shrugged into it then grabbed his cravat and tied it loosely about his neck.

With each layer he reapplied, her heart sunk farther past the hard planks of the floor. The sense of loss turned to one of helplessness while she stood there arms hugging her nudity.

Slowly, he stood upright, scrutinizing her with a sharp gleam in his eye. "For such a bold and forthright woman, I do believe you do not value your true self."

Her head jerked up as the familiar cutting rejoinders crowded her throat. Before a single one could spew forth, she was swept off her feet, carried to the bed, and set gently to her feet on the floor beside it. "I must leave. Pasha is sure to pound down the door at any moment. I will not have someone saying you trapped me—"

"*Trapped you!*"

"Yes." He swooped in for a hot, quick kiss that nearly knocked her off her feet. His lips moved to her neck. He pulled her hands from covering her breasts and held them out, looking at her until her body flushed with heat that started between her legs. "You are so beautiful. I want to crawl in the bed with you and show you exactly how much so." He brought her hands to his lips then dropped his hold and jerked the coverlets back, picked her back up, and tossed her in the middle of the mattress before tucking the covers about her.

Noah moved quickly to where her discarded garments pooled on the floor and grabbed them. He then shook them out and laid them across the settee. "Get some rest. I'll see you in the morning, love." One last touch of his lips and he was slipping out the door.

Geneva brought her fingers to her lips, stunned by the emotions roiling through her. A blossom of petals unfurling into full bloom. A cautious sense of bliss, exultation of euphoria? Perhaps it was the evaluative gaze he'd raked over her with its playful light that ignited the unfailing adoration and tender compassion flourishing through her.

She closed her eyes and reveled in the searing imprint of his hand on her skin. Delight. Joy. Hope.

For the first time since her mother's passing, it was *hope* that triumphed and allowed her to fall into a blissful slumber.

NOAH HAD NEVER felt so… so sated. So replete. So hungry for more. His entire body hummed with need and longing for a life that his uncle had managed to affect with his aunt. The sentiments felt so close, his fingers tingled with a desire to reach out, grasp, and cling to the possibility of such great happiness and contentment.

Sleep was as far from his reach as crawling in Geneva's bed tonight. He made his way down the stairs to the library and let himself in.

And stopped.

"Ah, Noah," Sander said. "Come, join us for a drink before the gentlemen take themselves off to Alnmouth for the night." Mr. Asher, Lord Martindale, and his uncle stood around the fire, warming themselves with heat and spirits. Sander filled then handed Noah a glass of Pender's best brandy.

Martindale eyed Noah over his own glass. "How on earth did Miss Wimbley come to land in Northumberland? She has a reputation as a bit of a rabble-rouser in some of the more questionable London areas."

"Is that so?" Sander said mildly. Dangerously.

Noah's lips tightened, but he refrained from speaking, seeing as how his uncle had picked up the gist.

Martindale, the daft prick, hadn't, and went on. "Oh, yes. I believe she's had a hand in stirring the masses for economic equality for the lower classes." He snorted. "And women. The idea is preposterous. As if Parliament would ever allow women to run the country."

"That sounds somewhat blasphemous," Noah said mildly. "Apparently, you've forgotten that Queen Victoria has successfully run the country now for a decade."

"Bah, that was Melbourne, Peel, and Russell." He threw out his hand.

Sander frowned. "Her nuptials to Albert in '40 solidified her position. Don't you agree?"

"What's that, Lord Martindale?" Mr. Asher threw in. "Why, Victoria's support's been a boon to the country's progress. Her endorsements to the rail systems will have England lauded as the greatest of technological advancements."

A notion with which Noah heartily agreed.

Martindale shot Asher a glare. "There have been pamphlets distributed all over London." His derisive sneer moved about the group. "The last one I read expounded the qualities of education for everyone. For the greater good of England. Absolutely ridiculous. I've never been able to prove it was Miss Wimbley, but I'd stake my life on the fact it's *her* who's putting out all that gibberish. When I catch that little harlot—"

Noah's hand tightened in a fist and he took a step in the marquess's direction before his uncle spoke up.

"Just a minute there, Lord Martindale. Miss Wimbley is a guest of ours and there's been no indication of her involvement in any such antics." Sander's mildness calmed Noah. "Perhaps considering what women are expected to give," he added with a thoughtful crease to his forehead, "or how they are expected to conduct themselves warrants a closer look in these matters."

Noah's tension may have eased, as Sander had likely intended, and Noah stepped back, flexing his hand. But the tension most assuredly had transferred to Martindale. Noah stifled an eruption of laughter behind a choked cough at the astonishment creasing the scoundrel's expression.

Asher clapped the marquess on the shoulder. "Best be getting on the road, eh, your lordship?"

Noah waited until Sander returned from seeing their guests to the vestibule and turning them over to Winfield.

"Is it true?" Sander asked him. "About the pamphlets?"

It wasn't Noah's place to enlighten his uncle, so he shrugged. "What would it matter?"

Sander speared Noah a contemplative look. As if Noah were

as transparent as the brandy he'd finished off. "It matters not to me. In fact, she sounds quite the reformer."

You've no idea.

Noah thought of that bold written essay he'd discovered. Its strong message for women, and men, if he recalled correctly, by women on their right to work, to care for their children. To remember that women were the future of the world because they were the ones who carried the sons and daughters for the future. It was a brilliant, well-articulated, call to action piece of work. How proud he was for his future wife. He would take great pleasure in creating a large, light-filled chamber for her to do her good works in. Whatever she required, he would build it with his own two hands.

Julius entered the library. "Is the bore gone?"

An apt description if Noah had ever heard one. "He is indeed."

"Docia gave Martindale quite the set down," Julius said. "Turned Asher on his head too. How is Geneva?"

"I was able to get her away with no incident." Noah went to the cabinet before his expression exposed that little fabrication. He poured a small measure of brandy for Julius, then, with his composure firmly intact, turned and handed it to him. "The credit with utmost gratitude goes to you and Docia."

"What do you suppose is triggering those megrims? They seem to strike without warning, don't they?" Julius took a sip of his brandy.

"I think perhaps it was too soon for her to be up and about," Noah said. Yet there *was* a pattern—he just hadn't quite been able to pin it down.

Sander took up the poker and stirred the fire. "I suspect you couldn't have kept her away with the entirety of the full British Fleet behind you."

Noah grinned, a little of the euphoric feeling seeping back through him. Scotland was but miles away. He and Geneva could be married by week's end.

After a bit, he took himself up to his chamber, forcing himself to steer free of the Blue Suite. God knew, he wouldn't have the wherewithal to stay out of her bed. She needed her rest and he was determined she would get it. But, oh, how he wanted just one more taste of those delicious lips.

CHAPTER THIRTY

"**B**LAST IT, ISABELLE, it's much too cold. And wet. Truly, dear, your parents will wish to do irreparable harm to someone, and that someone will be me."

Geneva had slept like the dead. For the first time in years, there had been no great weight of worry on her shoulders... or so she'd thought. She had no desire to go up against Sander and Verda when it came to their precious—and she was precious—only child. After all, Geneva was trying to fit into the family, not undermine those whose acceptance she sought. "Have you forgotten the person who pushed me over the cliff has not been located? And that he could be a *killer*?"

"Oh, yes. I see what you mean." The words were delivered earnestly enough, but it was the innocent blinking of her large, gray eyes that gave Geneva pause. She further threw Geneva off with a quick hug, enveloping her in her white, muslin dress, and went to the door. "Perhaps later, then. I'll see you at luncheon." She tossed a sweet smile over her shoulder then was gone. But the determined expression on her face was all too visible—Isabelle cared nothing of what anyone thought: she was going bug hunting.

Geneva glanced down at her wrap. She wasn't even dressed. *Blast.*

By the time she was donned in one of her own sturdy frocks Pasha would shudder at and Abra *had* shuddered at, Geneva ran for the stairs, but Isabelle was nowhere to be seen. Neither was

Winfield. Frightfully vexing. There was no time to lose, and Geneva dashed out the front door.

Of course the headstrong child had disappeared. Logic told Geneva Isabelle would choose a place near the laboratory; then again, she would not do what was logical. Stretched before Geneva, past the sweep of the drive, was a line of tall oaks that looked as old as the land itself. Geneva started to turn, but a flash of white hit the corner of her eye from that line of trees.

"Isabelle."

The response was a short, sharp scream.

Geneva ran, now thankful for her unfashionable yet comfortable boots and sturdy frock. She breached the woods and heard the low growl off to her right. The proverbial head-splitting axe pierced her skull. She fought through a vortex of blackness dotted with tingly spots that nearly felled her to her knees. The thrashing of leaves kept her on her feet. "Isabelle," she called out in a breathless and desperate rush. She burst through a canopy of low-hanging limbs that tore her hair from its fastenings and tripped over an exposed tree root. Pieces of the damp earth filled her nostrils—so different from the debris that blew over Berwick Street. Thankfully. She spat out the dirt.

"Please." Isabelle's whisper sent a chill weaving its way up and around her spine, raising the hair at her nape.

The heavy strands of hair blinded her and she shoved them away, coming face to face with none other than… "Papa?" She hadn't seen him in almost a decade. *No. That wasn't it at all.*

Starting at the crown of her head, the pain, agonizing and unbearable pain, moved to her temples and pounded with that ghastly visage that turned the fresh turn of the earthy fragrance about her into an instrument of immense torture. Even the slight breeze hit her face like shards of piercing glass. The ability to form a coherent thought fled her usually pragmatic notions.

Her vision was limited to silhouettes within the dark shade of the trees.

Isabelle whimpered. "Geneva?"

"Ah, the prodigal daughter of a seaman and his lady lives to face her adorin' papa," her father said. His inked arm sported a snake and flexed. The wicked-looking knife he held to Isabelle's delicate neck sent another wave of icy-black panic through Geneva. Sheer hatred permeated the forest and cleared some of the cobwebs—

Her eyes flicked to the chain around Isabelle's neck, where a corner of the locket for which she'd been searching exposed a large, red ruby.

The stakes had just heightened to an alarming degree. The compounding danger cleared every fleeting thought in Geneva's head. With a deep breath, she came slowly to her feet and met her father's seething malevolence. "It was you who pushed me over the cliff." That she was able to choke out the words was just as miraculous as her surviving the fall, along with the memories crashing through her. The battering rain, the shock of seeing that straggled hair, the outstretched, calloused and stained palm that had landed on her chest and pushed without the slightest hesitation. The actual fall and landing were still locked deeply away.

And Noah. His voice screaming her name over the pounding surf from below.

Geneva kept her eyes trained on her father, praying Isabelle would stuff the locket from sight, keep him from seeing it. Otherwise, they were both as good as dead. "Let her go, Papa. She's a child," she begged.

"I'll let 'er go, once I got you in me 'ands. Got just the place to stash yer bloody remains when I'm through with ye."

"Lord Chaston, the cave…" she whispered, edging within his reach. She had to save Isabelle. "Why, Papa? Why try to kill *me*? Your own daughter." She kept her tone low, placating.

"Yer no child of mine. She was done ruined when she married me." The stench of gin reeked with his menacing cackle. "'Er family cast her aside. Found 'er blubberin' like a squall at sea in one o' them fancy parks she done grew up near."

Geneva managed not to cast up her accounts. He shoved Isabelle aside too quickly for her to get her footing and she fell with a sharp cry.

Geneva stepped to the opposite side, drawing his entire focus on her. She had to keep him talking. But she couldn't seem to grasp his words. Not clearly... "Chaston? Lord Chaston and Mama," she said faintly, distractedly. He suddenly had a bruising grip on her arm as another, horrendous, thought penetrated. "You. It was *you* who killed Lord Pender, wasn't it?"

"That good-for-nothing dissolute had his way with *my* wife whilst I was at sea. She bore his bastard."

Julius. It was true. Julius was her brother. "But... but why wait twenty years? It makes no sense."

"I never 'ad a clean shot at 'em 'afore then. That's why. Bloody bastard was too quick. Too quick for a toff. Should'a been dead years ago."

Isabelle gasped.

He'd lost what little wits he'd ever possessed.

Geneva dare not pull her eyes from the glint of that blade. It was her attempt of willing him to drop it. She heaved in a deep breath as another horror hit her. "And... And the footman? You killed the footman." The question didn't require asking.

Without even trying his attention riveted on her. "Saw me, o'course. Now quit yer yappin—"

The revelations sliced through Geneva with the cut of the dagger he wielded, but there was also opportunity. "Run, Isabelle," she screamed. "Run!"

It was just enough of a distraction the girl needed.

Papa swung back to her, his fist dealing a whopping blow to her cheek. Somehow, Geneva managed to stay on her feet.

It hurt and she saw stars. But as she'd blithely informed Docia, she'd grown up in one of the more challenging London neighborhoods and struck back, quick like, with a knee to his groin. Hard. He dropped like a pile of stones in the middle of a turbulent sea. She snatched up the nearest weapon at hand—the dropped knife—and raised it, aiming for the empty cavity of his chest.

She'd threatened him years before and had failed in following through. A mistake she wouldn't make a second time.

"Set it down, Geneva. You're safe now."

"Noah?" she cried softly, sliding to the ground into a puddle of muck. "Isabelle…"

"She's all right, Gen. She's all right."

Her eyes raised to see him brandishing a pistol pointed at her father. "Kill him," she said, her voice trembling as bad as her hands. "He murdered your father and… and Docia's"

Her father let out a choked cackle that raised bumps over her skin. "'e ain't got the balls, gel."

"I don't think that will be necessary," Noah said. "On your feet, sir."

"Fuck ye." Her father was as belligerent as she could remember and remained where he was, on the ground. She'd known him too long to trust anything her father said or did. A person's mien spoke volumes if one took pains to observe.

Geneva came to her feet, clutching the knife within her skirts, this time, staying carefully free of his reach. "Don't trust him, Noah. He's wily."

Noah's eyes never wavered from him, the weapon steady in his grip. "I suspect he's been in the vicinity for years. Isn't that so, Mr. Wimbley? Or shall I call you 'Harlen'?" Noah asked. Papa's lips clamped tight, but Noah didn't let up. "It's been nigh on a decade, I'd wager."

Geneva stopped, her head taking on that incessant pounding that didn't bode well. "Since Mama's death. You left after she died. This is where you've been. All these years…"

"Your father has been insinuating himself in the community. Quite the regular at the tavern, aren't you, Mr. Wimbley?"

Papa let out another one of those skin-tingling cackles that grated over her.

"But why kill me? Why go after Julius?" she whispered.

Sneering, he said, "Ye think Pender was the only fool who done yer mama? 'E was jes the last in a string o' lovers she spread those legs for when I was at sea." He laughed again. "She couldn't hide her fancy notions. I found 'er letters. I ain't no fool. She owed me for givin' ye me name." Quick as a bolt of lightning, his arm shot from behind, a glint of metal piercing her vision.

But Geneva had prepared for this moment since the day of her mother's funeral when her father had dared come after her. The dagger flew from her fingers. "Noah, *fall!*" she screamed.

The blade struck the only man she'd ever known as her father in his thick, inked neck the same instant Noah's pistol fired, the bullet hitting Papa where his heart should have been.

She slid back down in the dirt and covered her face with her hands, ears still ringing with the thundering gunfire.

The gun thudded to the ground and strong arms instantly engulfed her. "It will be all right, darling." Noah's growl whispered against her ear. "He can never hurt you again. Never."

Geneva fell against his chest, needing nothing other than the steady beating of his heart to right her world. "I love you," she whispered.

CHAPTER THIRTY-ONE

NOAH RUBBED HIS hands over Geneva's cold arms despite the blazing fire in the library's hearth. "I have something for you," he said.

Her arms wrapped around his waist, her head lay on his shoulder. "I don't need a thing. I have you."

"I never found your locket, but I have something else I hope will suffice."

A startled laugh erupted from her. Then she started to giggle. Uncontrollably.

Noah shook her. "What the devil?"

Tears were filling her eyes.

Panic roared through him. "I tried, darling. Truly, I searched my father's chamber, but there was nothing there. I checked the trunks in the attic Winfield's had packed away. The safe only Father used. I'm so sorry, love. I couldn't find it. I was even going to rifle through Julius's private belongings. I'd given it to him when he was just a lad. As a keepsake from… his mother. But it was kept in the safe."

Still, she laughed until he realized she couldn't stop.

He crashed his mouth over hers. A move that sobered her in an instant. He licked her lips. They parted and he stroked his tongue against hers, one that felt of crushed velvet. The texture drove him wild, along with her response that drove every coherent thought from his head. Slowly, he pulled away and studied her. He tugged a handkerchief from his pocket and gently dabbed the tears from her face. "What was that, love? I don't understand."

"The locket. I found the locket," she choked out, taking the handkerchief from him.

"What? Where?"

"What is this about my locket?" Isabelle strolled in, Julius on her heels, startling him.

His brother's eyes narrowed. "More importantly, why would you rummage through my personal belongings?"

"Don't be angry with Noah," Geneva chastised him. "I came to Northumberland to find a ruby locket my mother had promised me when I was just a little girl. For the longest time, I'd thought I had dreamed it, but then Abra and I found a box under a plank in the floor of my flat. There was a letter she was writing to Lord Pender, er, the late earl—"

"Go on," Julius said.

Noah intervened. "I offered to help her find it. But it had disappeared from the safe."

A sheepish expression crept over Julius's face. "I, um, gave it to Isabelle, but I told her never to tell you. I thought it would hurt your feelings if you knew. It wasn't as if I could ever wear it."

Relief hit Noah in the chest.

Julius's eyes took on a distant gaze. "Sometimes I would see you take it from the safe and watch you studying it. You looked so… so troubled."

Noah led Geneva to the seating before the fire and dropped next to her. Isabelle and Julius followed.

"I didn't know the entirety of what happened until Geneva stormed Stonemare." Noah took her hand and squeezed it.

Julius laughed. "I gave it to Isabelle for her twelfth birthday."

Noah shook his head, touched in spite of the unfolding events.

Isabelle tugged at the delicate chain around her neck and displayed a large ruby encased in a gold filigree frame that resembled a wreath of leaves. "This is yours?" she directed to

Geneva.

"No, my sweet," Geneva told her. "It's yours now. I'm thrilled Julius gave it to you."

Docia, Sander, and Verda filtered in.

"Oh! Jewelry." Docia hurried over. She held the locket on her flattened palm, then turned it this way and that. "It looks remarkably like one my mother used to have. She was buried with it…"

Geneva's head tilted, her body stiffened. "Buried… How old were you?"

"Five or six. I don't remember." Docia's gaze never left the piece, one finger tracing the intricately woven leaves. "It's latched. Have you ever opened it?"

"It requires a key that I don't have. I didn't wish to break it." Isabelle's wistful tone broke Noah's heart.

"Perhaps I can help," he said.

"Key?" Geneva bolted from the settee like the cannonball that had nearly felled Wellington at Waterloo, as history recounted. She dashed from the chamber as if fire licked at her heels.

GENEVA BURST INTO the Morpho Suite and into her bedchamber, startling Pasha out of her skin. "Quickly, where is my reticule? The one from London," she demanded.

"Of course." Pasha hurried to the wardrobe and dug through, quickly returning with Geneva's dark-blue reticule. Made of a sturdy cotton, the dark color hid much of the wear, as Geneva had been using this same bag for years.

She snatched it from Pasha and loosened the drawstrings, dumped the contents on the bed. "It's not here."

"What are you looking for, miss?"

"A key." Geneva pilfered through the stack of pound notes, a coin purse, a small pamphlet on *The Importance of Educating the*

Masses, and another on *Women in an Economic London*. "It's not here."

Pasha pushed her aside. "You are too upset to see properly." She opened the coin purse and turned out the contents. No key. She picked up each pamphlet and the rusted key hit the coverlet from the *Women in an Economic London*.

Geneva snatched it up. "Oh, thank you." She hugged Pasha and was off again.

Within minutes, breathless, she stopped at the library door. She set an open palm, a fist, and her forehead against the cold oak and breathed deeply. The key cutting into her hand seemed to singe her skin. One more inhalation, then she entered.

Noah met her near the door. "What is it?"

She opened her palm. Raising her eyes, she met his where she detected a distinct sparkle.

"Let's see what we uncover," he said. He took her arm and led her to Isabelle.

"Try this," Geneva said on a rush of air, handing her the key.

"But..."

Geneva closed her fingers over Isabelle's. "Try it."

"All right," she said.

It took a few minutes with everyone hovering, but with some coaxing, the click, barely discernable, triggered and the locket sprung open.

Docia gasped. "Why, that's a miniature of Papa... and... me." Her words stumbled, her expression confused.

"Might I see?" Geneva pushed through the throng and took the locket from Docia. "That's you?"

"Yes, but—"

Geneva worked one of the miniatures free and turned it over. "There's something written here. It looks like a year." She leaned in closer. "1824." She glanced at Docia.

She turned absolutely chalky. "But that isn't possible. I would have been seven. Mother perished in '22."

Geneva met her eyes. "I think it's me." She had a sudden

need to sit, instead found herself swaying. Noah was at her side in an instant and guiding her to the settee.

Docia followed and lowered beside her. "Look behind the other one. The one of my father," Docia said in a cracked voice.

"*To Emily, the love of my life.*" Slowly, Isabelle raised her gaze, meeting Docia's and hers.

Geneva glanced at Docia. "I—I think we may be sisters."

Tears filled Docia's eyes. "That must be why he kept going to London for all those years after Mama passed."

Geneva clutched her hands. "I'm sorry."

"Why are you sorry? You have a brother, and now, a sister." Docia's fingers twisted about and tightened around Geneva's. "I've missed having a sister." A distant gaze softened her focus. "Someday, I shall tell you all about Eleanor." She blinked and turned back into her haughty, more familiar self. "And you *are* younger, which shall make it much easier to boss you about."

Geneva smiled through a blurred vision. "I doubt that you shall find it easy. Now more than ever, you'll have to treat my friend Abra with her due respect. Otherwise, I shall flatten you," she choked out. She threw her arms around her newfound sister's neck. So many questions flooded her. She withdrew, unable to meet Docia's eyes. "Somehow, Papa—Wimbley—must have learned the truth of my… heritage. That must have been what he meant when he said…" She looked at Noah. "When he said what he said about Mama."

"I think that was likely the case. There's also the possibility he confronted Chaston… the former Chaston," he said gently.

Docia gasped, her eyes going to him. "You believe he killed my father?"

"He confessed as much."

"He was an awful man," Geneva told her.

"I'm glad he's dead," Isabelle said with heartfelt emotion. "If I were already a doctor, I would not save him. I suppose I would have to, really." She paused, her gaze going to Noah, then said, "Perhaps you should crack his skull open and study his brain,

Noah."

Sander cleared his throat. "Good gads, Isabelle. The ghastly things you come up with…"

"Well," Verda interrupted. "I take it Miss Wimbley will be staying around awhile?"

"Of course she will be," Noah informed her. "She's already agreed to be my wife."

CHAPTER THIRTY-TWO

Six Months Later

STONEMARE HELD THE fresh strong scent of pine and evergreen as Noah made his way to the dining hall. He entered and found the whole of his family already seated and at different stages of breaking their fast.

A plate laden with kippers, bacon, and a gross amount of eggs sat before Julius. The latest copy of *The London Times* had Sander largely ignoring his own plate while Verda and Isabelle nibbled on slices of apples and pears.

The only persons missing were Docia, who'd left for London months ago, and Noah's adorable wife, who'd vacated their bed hours ago. Shocking, as he'd kept her up long after midnight, tasting and savoring every inch of her delectable body. But, alas, he'd made true the vow of creating an office with space and light for her to work to her heart's content. He'd chosen a large chamber in the west tower. One that could handle the tables required for all the newspapers and broadsheets her many cohorts sent to her that arrived daily.

He kept the fire tended to regularly in the event she dashed from their bed in the night with some urgent idea, as she'd explained in no uncertain terms, that must be taken down immediately "lest the sea steals the thought from my head never to return."

Of course, Noah had wisely inclined his head at her haughty and *bold* edict. Such brilliance was not to be contained. He loved her as she was. If and when they were ever blessed with children, he suspected she would have no notion how to raise them. But such worries didn't concern him.

He glanced at Julius attacking his eggs as if he hadn't eaten in a week. Yes, Noah knew all about raising an infant.

"Coffee, sir?" Fletcher startled Noah from his musings.

"Thank you." He took his seat at the table next to the empty chair.

"I don't think Geneva eats enough, dear," Verda said.

"She eats when she's hungry, Aunt," he said, silently agreeing. His coffee appeared along with Winfield, holding out a salver with two missives. Noah selected the one with his address. It was from Lucius.

The newspaper snapped. "Good God," Sander said. "Listen to this:

'A Consideration of the Gentle Sex in the Field of Medicine

Most recently, this Sapphire was approached with a most curious and progressive notion. The idea that women might not only partake in the healing arts, but indeed excel therein. Such an assertion is sure to raise eyebrows among the more traditionally minded, but this ideal should be considered with earnest reflection: the manifold of the presence of lady physicians. Just think, dear readers, what a service of this nature could offer, particularly to the gentler sex.

Possessing, as women do, their natural tenderness and compassion would bring a degree of patience and attentiveness that is particularly beneficial in the care of the sick to the practice of medicine.

The lady physician, endowed with such qualities, would excel in the gentle arts of nursing and caregiving, fostering an environment conducive to her patient's recovery.

'Tis unfortunate, however, that the path to becoming a physician is stacked with obstacles for women. The rigorous study of anatomy, the demands of clinical practice, and, mostly, the societal prejudices that persist against women in the learned professions. Yet should a lady succeed, the rewards for herself

and for her patients would be considerable indeed.

In conclusion, it is this Sapphire's belief that her presence in the medical field would prove a great advantage to the ladies of our society. With her unique perspective, compassionate nature, and the potential to ease the delicate sensibilities of her patients, the lady physician may well come to be regarded as an invaluable asset in the noble art of healing.

Yrs. One of the Clandestine Sapphire Society members.'"

Sander laid the newspaper aside and leveled a contemplative, accusatory eye on Noah. "Have you anything to say, son?"

Annoyance struck, with the quick lash of a performer's whip. "I suppose it bears repeating, Uncle, that I am no longer a child of ten to speak to in that belittling manner."

Isabelle snatched up the paper. She shoved her plate out of the way and smoothed it on the table, allowing Verda to share as they read the article through. A shimmer of excitement vibrated from his cousin.

Noah met the amused glint in Julius's eyes and realized at once, his brother was aware of Geneva's "clandestine" activities.

"I don't know why you are so annoyed, darling," Verda told Sander. "This is a wonderful article. This Sapphire, as she refers to herself, has the pulse of a nation influx."

The doors opened and Geneva entered in one of her old frocks Noah was certain he'd ordered burned. "What the devil are you wearing?" he asked her.

All conversation came to an abrupt halt.

"That dress looks vaguely familiar," Verda said. "I distinctly remember that brown shade. It hides dust remarkably well."

"Ink stains as well," Geneva said, taking her place at the table beside Noah. He would never tire of the burst of orange-blossom fragrance that assailed him with her presence.

Fletcher set a cup of coffee before her and Winfield reappeared with the salver, holding her missive.

"Oh, it's from Abra." Geneva broke the seal and unfolded the parchment. "Goodness. She and Baron Ruskin are to be wed. And, to celebrate, she is holding a musicale in March." Her gaze lifted to Isabelle. "It says here she wishes to have you play."

A hush fell over the hall. Then a scream worthy of an operatic aria from Isabelle filled the dining hall. "I must practice at once." She shoved from the table and dashed from the room.

"Oh, dear," Geneva said. "And it's only September."

GENEVA FOLLOWED HER husband to the west tower into their new abode—the Painted Lady—and fell onto the settee, her eyes tired from the strain of her latest essay to send to Hannah on the lack of social justice due to the circumstances of one's birth and gender. Such injustices and inequalities truly were abhorrent.

The settee jarred as Noah dropped beside her. He took her hand and used his thumb to stroke the base of her palm. "You woke early, Madame Sapphire."

Her eyes snapped to his. "What?"

His eyes danced with mirth. "Clandestine Sapphire Society? Makes sense, I suppose. You couldn't very well call yourselves the Secret Bluestocking Society."

Brief silence ensued while she gathered her composure, firmly set her jaw back in place. "Er, no, we could not." She narrowed her eyes on him. "Have you been going through my correspondence, sir?"

"Absolutely not. I'm not even ensuring the maids do their duty in keeping your study free of dust, despite doing my utmost to keep the fire burning. They are under strict orders to not touch a thing."

"Then how did you know?"

"Your latest article regarding women in the medical field appeared in the *Times*. Sander read the whole of it just before you walked into the dining room."

"Oh."

"Is that all you have to say? 'Oh'? By the way, Julius appears to know your secrets as well."

"Yes, yes. I told him months ago. He was suitably shocked… and impressed," she said, smiling at the recollection.

"You are a menace, Mrs. Oshea. Come here." He granted her no choice in the matter, scooping her up and straddling her across his lap.

She cupped his jaw in her hands. Ink-stained hands. "Do you regret marrying a woman bent on challenging the established order?"

He drew those ink-stained fingers to his lips. "Never," he whispered. His hand molded the base of her skull and pulled her to him. His breath heated her lips and the familiar fire ignited at her core.

She tugged up the bothersome skirts and wriggled against the hard length of him, wondering how she had ended up so fortunate in finding this remarkable, broad-minded man, whose love would sustain her throughout the course of eternity.

Within moments, the ugly yet serviceable gown was in shreds. The fire between them converged into an inferno as his hands framed her breasts, suckled her nipples, and surged his member into her. She held hard and fast to his shoulders, moaning. "Oh, Noah, what twist of fate blessed me with you?"

Stars shattered in the blackened skies behind her eyes in gold brilliance.

His climax exploded and his arms tightened around her, stealing the oxygen from her. "I'm the one Divine Providence smiled upon, love." He panted against her dampened skin.

Geneva laid her head on his shoulder, breathing in the very essence that was now a part of her soul.

A comforting quiet fell over her. "You never said what the earl sent in his note. Is Meredith well?"

He bolted upright. "I cannot believe I let you distract me so."

"Me!"

His manner had shifted to concern. Easing her to his side, he stood, then strode to a table near the door and picked up the missive.

Her stomach dipped, but she snatched it from his outheld hand and didn't hesitate in reading it over.

Noah, Felicitations on your recent nuptials.

She raised a brow at Noah. "Recent? It's been six months." Shaking her head, she silently read on.

I have every confidence your new wife will keep you firmly in line. I should have written long before now. Apologies. I've no idea what Rathbourne was about, Noah. The man is a cur, to be sure. My wife was not with child as he'd so blatantly announced to one and all—

Geneva glanced up, glaring. "Insinuated? The duke without the slightest hesitation accused her of taking a lover other than her husband. Bah! Those of us who know Meredith know she would never step out on her husband, no matter how abhorrent he might be." She dropped her gaze and continued.

I confronted her, naturally. And, naturally, we had a terrific row, as you can well imagine. But something dire is afoot, Noah, and Father was up to his neck in it, whatever "it" happens to be. Things are different than I initially believed, er, with my wife. Perhaps you and ~~Miss Wimbley, er~~ *Mrs. Oshea would consider visiting. I could use your expertise and I'm certain Lady Pender would enjoy a visit with her friend.*

The note went on regarding the horrid conditions of Perlsea Keep and the less-than-friendly nature Lucius was finding the Cornish natives.

"I do miss Meredith. She deserves better than Lord Pender."

Noah returned with a non-committal tone. "You really think so?"

"Certainly. The way he hovered about Docia. Why, it was insulting to my friend, who is his *countess*."

"He did mention things were not like he thought."

A deep sense of longing stole through Geneva. "I would love to visit her. Perhaps when we go to London for Isabelle's concert?"

"Of course. That is the perfect solution, my love. Will you search for your mother's relations?"

Geneva's stomach dropped at the thought and she didn't answer for a long time. "No," she said softly. "They tossed her to the curb for losing her heart. My mother was the most gentle person in the world. She didn't deserve such treatment."

His hand rubbed circles on her back and she leaned into it. "If you're satisfied with that, love, then I am as well."

She spun and threw her arms around his neck. "I love you."

"You can't possibly love me nearly as much as I love you," he whispered against her lips.

About the Author

Kathy L Wheeler writes historical and contemporary romance and has hit the Amazon Best Seller list several times over. In the face of danger, her heroines save themselves, their heroes just need to be there to catch them… after the fact.

Her many joys include the NFL, Musical Theater, travel (for example: she once spent twenty-one days going from Oklahoma City to San Francisco and back through Utah to Colorado. When her husband called to ask if she was coming home anytime soon, she then headed back home), and … karaoke.

Main sources of inspiration? Yes, well, they come mostly from an over-active imagination. She currently resides in the Pacific Northwest with her musically talented husband, Al, and their adorable dog, Angel who lives up to her name—*mostly*.

kathylwheeler.com
facebook.com/kathylwheeler
Instagram.com/kathylwheeler
TikTok.com/@kathylwheeler
YouTube.com/@kathylwheeler-author